D1050920

Praise for

THE BEST LIES

"A gripping story of love, obsession,
and the space in between."
—*Kirkus Reviews*

"Lyu . . . has created a powerful spiderweb of toxic
relationships in this intricate, page-turning thriller."
—*BookPage*

"A psychologically complex
story of an obsessive friendship."
—*BCCB*

"Highly recommended for fans
of complex psychological thrillers."
—*SLJ*

THE BEST LIES

By Sarah Lyu

SIMON PULSE

NEW YORK LONDON TORONTO SYDNEY NEW DELHI

This book is a work of fiction. Any references to historical events, real people, or real places are used fictitiously. Other names, characters, places, and events are products of the author's imagination, and any resemblance to actual events or places or persons, living or dead, is entirely coincidental.

SIMON PULSE

An imprint of Simon & Schuster Children's Publishing Division

1230 Avenue of the Americas, New York, New York 10020

This Simon Pulse paperback edition July 2020

Text copyright © 2019 by Sarah Lyu

Cover photograph copyright © 2019 by Jonathon Kambouris/Gallery Stock

Also available in a Simon Pulse hardcover edition.

All rights reserved, including the right of reproduction in whole or in part in any form.

SIMON PULSE and colophon are registered trademarks of Simon & Schuster, Inc.

For information about special discounts for bulk purchases, please contact Simon & Schuster Special Sales at 1-866-506-1949 or business@simonandschuster.com.

The Simon & Schuster Speakers Bureau can bring authors to your live event. For more information or to book an event contact the Simon & Schuster Speakers Bureau at 1-866-248-3049 or visit our website at www.simonspeakers.com.

Cover designed by Nina Simoneaux

Interior designed by Steve Scott

The text of this book was set in Scotch Text.

Manufactured in the United States of America

10 9 8 7 6 5 4 3 2 1

The Library of Congress has cataloged the hardcover edition as follows:

Names: Lyu, Sarah, author. ✳ Title: The best lies / by Sarah Lyu.

Description: First Simon Pulse hardcover edition. ✳ New York : Simon Pulse, 2019. ✳ Summary: Told in alternating timelines, seventeen-year-old Remy Tsai's boyfriend, Jack, is shot by her best friend, Elise, and while police investigate, Remy probes her memories for the truth of their friendship. ✳

Identifiers: LCCN 2018037017 (print) ✳ LCCN 2018043026 (eBook) ✳ ISBN 9781481498838 (hardcover) ✳ ISBN 9781481498852 (eBook)

Subjects: ✳ CYAC: Murder—Fiction. ✳ Best friends—Fiction. ✳ Friendship—Fiction. ✳ Dating (Social customs)—Fiction. ✳ Family problems—Fiction. ✳ Honesty—Fiction. ✳ Mystery and detective stories.

Classification: LCC PZ7.1.L99 (eBook) ✳ LCC PZ7.1.L99 Bes 2019 (print) ✳ DDC [Fic]—dc23

LC record available at https://lccn.loc.gov/2018037017

ISBN 9781481498845 (paperback)

FOR JEN FAN AND AMANDA YAO

1.

You never know when it's the last time.

You never think, *This is the last time I'll ever see his smile, shy and full of secrets meant only for me, the last time I'll ever hold his hand or kiss his face or lose myself in the warmth of his brown eyes.*

Jack's gone now and there was no time to say goodbye. To share one last smile, a final kiss.

I'll never see him again.

It's been three hours since I held Jack in my arms and I'll never hear his voice again, the way he laughed freely, the way he said my name, *Remy*, whispered like a prayer in the dark.

Three hours since strangers pulled me away from his body, and I'll never run my fingers through his dark hair, never feel the heat of his touch against my skin.

Three hours since Elise pointed a gun at him, and I'll never taste his kiss again, breathe in the scent of his peppermint shampoo.

"We need to come up with a story," my parents tell me. Something to give the police, something to explain what happened, what I was doing there.

They want me to lie but they won't say that word, they won't say *lie*. My parents, they want to protect me. I can see the fear in their eyes. They fear for me, what might happen to me. But there's something else too, a different kind of fear.

They're not just afraid for me, they're afraid *of* me.

Here is the truth.

I was born Katherine Remy Tsai, but everyone calls me Remy. I used to know how my story would turn out, but now I have no idea what tomorrow will look like. I used to know what laughter felt like, but now I can't imagine smiling ever again.

I live in the north suburbs of Atlanta, in a town called Lyndens Creek. There is no creek, though, none I've ever heard of, and I was born here. It used to be farmland, just hills and animals. Now it's a nice town, with nice people, the kind who could never, ever fire six bullets into someone's chest.

There are nice schools here, and we went to one of them, Riverside High, known for its terrible football team and soaring SAT scores. The kind of school funded by sprawling golf-course communities where retired lawyers and men of business putter around, and where I fell in love with Jack under a blanket of stars.

Yes. This is a nice place, and I used to be someone who belonged here.

In my bathroom now, I look into the mirror to find a stranger staring back at me. Steam from the running water consumes the bathroom until the glass fogs over and I am suffocating.

The clothes I was wearing only hours ago are stuffed in an evidence bag at the police station. The Superman tee Jack gave me on the first night we met, my favorite pair of jeans, my once-white espadrilles. All ruined.

My body is an afterimage of the damage, a map of dark red told in streaks and smears. Jack's blood is on my face and in my hair, on my arms and under my fingernails. There was so much, the paramedics had rushed to me, checking for signs of trauma, but they couldn't see the hole in my heart.

My name is Remy.

I am seventeen years old.

This won't last forever.

Elise taught me that once as a way to keep myself grounded. These are things I can hold on to. A reminder that how I feel now won't be how I feel forever.

Standing in the shower, I let the water burn the last of him off my skin, watch the blood swirl down the drain until it runs clear.

But I can't get clean. Even with every last drop of shampoo and soap gone, I am still scrubbing, until my skin and scalp are raw and angry.

Until the only thing left is a shaking, sobbing girl on the shower floor.

A shaking, sobbing girl who has to face a loss she's not ready to accept. Part of me knows Jack's no longer here, but I just don't want him to be gone.

2.

They're arguing again, my parents. It's the only constant in my life. The sun will break over the horizon in the morning, and like clockwork, my parents will fight.

"What are you doing?" Dad shouts, following Mom as she paces around the living room. The phone is pressed against her face as she shushes him. Her eyes hold nothing but contempt.

"I'm calling a lawyer," she says, her voice a sharp hiss.

"No one's awake right now. It's three in the morning." He is exasperation and she is anger. These are the roles they've played for years.

My brother, Christian, and I sit quietly on the couch, my hair dripping, still wet from the shower. The sound of water hitting leather punctuates their screaming, a steady drumbeat to the crescendo of their anger. We don't look at each other, we don't look at them. This is so familiar it's almost comforting. I can't handle what's happened, but this I could manage all day long, the shouting and cutting words, my parents at each other's throats.

"Hi, hello," Mom says when someone answers the phone. She shoots Dad a look: *See?* His mouth flattens into a thin line.

They pick up right where they left off after my mother ends the call. They argue about the lawyer—*when will they be here, who is it, where did you even find them*. They argue about how tired they are. They argue about what happened.

"Did you know?" Mom asks him.

"Know what, Helena?" Dad says, palm pressed against his temple.

"Where your daughter was. What's been going on with her. *God,* Stephen, how useless can you be?"

I am right here but I say nothing. Christian peeks over at me. If he's concerned, he doesn't say anything.

I think maybe I'm the one who died, maybe this is my own special version of hell, watching my parents snipe at each other on loop for all eternity. Maybe this is what I deserve.

A knock on the door finally interrupts them half an hour later and they pause when it grows louder. It's the lawyer.

"I'm Vera Deshpande," she says once she's in the living room, eyes searching our tense expressions. "Tell me what happened."

Everyone looks to me. When it becomes clear I am too wrecked to speak, my parents start up again all at once.

"Her boyfriend—"

"Her best friend—"

"He's dead—"

"She shot him—"

"Not Remy. *Remy* didn't shoot anyone—"

"That's what I meant—"

"It was that girl, Elise—"

"It was all *her*—"

"I don't even know where she got a gun—"

They're talking over each other, and I would feel vaguely sorry for Vera if I could feel anything at all. Finally, they catch themselves and pause.

"Where *did* she get a gun?" Mom asks, and all eyes turn to me again. I study the floor, wish I were invisible, wish I were anywhere but here, anyone but me. "This is serious, Remy," Mom continues. "You could go to prison. Do you understand?"

Condescension coats her voice, but there's an edge there too, sharpened by fear. "Someone's *dead*." They don't say his name. They don't care about him, and they don't care about Elise either, even after everything.

And I can't tell if they really even care about me and what happens to me or if what they really care about is how this will look for them, if their daughter goes to prison. How this will affect my mother's nomination to the hospital's board, the promotion my father's gunning for at Coca-Cola. How it'll ruin the perfect image they've worked so hard to craft. We never talk about it but this is why they're still together, after all these battle-worn years. It's not important that their marriage is a failure, what's important is that no one *knows* they've failed, and so the charade continues no matter the cost.

"Remy, please," Dad says, eyes pleading with me. "We're trying to help you. We love you."

Love, that old excuse. They love me the way they love the Mercedes in the garage, the way they love an expensive timepiece on their wrists. They love me only for what I could be to them. I am to be seen but not heard, to be had but not understood. Love is the weapon they wield when it suits them, the justification for everything they do.

"Remy," Dad tries again.

"Don't be stupid," Mom says, cutting him off. "Tell us everything."

I hug my knees in and hide my face. It's a reflex to ball up, shield myself from the world when it's all too much. Part of me knows they're right to panic. I have no idea what'll happen to me, and underneath the shock and grief, I'm terrified too.

"*Remy*," Mom says, her voice like a slap to the face. "This is not the time to play the sullen teenager." She always knows exactly what to say to get a rise out of me.

"I'm not playing. This isn't a *game*," I say, head still buried, hidden behind my legs. "Jack's dead."

Words that I haven't allowed myself to even think now hang in the air. He's really gone.

"Yes. And I know you're sad," Mom tries again. "But—"

"*Sad?*" I can't believe her. She's always been like this. Cold, uncaring. I used to think maybe she had to cut off her emotions because she's a surgeon, but now I think maybe she never had any to begin with and that was precisely why she was such a good surgeon.

She pushes on. "But you have to think about yourself at this point. There's nothing you can do for him now. And do you think Jack would want you to—"

"Is that what you think when someone dies on the table? That there's nothing you can do for them now?" I am screaming, struggling to contain myself. "You would. You don't give a shit about anyone but yourself." I release my legs and grip the couch seats, knuckles white. I start to cry and it's a capitulation. I've lost.

"Yes," she says without flinching. "That's exactly what I do. I have to. Because the next person I operate on deserves my best. You can't just crawl into bed and shut out the world." She's right about one thing—all I want to do is crawl into bed and shut everything out. All I want to do is sink into my pain, let it drown me. "You have to think about what's in front of you."

"Well, of course, that's you. You're perfect. A machine. How can any of us ever measure up? No one was ever good enough for you. Not Dad, not me—" This is an old argument, these are all

7

words I've flung at her before. It's a strange comfort, being back here with her. Surreal but almost normal. The boy I love is dead and it feels like the world is closing in on me, but here we are sparring like always.

"I do what I do to survive." Her voice has turned deadly quiet and it's more terrifying than when she's screaming at the top of her lungs. "I have to make hard decisions every single day. Life-or-death decisions. All you have to do is go to school, get good grades, avoid getting caught up in a murder investigation. How do you fuck that up?"

Christian's eyes are wide, but I know he won't step in on my behalf. He can barely look at me, eyes down on his phone. Maybe he thinks I'm hopeless, stupid, a lost cause—the way Mom sees me. Maybe he thinks I'm something worse, a monster, and he can't stand to be in the same room as me.

"Helena," Dad says.

Before this escalates any further, Vera cuts in. "Why don't I talk to Remy alone," she says. We all stare at her blankly. We'd forgotten she was there. "Let's go for a drive."

In her car, she doesn't say anything when I lower the window and light a cigarette, doesn't tell me to put it out or ask me if I'm old enough to have them. My hand shakes as I smoke, my entire body unsteady. It hurts to breathe. It hurts to *exist*.

"They're just worried," Vera says about my parents as she starts her car. We can still hear them from the driveway, their words faint but heated.

"No, that's pretty much how they always are," I say, my voice flat. I am on the edge of falling asleep but I am also wide-awake. I feel dizzy, spinning between the two states.

Vera doesn't respond, pulling out of our driveway. It's almost four in the morning and we're the only car on the road. The world seems both dead and infinite. We have four hours, five tops, before we're due at the police station. Elise was held for questioning, but they released me into the custody of my parents. I was covered in blood, I wasn't the shooter, so they allowed me to return for questioning in the morning.

"So, Remy, why don't I explain what we can expect this morning when we go in?"

Somewhere in the back of my mind I remember that today is Monday. I have a physics test I didn't study for, on classical mechanics, the laws of gravity and motion—the laws that govern how the stars in a galaxy move and how a gun discharges.

"They'll start by reading you your juvenile Miranda rights." Vera briefly recites the lines that remind me of crime shows on TV, and I can't believe this is real life. "Then someone will take your statement," she continues. "A detective, usually, but possibly a police officer. It's important to remain calm. First impressions do matter."

Her voice comes in and out of focus as I smoke and stare at the streetlights that glide past us. The air is cool on my face and the tears fall freely. I am wrung dry, inside and out, incapable of feeling anything and overwhelmed all at once. My mind has shut down in self-preservation. I feel nothing but still the tears come.

"Tell me what happened. All of it. Don't leave anything out. I'm on your side," she says. "What you say to me stays in this car. But you have to tell me everything."

I don't answer.

"Remy?" Vera says, her voice a soothing balm. I turn to face her. She looks tired but her thick, dark hair is pinned into a knot and her blouse is free of wrinkles, lipstick perfect. I wonder where my mother found her, why she picked up the phone at three in the morning, why she's *here* with me instead of in bed. "I know we just met but I need you to trust me. I need you to help me help *you*. I need you to tell me what happened."

"Okay," I finally say, swallowing. I wonder where Elise is now. If they took her to the police station, if she's at the Pink Mansion, all alone, if anyone's called a lawyer for her too. If anyone's looking out for her. I'm scared for her, I realize. I'm scared for both of us.

"And don't lie," Vera says. "I need to be prepared. The truth always comes out with these things."

3.

At the heart of every good lie is the truth, that's what Elise told me once. *The best lies are at least half-true*, she said, like it's just a matter of mixing paint, two different colors swirling together until no one can tell where the truth ends and the lie begins, a new color emerging.

When the police pulled me away from Jack's body, they sat me at the back of an ambulance, wrapped a blanket around my shoulders, and asked me what happened. *I don't know*, I said. They didn't believe me, but I wasn't lying.

The answer the police are looking for does not contain multitudes, the answer they want leaves no room for interpretation. They want cold, hard facts where none exist. Everyone does, Vera included.

Yes, it's a fact that late Sunday night Elise, Jack, and I were at her house, known to most in the area as the Pink Mansion, named for its blush painted exterior and its massive grounds. It's a fact that Elise, with her grandfather's revolver, shot and killed Jack. It's a fact that I called 9-1-1, kneeled by his side crying as I held him in my arms, as if I could keep him there if I only held on hard enough.

These facts tell a story, but not the whole story—the *real* story.

Trauma has a gravity of its own, powerful enough to distort everything that came before and everything that comes after. Each wound a landmark on the road of your life. Each wound a signpost marking an end, a door slammed shut, forever closed to the person you could've been, the life you could've had if only, if only—

But then there is the first one, the very first trauma, and isn't that where everyone's story begins?

For Elise, it began eleven years ago, at the age of six, when her mother packed her bags at Christmastime and left. Elise didn't see her again until seven years later, at her funeral. She was gone forever, no calls, no emails or letters, and then she died on impact when her car hit a highway median at ninety miles per hour. Elise was only thirteen.

The night her mother left, never to be seen again, was the night Elise discovered that the person who was supposed to love her best in the world was capable of driving away without ever looking back, excising Elise out of her life like a tumor.

For me, it was a voicemail. I was four, maybe five, hiding with Christian in his closet. We'd been watching TV when it began—low, irate voices turned into loud, angry yelling. Christian took me by the wrist and we went upstairs, closed his bedroom door, and sat on the floor, leaning against the foot of his bed to wait out the storm. Eventually, we ended up in his closet, comforted by the small, dark space, the softness of his clothes piled around us like blankets.

Outside, the hurricane raged, but in there, we were sheltered.

Despite the cold, clammy fear that ran through me, I managed to fall asleep, waking only when the house settled into an eerie silence. I tried to leave, thinking it was all over, but Christian tugged on my sleeve and shook his head.

I had to go to the bathroom but I sat back down, hugging my knees in tight. Then I heard her voice downstairs, so far away but all too close, my mother: *"It's me. Pick up the fucking phone, dammit. It must be nice being you. It must be nice to go on business trips and sleep with other people's wives. It must be nice to just leave whenever you want. Leave me with the children. You know, I used to watch all those pathetic mothers on TV, the ones who were in orange jumpsuits because they'd drowned the kids in the pool and I used to think, Who the fuck does that? And now I think I know. Now I understand. Their husbands were off fucking other women."*

Over the years I grew familiar with the types of voicemails Mom left for Dad, designed to get his attention, to get him to come home. But back then, I didn't know any of that.

Back then, I only knew that I wasn't safe, that the person who was supposed to love me best in the world spoke of destroying me like it meant nothing at all.

It was my first memory, and in some ways, my beginning, the first brick in a long road that's led me here.

I'm as alone now as I was then.

4.

We are driving aimlessly through the area and I'm not sure where we are or how we got here. Everything is a blur in the dark. Vera's car has a moonroof and I stare up at the sky but all the stars are gone tonight, tucked behind a thick blanket of clouds. There's electricity in the air, it's going to rain soon.

"Remy?" Vera asks, bringing me back.

"I don't know. I don't really remember what happened," I say, and that is the truth. It was all only hours ago but the night comes in and out of focus. Brightly lit, then shrouded in darkness.

"I wasn't there," I tell Vera, and that is also the truth. Snapshots of the night dance in my mind, a broken record on repeat. Little moments shuffling and reshuffling themselves, everything chaotic, tangled.

I close my eyes and I can still hear the gunshots ringing in my ears but they sound muffled, far away. I remember Jack at the front door of the Pink Mansion, saying, "Maybe it's better if I talk to her alone." *Blink.* Elise is out on the balcony and I'm sitting on the stairs and we are not speaking. *Blink.* Elise puts a comforting hand on my shoulder, saying, "Everything's going to be okay, Remy." She says something else, but it's too quiet, just out of reach. It's all jumbled, out of order, and I feel disoriented. I've been awake for over twenty-four hours, I realize, shaking my head hard. No, it's been longer, thirty hours, forty maybe.

"Which is it?" Vera says, frowning. "You don't remember, or you weren't there?" The rain begins to fall softly, little sprinkles from the sky. Tossing my cigarette out before I close the window, I look up through the moonroof and watch as rain hits the glass, as it obscures everything.

"I wasn't there when it happened."

"When did you arrive? After he'd been shot?" Vera's voice is detached, clinical. She could be ordering a turkey sandwich, not asking about a fatal shooting.

"No." I have to focus. I *will* my mind to focus. I feel untethered, swept into a storm of uncertain memories. I need the truth. I need something to hold on to. I try to rub the sleep from my eyes, and finally, the moments stop shuffling.

Here, again, is the truth.

We were arguing, the three of us, about the pranks. It always goes back to Elise's pranks.

At that point, Jack and Elise were no longer pretending to be friends, not even for my sake. They couldn't even stand in the same room without setting off an explosion. She was gunpowder and he, a lit match.

I acted as an intermediary, defending one to the other, keeping them apart. If you'd asked me Sunday morning, not twenty-four hours ago, I would've told you it was just a rough patch. A spat, a series of misunderstandings.

"It was harmless," I told Jack over the phone on my way to Elise's house.

"You know it wasn't, Remy. It never is," he said, and I could just picture him shaking his head sadly.

"No one got hurt."

"That's not the point, and you know that," he said, sighing.

"It was an accident." It was. "Fireworks can be dangerous."

"Exactly," he said. "They're dangerous. And she knew that."

Silence stretched tight between us.

"I'll talk to her."

"Remy—"

"I have to go," I said, ending the call.

Elise was outside when I arrived at the Pink Mansion. "Did you talk to Jack?" she asked.

"I did." We entered the foyer and I slipped my espadrilles off by the door.

"What'd he say?"

"He hasn't changed his mind," I said, not meeting her eyes. "But he will. I'll explain and—" It was all just a big misunderstanding, I thought. If I could just get them to listen to each other.

"You told him it was an accident?"

"I did." We walked out onto the balcony, the air thick with humidity and still warm from the day.

"Why did you even tell him?" she snapped at me. "If you'd only—" She saw the surprise hurt on my face and exhaled in frustration.

"What are you going to do?" I asked.

She looked out at the water below. It'd been raining a lot recently, leaving the river swollen, its violent current a symphony filling the air.

"You've put me in an impossible position," she said.

At a stoplight, Vera glances over at me. My fingers play with the lighter Elise gave me for my birthday, flipping the top open and closed. Heavy in my hand, the metal feels warm to the touch, and I am itching for another cigarette.

"I was there first and it was just me and her."

"You and Elise," Vera confirms.

"Yes." Elise had put her hand on my shoulder, told me everything would be okay. "We got into an argument. Over something stupid."

"Something stupid?" she asks, studying me.

15

I nod slowly. "I don't even remember what it was," I say, but I do. The last prank, our big finale the night before. What happened after we split from the group. What we did when it was just the two of us. But I don't want to tell Vera about it.

She accepts my answer, at least for now. "And then?"

Then Elise went out to the balcony alone, staring down at the river below. I sat by the front door, at the foot of the staircase. We were fighting, too angry to speak.

"When Jack came, I let him in. He told me to go home, that he'd talk to her. So I left." He'd kissed me on the forehead, his hand lingering in my hair before he let go.

"Elise was out on the balcony. Maybe the door was closed and she didn't hear him come in, and when she came back inside—" I break off, choking on a sob, the tears coming hard and fast. My eyes ache and burn, swollen and sore from the never-ending tears.

Vera pulls over to offer me tissues and turns on her yield signal even though no one else is around or awake for miles. She doesn't put a hand on my shoulder or squeeze my elbow. She doesn't touch me, and I'm grateful. The drizzle outside begins to slow, so she cracks open the windows and the cool air helps.

"He must've startled her," I say. "I'd just turned on my car when I heard the gunshots." It happened so quickly. All within the span of a minute or two. I rushed out, leaving the car door open, my keys still in the ignition.

Vera stares at the road ahead. She's not taking notes but I can see the wheels turning in her mind, taking the words I say, the threads I spin, and spooling them together tight.

"So it was an accident," she says finally, but she doesn't sound convinced.

"That's what must've happened." I nod immediately, lighting another cigarette with a shaky hand. I wasn't there. I didn't see it. But this is the only explanation I have, the only one that makes any sense. She has to believe me, she *has* to.

It was a horrible, tragic accident.

"So your friend had a gun on her in the house."

"If you knew her story, you'd understand why she had that gun." I try to steady my voice, sound confident when I feel like I might crumble.

"And you just let him in and left without saying anything to Elise. You're not leaving anything out? You're telling me everything?" She sounds like she doesn't believe me, sending doubt straight to my heart.

"I am," I insist. "That's the whole story. That's how it happened." That's how it *must* have happened. That much I know.

She looks like she's about to challenge me again, but instead she returns to an earlier question. "You said you were arguing. What about?"

The last prank. Or maybe it was really about all of them. Everything always leads back to those stupid, stupid pranks.

5.

The night I met Elise was also the night of the very first prank. It was nearly a year ago, when I was a sophomore attending the homecoming dance with my then-boyfriend, Cameron. He'd graduated in May and was now a freshman at Georgia State.

That summer we ran wild, staying up late, going for joyrides in his Mustang. Before he left for college, we were inseparable. We were free and in love.

We watched movies in my basement, stole a bottle or three of wine from my parents' collection. Snuck up to his room when his parents were gone. Kissed and promised each other we were forever.

But at the dance, what was supposed to be a blissful night was nothing but heartbreak.

The cafeteria had been cleared, tables and chairs stacked halfway to the ceiling to make room for the dance floor. "Have I told you how much I love you?" I said as we swayed to a slow song, my hand in his hair.

"Mmhmm," he said, but there was no warmth in his voice.

Desperate, I kissed his neck. He pulled away.

"What's wrong?" I said.

"It's just hot in here."

"Do you want some water?" I asked.

"No."

"They have Gatorade."

"No."

"I think the PTA baked brownies this year," I said, just trying to get him to say yes to something—anything.

"No."

I paused. "Did I do something wrong?" Lost and confused, I felt like crying. All I wanted was to go back to the way I thought we were.

"No." He sighed. "Let's get some air." The halls were crowded, the courtyard full. He pulled me by the wrist to the back of the school, out to the empty bus bay.

"Look, Remy, I like you, I do," he began, even though he'd told me he loved me only weeks ago, the weight of his body over mine, the press of lips on lips, hips against hips. "But it's different now. I graduated, and you don't know what college is like, and I don't care about all this high school crap."

"You were the one who offered to take me to homecoming," I said, feeling panic swell inside me. "We didn't have to go."

"It's not about that. Look, I'm sorry."

"Was it something I did? Something I said?" I asked, wrapping my arms around his neck, pinning him there. Maybe I could do something to salvage the night, to press rewind.

"No," he said.

"Tell me what I did wrong. Tell me how I can fix it," I begged.

He pulled me off of him, his hands tight around my wrists. He touched me like he couldn't stand to be near me, pushing me away, holding me at a distance.

"I said I was sorry," he said, as if saying *I'm sorry* was absolution enough no matter the crime. The lines of his face hardened. "I have to get going. Do you need a ride?" He knew that I did, but I could tell he couldn't wait to leave, so I shook my head softly and let him go. Crushed, I watched as he walked out of my life without a second glance. The first tear rolled off my face, hit my chest. He was lost to me and there was nothing I could do to make him come back.

Not wanting to return to the dance, I sat on the cold ground against the doors, heard the music rage on behind me. My friend Melody texted asking where I was, but I ignored her. She never liked Cameron, and the last thing I needed was to see the relief on her face when I told her he'd left me. Instead, I curled in on myself and waited for the unbearable pain in my chest to turn into breathless sobs.

That was when I heard it. The click of a lighter striking a flame. I looked up and there she was, perched on a metal bench with cigarette in hand, an angel of the night. The patron saint of the wronged and my savior, Elise Ferro.

"Want one?" she offered, hand outstretched, a pack of cigarettes in her palm. There weren't a lot of smokers at school and I'd only smoked one or two times before with Cameron and his friends, but none of them were regular smokers. "It calms me." She made it look so glamorous, the wisps of smoke framing her face against the dark of night.

"Thanks." I took one and she gave me a light. Leaning in, I got a closer look at her face in the glow of the flame and didn't recognize her. She had to be new, sitting out here in the bus bay, smoking alone.

"What an asshole," she said, eyes flicking in the direction where Cameron went. She'd been there the whole time, heard everything. Heat and mortification spread over my face. I wanted to crawl into bed and never get out, just sink under the covers and disappear forever. To a place where Cameron still loved me and there was no pain.

"Do you want to get out of here?" she asked, eyes softening when she saw my stricken expression.

I looked behind me at the double doors that led back to the dance, the loud music and happy faces, to Melody and all the people who knew me. They'd know I'd been dumped soon enough.

Blinking back tears, I nodded. *Please*, I wanted to say. Anywhere but here.

"I'm Elise, by the way," she said on our way to her car.

"Remy," I said, and her smile was warm.

Elise had long, inky hair, and even in the dark I could tell she was beautiful. Small mouth, delicate nose, high cheekbones. Thin, with wrists like twigs, she looked fragile, breakable. She had a single scar near her left eye, extending into her hair, a soft crease in her otherwise smooth skin. But it was the sharpness of her blue eyes that I noticed the most—every glance a spark, like they held a live current behind them, a glimmer of something thrilling and a little scary.

6.

Halfway down to the student parking lot, Elise and I tossed our cigarettes, watched the ash break off and the final glow extinguish.

"Which one's your car?"

"It's pink, you can't miss it."

"No," I whispered when we stopped in front of a powder-pink Cadillac convertible.

"*Yes.*"

"I didn't know they still made these things."

"I don't think they do. It was my grandmother's," Elise said, hopping in.

"You're kidding," I said, getting in next to her and dragging the seat belt across me. We sat on one long connected seat with no center console or cup holders to separate us. I'd only seen cars like this in movies or TV shows.

"She was a top saleswoman at Mary Kay or something, and this car was what they gave her one year." Elise shrugged and started the car.

"It's awesome," I said, running my fingers along its side.

"She's kind of a pain in the ass," Elise said, but she was smiling. "But she's tough and I like that."

"She?" I asked, confused. "The car?"

"Yep. This is the Pink Caddy," she announced with a small wave of her hand like she was introducing us. "So, where do you live?"

I began to direct her but stopped. "Are you hungry?" I asked, not wanting to go home, not wanting to be alone. We drove to get bubble tea and sat in her car staring out at an empty strip-mall parking lot.

"Do you want to talk about it?" Elise said. "About what happened with that guy."

"Not really." I looked down at my lap, thumb running over the edge of the cup lid, taking slow sips. "I don't know. I thought he was really happy. I thought we had a great summer. He said he could see us together forever." I wiped a tear away. "I guess not."

"Why was it all about him?" Elise asked, incredulous.

"Huh?"

"What about you?" she said, a spark of anger in her eyes. "Were you happy? Did you have a great summer? Did you love him? Did you want to be with him forever?"

"Of course," I said, though suddenly I wasn't sure anymore. "I think so."

She stayed silent.

"I don't know," I said finally. "I guess I was always just focused on him."

"So it *was* all about him. About what he needed, what he wanted, what he decided, wasn't it?"

"Well—" The thing was, I didn't care. I didn't care if everything was about him, I just wanted him to *stay*. I started to cry again, the tears dripping off the curve of my chin and splattering onto my dress.

Elise unbuckled her seat belt, reaching a hand out.

I put down my bubble tea and hid my face behind both hands, starting to sob. Pathetic.

"Come over here," Elise said, arm still extended. "Come over here and stop making dying whale noises."

A laugh bubbled through my sobs and I coughed. Scooting over, I leaned my head on her shoulder. She felt safe, even though we'd just met. She felt solid, like she'd stay if I asked.

"Boys are stupid," she said.

"Boys are stupid," I agreed.

"There was this guy at my old school. He *knew* I liked him, you know? And I think he enjoyed it, having someone fawn over

23

him, laugh at all his jokes, hang on to every word. He asked me to prom last year and I was just so happy. I bought this red dress, new shoes, new makeup. But then the day before, he texted me that he wasn't feeling well, that he was going to stay home.

"He lied, of course. The girl *he* liked had just been dumped by her boyfriend and was suddenly without a date for prom. And as soon as he heard, he dropped me, just like that. He didn't care if I'd bought a new dress, he didn't care if he'd broken my heart. He was casually cruel because he didn't need me anymore and I was now an inconvenience." She sounded bitter but also strong. This thing that had hurt her couldn't anymore, and nothing would penetrate the armor she'd forged for herself. I wanted to be like that. I wanted to stop hurting.

I turned my head to look up at Elise.

"Fuck boys," she said, rolling her eyes.

"Fuck boys," I agreed.

"Come on," she said, sitting up. "Let's go."

"Where?"

"I know just what you need."

7.

When we pulled into her driveway, I gawked at the house.

"You live in the Pink Mansion?" I said, still staring as we pulled to a stop.

"What?"

"The Pink Mansion. This was on my bus route to middle school and that's what we called it. I didn't know if anyone lived there, though we'd see gardeners once in a while." It was one of the last remaining estates in the area, the rest all carved up into gated subdivisions or remade into lush golf courses.

We went in and climbed all the way up to the attic. The house was dark and a little too quiet. The pink, soft in daylight, took on an almost sickly mauve. The grounds looked a little neglected, grass unmowed and weeds in the flowerbeds.

"My dad's at his girlfriend's house," Elise said by way of explanation, not saying anything else, just shrugging and turning away like she didn't want to talk about it. I wondered about her mom, where she was.

Elise walked around the attic through the clutter of boxes, ducking her head under low beams. "I know it's here somewhere."

I followed her around, sneezing from the dust, touching the odd Christmas ornament or picture frame.

"Who is this?" I asked, picking one up, wiping away a layer of grime from the glass. A black-and-white photo yellowed with age, it looked like a stock picture sold with frames, a happy family of three: mom and dad smiling down at a young girl with blond curls.

"Probably my mom and her parents." She didn't even glance over.

I examined the attic more closely. "When did you move here?"

"A few weeks ago, why?"

All the boxes were covered in dust and looked like they hadn't been disturbed in ages. The house as a whole didn't look like a family had just moved in. All the old boxes in the attic, all the nice furniture, perfectly placed like someone had been living there for years, not weeks.

"This was my grandparents' house," she explained after noticing my confusion. "My mom's gone, so it went to me when my grandmother died." It took a moment for that to sink in.

"Oh." I set the photo down. "I'm sorry."

"It's fine. Anyway. My grandfather *loved* fireworks. I know they've got to be here somewhere."

"Okay." I was still unsure of what she was planning, but it didn't bother me as long as I was with her. I helped her look through boxes, but eventually I got tired and sat on a box in my homecoming dress.

"Jackpot," Elise said, lifting up a string of firecrackers.

"Maybe we shouldn't do this," I said when we were about to get on the highway. My palms began to sweat, my heart beat faster at the thought of seeing Cameron again. I wanted to go home.

"It'll be cathartic," Elise said.

"I don't know."

She sped up on the highway. "Look, we can turn around, I can take the next exit and we can just go home. But is that what you really want? This guy made it all about him for—how long were you together?"

"Almost a year."

"A whole year! And then he just dumps you like that, at home-coming, and doesn't even offer to drive you home?" She began to wave an arm around as her voice rose. "Are you just going to, what, crawl into bed and call it a night? Curl up and cry yourself to sleep, all over some asshole?"

"No?"

"Or, are you going to do something about it? Do something you never thought you could do? Do something *he* would never think you could do? Something no one could imagine you doing?" She was breathless in her rage.

26

"Okay," I said after a moment. "Let's do it."

I directed her to his dorm and we parked in a loading zone. I'd been there with Cameron weeks ago, boxes of his things in the trunk of my car. I had kissed him goodbye, not wanting to let go.

"Ready?" Elise gestured grandly all around us at the buildings, the trees, the skies, twirling on the ball of one foot like a ballerina. She wasn't just magical. She was magic itself and I was completely under her spell.

"Okay."

"It's going to be loud," Elise whispered. "But don't get scared. They're asleep. And they're going to be confused and they're going to want to climb down from their bunk beds and come outside to see what's going on. We'll be long gone before they even think about calling the police." I nodded and we split up. I tied the firecrackers to one of the security bars and stood under them almost in a daze. I remember my racing heart, the matches slipping from my hands.

The firecrackers were supposed to go first, waking everyone before the show, but when I looked up, Elise was already heading toward me, which meant the fireworks were lit. I heard the first one shoot up into the sky, staring as it exploded, mesmerized at the *pop, pop, pop.*

It was loud enough to wake the entire building and all the buildings within five blocks.

"What are you doing?" Elise gripped my arm. She pulled out her lighter, struggled to get a flame, shook it. I'd never done anything like this before—getting payback. This was the kind of thing Cameron couldn't imagine I'd be capable of doing.

Never think I *could* do.

The third rocket whistled its ascent before bursting in the sky. "Wait," I said, taking the lighter from her and flipping it shut. Windows of the dorms closest to us shot the trees with slants of light, but Cameron's room was still dark.

"What are you doing?" Elise asked again. "We have to go." I knelt to the ground, fingers running across a single match. It was all I needed. I struck a weak flame and touched it to the fuse long enough for it to catch, burning my fingertips.

"Okay, let's go." We ran into the trees for cover but I stopped, turning back to see Cameron's window light up, to see the shock on his face as the firecrackers burst with the sound of gunfire.

That was the first prank. The beginning.

We laughed and whooped on the drive back and I felt alive in a way I hadn't in a long time, maybe ever. Looking over at Elise, her long hair whipping around in the wind, I remember thinking that this was the start of an adventure, the beginning of the rest of my life.

We were a forest fire, wild and full of rage. We were a galaxy unto ourselves, a million stars blazing bright.

Everything was possible then.

8.

Sitting in the car outside the police station, Vera and I rehearse what I'm going to say one last time. It's morning and I haven't gotten any sleep. After Vera drove me back to the house, I lay in bed staring at the ceiling and alternated between sobbing until I couldn't breathe and feeling completely numb, my mind wiped blank.

As Vera speaks, I stare out of the window, not really listening. I catch my face in the side mirror and I look awful, my eyes swollen and bloodshot, my skin splotchy and raw, my hair rough like straw from repeated washings. It's definitely been at least forty-eight hours since I last slept. My heart spasms wildly in my chest, pumping desperately, and I feel like I might faint.

"Here." Vera hands me a small cup of coffee.

I take a sip and let the hot bitterness hit my tongue. Jack loved coffee, drank it black by the gallon, called it his only vice. Fancy coffee shops, McDonald's, Starbucks, gas stations, it didn't matter as long as it was dark and hot.

"Remy?" Vera yanks me back. "Remember, keep it simple. It

29

shouldn't take longer than an hour, two tops. Just tell them what happened and stick to simple yes and no answers when they ask questions." Her voice sounds so far away, an echo of an echo of an echo. "Remy?"

"Hmm?" I say.

"Let's go over it one more time." We've been through this. Last night, and again an hour ago this morning.

My mind strays, unable to focus. I wonder where Elise is. I wonder where they took Jack's body, if his aunt and uncle have seen him, if his mother's landed yet. *Oh God*, I think, covering my eyes and pressing them closed. And Evan, Jack's cousin. Lola, his dog. More tears burn their way out of me, salt to the wound.

Doubt cuts through me and I close my eyes, trying to call the memories back. They dance before me, disjointed and unfocused once again. I am so tired and the coffee has only made me more jittery. I think about the night and the memory has a strange finish to it. Surreal, like I'm seeing myself from afar, like I'm watching a movie.

Me, sitting alone on the staircase, smothered in the silence of that big pink house. Jack coming through the door, saying, *Maybe it's better if I talk to her alone.* Elise saying, *Everything's going to be okay.* Her voice distant, fuzzy. I squeeze my eyes shut. She says something else, but I can't make it out, her voice warbled and distorted.

And then finally, the gunshots, still ringing in my ear.

"You said you were at the Pink Mansion and it was just you and Elise," Vera supplies helpfully.

I nod and swallow.

"And you were arguing over something," she continues. "What was it?"

"I don't remember. It was something stupid." It's what I said

30

last night, but I still watch for her reaction, see if she believes me. If I tell the police that they were arguing about the pranks, they'll find out all about them. I'm not trying to lie, but the truth is complicated and this is easier.

"Okay, then what happened?" Vera asks.

"Then I called Jack, and he came over. He said he'd talk to Elise alone. I went to my car and just as I was about to leave, I heard the gunshots." Now I'm the one who sounds far away, like the words are coming through the car speakers and I'm trapped here and forced to listen to them.

"Then?" she asks softly.

"Then I ran into the house and—" I choke on a dry sob. "I saw Jack and he was—" Another sob shakes my whole body and I can't keep it under control. "I called 9-1-1."

Vera hands me tissues and I wait for the tears to come but they don't. Instead, I'm heaving from the sobs, the coffee burning its way back up.

"Okay," Vera says. "It's going to be all right."

I ignore her and she leaves me alone. I stare out of the window as the sobs turn to hiccups. She parked in the far corner of the parking lot and all I can see are trees, their leaves moving with the wind. It's strangely hypnotic, numbing.

If I'd announced Jack's presence—

If I'd said goodbye to Elise first—

If I'd stayed—

Everything would be different.

I remember the first night Jack and I met, back in April, when I got on his motorcycle, hugged him tight, my right cheek pressed between his shoulder blades. We'd gone to the lake, and after,

31

we climbed a jungle gym in the park and stared at the stars. We smelled of earth and water, and he tangled our fingers together loosely. We were too big for the platform, had to lie with our knees bent like little pyramids, thighs resting against each other.

"Do you think there's anyone out there?" he asked me, eyes looking up.

"Out there?" I said, lifting my free hand to point at the sky.

"Sometimes it's easy to forget how little we are here. Stuck on this tiny rock revolving around a small star, stranded in the middle of the Milky Way. Sometimes it's easy to forget how big the universe is. How little it cares about the lives we live, how little any of it matters." His voice held no sadness, only an awestruck reverence. His eyes shone even in the dark, the light of the stars reflecting back out to me. He was so beautiful.

"Don't say that," I said, turning fully to face him. "Your life matters."

He turned too and smiled. We were only inches away from each other. I could feel his breath against my skin, warm and cool at the same time.

"Can I?" he asked softly, and I loved the way his eyelashes fluttered, like he was nervous, like I might say no.

"Yes," I said, and then he pressed his lips softly against mine and stole the air out of my lungs.

I don't think I've been breathing right ever since.

9.

It's cold inside of the station and I wrap my arms around myself tight. I pinch the sleeve buttons of my shirt around my wrists, running my thumb over and over them, popping one button in and out.

"It won't be long," Vera tells me, and I know she wants to reassure me, keep me calm.

My parents sit on the other side of her, Christian next to them. Our eyes meet briefly, and for a moment, I think I see real concern on his face, but I blink and he's already turned away. Everyone is dressed up, everyone is quiet, exhausted but nervous. I keep looking at the door, waiting to see Evan or Jack's mother show up.

Or Elise.

Or Jack himself, here to tell me it was just a nightmare and he was fine all along and that everything would be okay. Or that this was actually a prank gone too far and I was just too gullible.

"Do you need to use the restroom?" Vera asks me. "Now's the time."

With everyone's eyes on me, I just want to disappear, but I can't make myself move. Elise would never freeze up like this. She always knew what to do. Part of me longs for her to tell me how to feel, what to say. I need her, I need her.

But the thought of seeing her again twists my stomach and I feel sick.

"Remy?" Vera says, concerned.

I shake my head, *no*, too afraid of what will happen if Elise is waiting for me in the restroom, what I'll say if I see her now.

The heel of my foot taps and taps the floor, faster and faster, matching my heartbeat. My hands are unsteady, fingers vibrating.

Exhaustion and fear tighten their grip on me, but there's something else too, right under the surface, and it takes everything I have to keep it there.

I can't believe it. *I can't believe it.*

Jack's really gone. One last time, I think. Just one more time, let me hold him in my arms. It's all I ask, all I want.

But even as I whisper the words in my mind, I know it's a lie. If I had him in my arms again, I'd never, ever let go. As desperation claws at my throat, I shiver and shake—anything to keep a scream from escaping.

Knowing what happened doesn't help. Knowing it was an accident doesn't change the fact that he's gone and Elise is the one who took him from me.

I glance at the front doors, then down the hall. I know she's here somewhere. I can feel that invisible push and pull whenever she's near, like she is a star and I am a captured object.

If I had any sense of self-preservation I would cut the tether and leave her behind. I would follow the plan Vera has set out for me. Give my bare-bones statement. Tell my story in as few words as possible. Maintain my innocence and cooperate without giving them anything that could be used against me. Protect myself and only myself.

"You don't understand the trouble you're in," my mother said that morning before Vera arrived.

"This is the rest of your life we're talking about. Do you want to spend it in prison? Do you?" Dad said, but all I could think about was how I'd lost everything already. How I'd spend the rest of my life without Jack, without Elise. How impossible and lonely the future seemed.

"Do you know what it's like in prison? It isn't summer camp."

"You have to remember: You didn't do anything wrong. You weren't the one who pulled the trigger and you weren't anywhere near them when it happened."

"Don't do anything stupid out of some fucked-up sense of loyalty. You don't owe her anything. You don't owe anything to anyone but yourself." They were wrong, they didn't know. Some debts you can never repay. Some things you can spend your whole life making up for and it still won't be enough.

"And don't trust whatever the police say. Don't lie, but don't give them anything they can use against you later, and you don't know what that could be, so stick to short yes and no answers," my dad finished.

Maybe they'd watched too many police dramas, but my parents were relentless. They drove fear deep into my heart. Glancing at them now, I can see that they're terrified too.

And as much as I hate them, part of me knows I'm lucky to have people who worry about me, people who want to protect me.

But Elise is alone. And probably even more terrified. She doesn't have anyone to warn her about these things, to tell her what to do. To protect her.

She has no one.

Only me.

You don't owe her anything. But don't I?

It'd always been just the two of us from the moment we met. The night Elise collided into my life was the night the world burst ablaze with color. Cameron and all the boys before him were just distractions, someone to make me forget about my parents, my life. An escape.

No one else could ever compare. With Elise, I didn't need to forget. With Elise, I didn't have to hide my wounds, because she had them too. Because we both needed love and discovered we could give it to each other. Together we reinvented our pasts and were reborn soulmates. Complete, whole.

Elise takes the terrible things I've done, takes the ugliest parts of me, and loves me anyway. She always forgives me, no matter what.

I don't know if I deserve it.

My name is Remy.

I am seventeen years old.

This won't last forever.

It feels like I'm crumbling from the inside out, but I have to be strong, I have to hang on.

What doesn't kill you makes you stronger: Elise and I, we believed that, breathed it, lived by it. And I still believe—I *have* to believe—because there has to be meaning to all this pain and suffering.

There has to be a reason. There has to be.

"Remy?" Vera says, jolting me out of my thoughts, alarm in her voice.

Immediately, everyone's eyes are on me.

"What?" Then I feel it and touch a hand to my cheeks, pulling back to see my mother's foundation mixed with tears.

"Let's—" She looks from me to my family, hovering over me like hawks. "Let's go for a walk."

Outside, I dry my face and try to breathe. We're standing behind the station but I'm still skittish, afraid of what's waiting for me just around the corner.

"What's going to happen?" I ask. "To me, to Elise." *To us.*

Vera hesitates. "I can't say."

"What *could* happen?" I ask with a sniff.

"Well, it's hard to predict what'll happen, but the DA will decide whether or not to bring charges against her. And potentially you as well. If the evidence corroborates what you described, then they might decline to prosecute."

"Really?" I am breathless with shock as her words sink in.

"In Georgia, you have the right to shoot someone who enters your property without your permission."

"Like self-defense?" I cough, my throat raw from all the crying.

"Not quite. In a sense it's self-defense but the burden of proof is nowhere as high. You don't have to be in imminent danger. You just have to *feel* threatened." She's careful to keep her voice neutral, steady, but I can sense she disagrees with the law.

My head spins and I have to lean against the wall for support. Though scratchy and rough, the brick wall is cool to the touch and I want to press my cheek to it. I think about last night, close my eyes. I can see Elise out on the balcony still. She turns with heavy shoulders and walks back inside. Then she hears footsteps, sees the shape of a man approaching her in the dark, sees *her father* approaching her and doesn't think, can't think. Just points and shoots.

Her fear is palpable to me even now, even though I wasn't there. I take a shuddering breath and cough again.

"It's time," Vera says, checking her phone. "Are you ready?"

I'll never be ready, but I have no choice.

"Listen, Remy." Vera looks serious, grim even, as we begin the walk back. "What you say now is important, do you understand?"

I nod, my heart racing. Everything depends on me. It feels like I hold both of our lives in my hands, the weight of it threatening to pull me under.

"You need to worry about yourself right now," she says. "Don't worry about your friend or what might happen. Just focus on what you're going to say."

"But they could choose not to prosecute?" I ask, voice low. I feel weak, like my legs could collapse at any moment. Elise was always the strong one of the two of us. She was always the one who knew what to do, who had answers. But now it's up to me.

"It depends," Vera says as we're about to round the corner to the main lobby where my family waits. She stops, places a firm hand on my shoulder. "It'll depend on what the evidence suggests. It'll depend on a lot of different factors—the strength of that evidence, if they can establish not just means but motive, public perception of the case, even. Prosecutors only like to try cases they think they'll win, which means they're very cautious about which cases they try. So it'll depend on a lot of things."

"Like what I say?"

Vera frowns, and I can tell my question doesn't sit well with her. "Just stick to the truth, okay? Keep it simple, like we talked about. Tell them what you told me last night." She looks like she has more to say but then someone turns the corner, almost colliding with us.

"There you are," the stranger says. "I'm Detective Sloane Ward."

I feel like I'm going to throw up.

"We're ready for you now," the detective says, her smile quick, a flash of teeth.

10.

The camera behind Detective Ward is pointed right at me, its red dot blinking steadily. I try to stamp out my growing panic but I can't—it's wild and burning through me like poison. My chest squeezes unbearably and I can't breathe.

I tear my gaze away from the blinking light to focus on the person in front of me. A middle-aged white woman, all business, lips flattened into a severe line, a permanent crease between her eyebrows. She's flipping through a thin file, pen stuck behind her ear, frizzy brown curls brushing her shoulders. Her white dress shirt is crisp underneath a royal blue cardigan. She wears a simple gold wedding band. Her nails are filed down, neat but bare. Without makeup or flashy jewelry, she doesn't look like she belongs in a town like Lyndens Creek—she's different, an outsider. Maybe she'd understand us. I press my palms against my knees, rub them dry. Vera glances at me, concerned.

I think about everything I'm going to say and everything I can't say. The words I practiced with Vera are right there, fresh on my mind: *Elise and I were at her house. Elise and I were arguing but I don't remember why. We separated and I called Jack. He came over and said he'd talk to Elise alone. I went to my car and was about to leave when I heard the gunshots.*

"Okay, Katherine," Detective Ward begins, and it's jarring to hear my own first name. It feels like she's talking to someone else. I never liked it and fought with Mom to go by my middle name, and now I can't help but think *Katherine* belongs to another life, and maybe it does. To someone like Christian, obedient and loved.

"She goes by Remy," Vera corrects gently.

"Oh. Okay, Remy," she starts again. "I'm going to ask you some questions and I want you to answer them to the best of your ability, okay? This isn't like in the movies or on TV. You're not in any trouble. It's not an interrogation," she says, even though it feels like one. "I'm going to read you your rights, but it's just a casual conversation, really."

As she delivers the same short speech Vera did, my gaze shifts back to the blinking red light.

The detective notices. "Don't worry about that. It's there to make sure we don't miss anything and everything we talk about is aboveboard."

"Okay," I say, my voice barely higher than a whisper. My throat is still scratchy. I cough, and it makes it worse.

"You all right?" Detective Ward asks as I try to clear my throat. She's trying to sound warm, to make me think she actually cares. When I manage to nod, she moves on: "Please state your name."

I open my mouth but nothing comes out. The room suddenly feels too small, like it's closing in on me. The light is too bright, the air too cold. My heart rattles against my rib cage, urging me to run, and all I can think about is making it out of this alive.

This won't last forever.

It helps, and I take a deep breath before I speak: "My name is Katherine Remy Tsai. Everyone calls me Remy."

"Good. See? Nothing to worry about," she says, her smile purposefully friendly. "How old are you, Remy?"

"Seventeen."

"When's your birthday?"

"November nineteenth."

"Can you tell me what happened last night?"

Behind Detective Ward and the camera is just a wall. No one-way mirror like on TV shows, just concrete cinder blocks painted in a thick, glossy white. It reminds me of the walls at school, but I am acutely aware that I'm no longer in a classroom.

When I remain frozen, unable to answer, Vera steps in.

"Can we start with simpler questions?" she asks.

Detective Ward doesn't argue. "Did you know that your friend had a gun? Or where she might've gotten it?" she asks.

I was there when she found it in the attic filled with all of her grandparents' things. *Don't lie, but don't give the police anything they can use against you.* "I think it was her grandfather's," I say, and it's the truth.

"Really," she says, putting her pen down. "Do you know where the gun is now or where it could be?" Detective Ward leans forward, elbows on the table, fingers coming together to form a peak.

"You don't know where the gun is right now?" I ask, shocked. After Jack had been shot, the last thing I would've paid attention to was the gun and what Elise did with it. Before Detective Ward told me it was missing, I just assumed the police had it.

"No, we don't," she says, eyes so piercing that I flinch. It feels like I'm trapped in some kind of game but I don't understand the rules.

"I don't know," I say, still in shock. For a moment I'm scared of what this means, that it's still out there, the revolver that belonged to Elise's grandfather, but then I think maybe they just haven't found it yet, that it was lost in the chaos of last night and probably under a couch or TV stand.

"What can you tell me about last night? Anything at all." Ward frowns, growing impatient. "Think about Jack," she says like I've forgotten about him, like I need to be reminded of the wound in my chest.

I do think about him, I want to scream. I'm always thinking about him. I wish he were here, I wish I could see him again. I loved him. I love him still.

Think about Jack.

"I loved him," I choke out, and it's all I can say as tears stream down my face.

But I feel fear closing in. It spreads to every inch of my body until there's no room for the love that I have for Jack. It hijacks my brain until I can't breathe, until I can't think about anything other than survival.

It feels like I'm dying.

"Let me tell you what I think happened," Detective Ward says, ignoring my tears. "I think this was a romantic entanglement that went sideways." Her voice is matter-of-fact, almost soothing in its neutrality. "The only question in these situations is who played what role. We know Elise was the shooter. We know Jack was the victim. What were you?"

Her words coil around me. For a moment, I think the earth is quaking, but it's just me shaking uncontrollably in my hard plastic chair.

"There's no need for any aggression," Vera intervenes. "We came in here to cooperate."

Detective Ward takes a pause, looking down at her notes, giving me a moment to dry my eyes. My hands are coated in streaks of my mother's foundation, my mask coming undone.

When I've quieted, she leans in even closer and changes the subject. "Tell me about Elise."

"What do you want to know?" I say.

"Was she ever violent around you?"

"What?" I don't like the way she's talking to me. I don't like what she's implying.

"To your knowledge, has she ever hurt anyone before?"

"No!" My mind screams with panic. She's asking leading ques-

42

tions, like she's already decided what kind of person Elise is and what really happened last night.

"Has she ever hurt *you*?"

"No! Of course not," I say.

She examines me and leans back, clasped hands resting on her lap now. "Sometimes we think we know someone and we think the world of them, but maybe they're not always what they seem. You never really know what someone's capable of."

"Elise would never do something to hurt anyone. I know she didn't murder Jack because I was there." The words fly out of me before I can stop them.

The entire room quiets. There's just the sound of the air-conditioning clicking on, the sharp cold hitting the back of my neck.

What did I just say?

"You were there," Detective Ward repeats slowly.

What have I just done?

"Wait," Vera says, confusion and panic in her eyes.

"Are you certain? Are you sure that's the statement you want to give?" she says as Vera interjects again. She wants some time with me, alone.

"We'll answer any questions you have but Remy just lost her boyfriend and hasn't slept. She needs a minute." Vera doesn't wait for an answer. She takes me by the wrist and pulls me down the hall to the restroom.

Splashing cold water on my face, I watch as the rest of my makeup runs down the drain. War paint, that's what Mom called it once, like going to work required battledress. She always looked perfect, not a hair out of place, face bright and never tired. Appearances always mattered more to her than anything else.

43

Looking up, I stare at the girl I see in the mirror. She looks wrecked, eyes swollen, skin patchy and rough. She looks like she went into battle and lost everything.

Why did I say I was there? I splash more water on my face, too ashamed to look at myself anymore.

"Remy," Vera says once I've turned the water off. "We need to talk."

I dry my face, lean on the sink with both hands against the counter.

"You told me you *weren't* there."

At the heart of every good lie is the truth, that's what Elise told me once. *The best lies are at least half-true,* she said, but what if she had it wrong? What if it was the other way around? What if it was the truth that required a lie? Not the facts but the truth, and the truth is that it was all a horrible accident.

I collapse to my knees, fingers still gripping the edge of the sink, head heavy.

"Remy!" Vera tries to catch me but she's too late.

Letting go of the counter, I ball up into myself like I've been punched in the gut. It becomes more and more difficult to breathe. I'm gasping for air until I vomit onto the floor, my morning coffee coming up bitter and burning.

"Oh my God," Vera says, but her voice barely reaches me. She leaves my side to return with fistfuls of paper towels.

Despite the coughing and choking, I feel strangely better. Empty, but lighter, like I have a new sense of clarity. I know what I have to do, how I'll save us. And for the first time, I have direction.

I wasn't there but if that's what I need to say to make sure they know the truth—that Elise would never have killed Jack if she'd known it was him—then I'll say it. I'll lie, but only so they'll know the truth.

I stagger up and hold on to the nearest wall to steady myself. Vera is saying something but it's hard for me to hear.

Finally, her voice comes into focus. "You said you weren't there," she says again.

"I'm sorry," I whisper.

"Why didn't you just tell me?" she asks, not angry, just perplexed, and I'm relieved. "You know I'm on your side, right?"

"I'm sorry," I say again, and I am but only for the trouble it's causing her now, not the lie.

"Were you just scared to tell me?" she asks.

I nod.

"So you *were* there," she says. "And you saw all of it."

Jack's gone, but Elise is still here.

"Remy?"

I nod again, struggling to find my voice. I've already lost him, I don't want to lose her.

"But everything else is true," she says, searching my face.

"Yes," I manage to say. I wash my hands, watch them shake under the water. After I wipe my face, I look at myself once more. There's no war paint, no mask to hide behind. This is who I am. I know what I have to do.

"We don't have to do this right now," Vera says. "We can ask to reschedule, come back tomorrow."

"No. I'm okay," I tell her, and though I'm not sure either of us believes that, she sees the determination in my eyes and relents, leading me back.

Detective Ward isn't in the room when we return. Vera keeps

asking me if I'm okay, telling me that we really could come back tomorrow, but I just shake my head. I'm exhausted and shivering and in pain, but if I don't do this now, I'll lose my nerve. I always wanted to be more like Elise, who never second-guessed herself. I thought it was pure confidence, maybe even arrogance, but that wasn't it. She simply trusted herself and that's what I have to do now, trust myself. Trust her.

Taking a deep breath, I sit down at the table and press my palms against the cool surface. When Detective Ward finally comes back, she pauses at the door, leaning against the frame. "Ready?" she asks, one eyebrow raised. I nod. Detective Ward turns on the camera and sits down in front of me, crossing her legs, examining me. "Why don't we start over at the beginning."

Is it really lying if it's in service of the truth? The truth is complicated, this lie is simpler. But both roads end in the same destination: This was an accident, pure and simple. One is long and winding, the other is a straighter line.

Jack, I think, would understand. He didn't believe in revenge, an eye for an eye, and I can't imagine that the Jack I knew would want Elise to go to prison for the rest of her life for a mistake— something that couldn't have been her fault.

I remember what he said to me once: "You're still here, you've survived so far, and you'll survive this, too, and whatever else comes your way." I'm just trying to survive. I'm just trying to hold myself together.

The camera glares at me, its red light blinking steadily, a time bomb counting off the seconds before detonation. I stare back, unflinching.

I can't save him, but maybe, just maybe, I can save her.

11.

The night of homecoming, Elise pulled up to my house in the early hours of Sunday morning, the windows dark, everyone asleep. We were still giggling in the Pink Caddy, and feeling a little starstruck, I didn't want to leave her side.

I felt light, like I was floating, like I could fly. Her spark was contagious, brighter than the fireworks we'd set off earlier.

"Come on," I whispered, leading Elise around the house, down to the backyard. We sat by my pool to smoke, lighting matches and tossing them into the water.

When the night grew too cold, we ducked into the basement for blankets, and that was when I heard their voices upstairs.

"You can't be fucking serious!" my mom screamed. "How dumb do you think I am?"

"It happened one time. You're never going to let it go. One time and you're never going to forgive me, are you?" he shouted back.

I looked at Elise and panicked. Coming back here was a bad

idea. All the lights were off—I thought they were asleep or I would never have let Elise stay.

"You promised it would be different," she said, and I could tell she'd been crying. I almost felt bad for her but she didn't deserve my sympathy, not after all the things she'd said and done.

"It *is* different," he said. "It's been different. I'm different. You're the one who hasn't changed. You're the only one stuck in the past."

"Fuck you, don't lie to me! Just. Don't."

She was disdain, and he, resentment. The things they argued about changed, but the script remained the same.

Angry stomps. A frustrated growl from Mom. Glass shattered against the floor.

I felt a tug on my wrist and was surprised when I turned to see Elise. Shame burned through me. They aren't usually like this, I wanted to say, the lie locked and loaded. Everything's fine, everything's fine, I wanted to tell her.

I'm normal, I'm happy, I'm like everyone else. That's what I wanted people to see, what I allowed them to see.

By this point, Christian and I were both experts at keeping our two lives separate. The unspoken rules were simple: always hang out at other people's houses and avoid bringing friends home, especially if we knew they'd be there.

I hadn't even let Cameron pick me up unless they were both at work. Melody lived on the other side of town, but when we were kids I went to her house almost every afternoon and her mom or dad would drive me home in the evening.

Cameron had no idea, and while Melody may have suspected something was wrong, she never explicitly said anything.

A slipup, that's what it was. Bad luck that we went inside when we did. They weren't supposed to be awake. And now someone had glimpsed the truth about them. About me.

Elise's expression was unreadable. Our eyes locked and I winced at the sound of more glasses and plates being shattered above us, punctuating angry screams that tore through the house. I wondered if Christian was home, if he was upstairs in his room, headphones squeezed on tight in the dark. If it even bothered him anymore or if he was now immune, safe in the knowledge he'd always have Mom, protected by the only person who had any real power in this family.

"Are they always like this?" she asked.

Elise's eyes were kind. Soft, warm. A safe harbor.

"Come on," she said, two fingers still hooked around my wrist. "Let's go."

"Go where?" I said, feet heavy, limbs frozen. I wanted to disappear, hide in my room, crawl into my closet until the storm ended. I wanted to escape Elise's searching gaze.

"To my house."

"No, it's okay." But I did want to go with her. I wanted to escape that house. Though maybe what I wanted to escape most was that life.

"I think you like it," my mother said upstairs, breath hitching. "I think you like me like this. Weak, powerless. Begging."

"You have all the power," my father said. "You've always had all the power."

"Don't you dare leave!" she commanded, but I heard the door slam and the car start.

Elise squeezed my wrist.

"I don't have any of my things." I looked up at the ceiling in the direction of destruction and madness. I wanted her to leave but I couldn't stand the thought of being alone.

"I have clothes. And a spare toothbrush."

"Okay," I finally said.

She put an arm around me, lightly, as if she didn't want to scare me away. As if I were fragile, and I guess I was. As if I needed protection, and I guess I did.

I followed her out and she pulled the door closed silently behind us. Together we slipped away into the night.

12.

After we left my house that night, Elise never brought up what she'd witnessed. She didn't ask about my parents, or look at me the way Melody would whenever I deflected questions about my family, like she was worried about me, like maybe she pitied me.

That's what I loved the most about Elise from those first days. She made me feel safe. She understood what it was like, having to keep part of yourself hidden.

At school, we discovered we only had two classes together. I gravitated toward her in both and sat next to her, sharing small, secret smiles. We walked to lunch together after fourth period World History and I tugged her along to Melody's table.

"This is Elise," I said, sitting down and dropping my back-pack onto the floor. "She just moved here." I introduced Elise to Melody and two other friends, Danielle and Anjali. They were really Melody's friends, and the three of them did almost every-thing together—all honors and APs, Speech and Debate, soccer team, National Honor Society.

"Hey," Melody said. Danielle and Anjali glanced up with polite smiles.

They were nice, always trying to include me in everything they did, but I wasn't really like them. I didn't get straight As, or give up my Saturdays to teach little kids how to read. No one ever said it, but we all knew they kept me around because of Melody, and Melody kept me around because of how long we'd known each other.

The only two Asians in kindergarten, we glommed onto each other and became best friends. But over the years, our interests diverged. Melody had still never been kissed; Cameron was my third boyfriend. Melody got special permission to take AP Chemistry early; I was in only two honors classes and had racked up a grand total of zero APs.

Even though our school system grew more diverse over the years and we were no longer the only Asians in class, Melody was loyal and stubborn, as persistent in her friendships as she was with building her resume, and that, along with our shared history as outsiders, was why I liked her.

"So where are you from?" Mel asked Elise.

"Chattanooga," she answered.

"Oh, I think I've been once," Danielle said. "The Tennessee Aquarium's there, right?"

"Yep," Elise said, biting into an apple.

"Do you miss it? Your old school, your friends?" Anjali asked, and Elise just shrugged.

"Did your parents get transferred for work?" Danielle said.

"Something like that."

It went on for a while—polite questions and short answers. I grew nervous, unsure why Elise was so reserved. She wasn't rude, just quiet, like she didn't like all this attention on her. She only seemed to relax when the others moved on, shooting me a small smile that didn't quite reach her eyes as Melody, Anjali, and Danielle talked about a bake sale they were organizing for that Thursday.

By the end of lunch, Melody had pushed me into baking muffin tops and asked Elise to contribute too.

"I'm not really good at that kind of stuff," Elise said.

"Oh, I'm not good at that kind of stuff either," Melody said, even though that was a lie. For each of our birthdays she'd bake our favorites: coconut cake for me, brownies for Anjali, and red velvet cupcakes for Danielle. And she'd do it all *from scratch*.

"I just get mix or frozen cookie dough," she continued, waving Elise's concerns aside.

"I'd burn them," Elise said with a forced laugh. I looked between the two of them, just trying to think of a way to prevent a fight over some stupid cookies.

"I could come over and help Wednesday after school if you want," Melody offered, still oblivious. I knew they were different, but I still wanted Elise to like her, or at least give her a chance. Though I think I was also secretly impressed—most people had a hard time saying no to Melody when she was this determined, but not Elise.

"No, thank you," Elise said firmly, not making an excuse this time. Melody frowned in confusion.

"But—" she began to protest.

"I can do cookies too," I said, trying to defuse the situation. "If you want."

Melody stared at Elise's stoic expression and answered me without looking over. "Sure, I guess."

After lunch, as Melody and I walked to honors language arts, the one class we still shared, she asked how I'd met Elise.

"Why?" I said.

"Just wondering." She adjusted her backpack straps.

"At homecoming." Cameron had broken up with me only a couple days ago and I hadn't had a chance to tell her yet, so I didn't elaborate.

"So that's where you were," she said. "I texted but you never got back to me."

"Sorry," I said. "She gave me a ride home." That was technically true. There were just a few detours.

Melody paused outside of our classroom, tapping her chin as she considered this.

"Why?" I asked.

"No reason. She's just a little weird."

"Because she didn't want to help with the bake sale? Come on, Mel," I said. Elise hadn't acted weird, she just didn't want to give in to Melody's demands.

"No, it's not that," she said. "I don't know, I tried so hard to talk to her and she just seemed so . . ."

"Yes?" I said as the one-minute warning bell went off.

Melody finally settled on a word: "Cold."

"What?" Maybe she'd been a little standoffish at lunch, but Elise wasn't cold. She'd been there for me even though we were just strangers.

"Yeah, that's it. She seemed cold."

"Okay, so not wanting to bake cookies makes her cold?" I said, my irritation growing.

"No, it's not about the cookies."

"Miss Tsai, Miss Moon," Mr. Hunter called out to us in the hall. "Are you planning on joining us today?"

"Sorry," Melody said, rushing inside.

Even after class, Melody didn't want to let it go. She seemed genuinely confused, like she'd never encountered anyone like Elise.

"Why didn't she want to answer any of our questions?" she asked as we walked to our lockers. "It was just weird. That's all I'm saying."

I didn't know what to say because I wondered the same thing. Elise hadn't minded the attention two days ago when we were setting off firecrackers outside Cameron's window.

Elise was a mystery, but I liked that about her.

I liked that she didn't care about fitting in, that she kept parts of herself locked away. That she made being different look so easy.

13.

With little effort, Elise could've had her pick of friends. She was beautiful and electric, fearless and uncompromising. She didn't follow, she didn't act like anyone else I knew.

Elise was everything I ever wanted to be.

She dropped by our lunch table a couple times after that but seemed to like floating better, changing tables often, sitting in the senior section one day and with the gamers the next. But soon she had her own table, and was gathering people up like strays. Lance Krasinski, who had bright red hair and wore ironic T-shirts that said things like CECI N'EST PAS UNE PIPE; Julie Adichie, who was the captain of Science Olympiad and wore her hair cropped; Mark Ransom, who modeled for department store catalogs on the weekend and rode a Vespa to school; Jae Park, who once performed magic tricks on *Good Morning America* when he was in middle school.

And for a little while I thought maybe that was it for Elise and me. One bright, explosive night of abandon, a comet lighting up my sky for a brief moment.

I couldn't keep the news about Cameron from Melody forever. When I told her later that week, we went to her house and marathoned *Law and Order: SVU*, her favorite show, and got sick eating an entire carton of ice cream. Everything Mel knew about love she learned from the movies, including the parts about how to handle breakups—bingeing on ice cream and TV. It made talking to her about it difficult. I never knew how she'd react.

She never liked Cameron, but then again, she never liked any of the guys I liked. Whenever I tried to talk to her about them, she'd end up lecturing me about how immature high school boys were and how they weren't worth the distraction.

So I learned to keep most of it to myself rather than risk more I-told-you-so's from her. And of course I never told her the rest of the story, the fireworks and the surge of satisfaction I experienced when I saw that look of genuine fear on Cameron's face. It felt like a secret, and Melody would never understand. I could just hear the panic in her voice: *But that's illegal.*

The call came late Friday night. I was surprised when I saw her name lighting up the screen of my phone. "Hey," I said, my heart skipping a beat.

"So here's the plan," Elise said without preamble. "Can you get some peanut butter and go to the address I just texted you?"

"What?" I looked at my phone and saw her message. "Why?"

"You'll see."

I didn't hesitate, grabbing the peanut butter out of the cupboard and jogging to my car, easing it out of the driveway with the headlights off to avoid waking anyone up. I had no idea what I was doing or why. I wasn't really sure if she'd even be there when I arrived, but I had to find out. Whatever it was, I knew it'd be fun and thrilling, a hammer to break the monotony of school, sleep, repeat.

I pulled in behind a white Camry parked up the street from the address Elise sent. She and a few others stood by the car in dark clothes, huddling over something.

"Hey," I said as I walked up to them, my heart racing.

"Remy!" Elise gasped, and enveloped me in a tight hug like we were the best of friends. We hadn't talked much lately, so I was surprised, but I was also secretly thrilled to see her so excited by my arrival. Even though we weren't best friends, it felt like we *could* be someday. "Did you bring the PB?" she asked once we separated.

Nodding, I held up the jar. "I wasn't sure how much you needed. If you want, I can go get some more," I said, ready to do anything for her.

"No, this is perfect," she said with a big smile that lit up her eyes before turning to introduce me to Julie, Mark, and Jae. I knew *of* them, but I'd never exchanged more than two words with Julie or Mark, and Jae was a junior, so we'd never even had a class together. "Lance's home with the flu. Thanks for helping us out—I knew you'd come," she said like I'd saved the day.

"Of course," I said, a little dizzy with anticipation. "What are we doing?" Then I noticed the thing they'd all been hovering over, a small box Julie held gingerly. When everyone quieted down, I could hear light scratching and tiny squeaks. "Is that—"

"Mice?" Elise finished for me. "Yes, and that's what we need the peanut butter for."

I looked at her in confusion.

"I told them what we'd done to Cameron," she said, and I felt surprisingly hurt. I thought it was our secret, I thought that night belonged only to us. "Jae just found out his girlfriend, Dana, was sleeping with his best friend."

"Oh shit," I said before glancing up to see his jaws clench. Anger was coming off his body in waves. He was clearly hurting, just like I was homecoming night, and Elise was here to fix it—to right a wrong.

"I don't have any more firecrackers, but I had another idea," she said, that familiar glint in her eye.

Dana Wolfert occupied the basement suite of her house. We quietly marched around to her backyard and tried the door. It was locked. Then the four of them fanned out, trying the windows one by one. I stayed close to Elise, unsure of what we'd do if we couldn't get in.

"This one's open," Elise whispered. "Thank God, or we would've had to break a window."

That surprised me, but I remained quiet because I didn't think she would've actually broken into the house for something as silly as a prank. But then I saw that spark of determination in her eyes and wasn't so sure anymore. It didn't scare me though. I found her dedication kind of romantic, that she'd be willing to risk getting in trouble for her friends.

Inside, Elise took on the riskiest job, smearing peanut butter around Dana's bed, her pillows, her nightstand.

"Dana sleeps like the dead," Jae had assured us.

Mark stood by the stairs to keep watch for any movement above while Julie pulled out a small bottle of cooking oil and coated all the doorknobs. Then Jae dealt the final blow, walking in with the box of mice and tearing it open just enough for the mice to climb out. Then they closed the door behind them and ran, trying to stifle their laughter.

"Are you sure she's going to wake up?" Elise asked Jae when they were outside.

"Fuck," he said. "I don't know."

Dana answered the question with a terrifying, high-pitched scream. The mice must've found the peanut butter—and her.

"Oh my God," Julie said, eyes wide, hand covering her mouth in an attempt to keep from laughing.

"Run, run, run," Elise whispered sharply, taking me by the wrist. Once we got to the cars, she said, "You guys go ahead. It's too crammed with all of us. Remy can drive me home." I looked at her in surprise, so happy that we'd be alone, even if it was just for a car ride.

More screams pierced the night. Lights began to flood the street.

"Shit, guys, we have to go," Mark said, jumping in the driver's seat. The others scrambled in and tore out of the neighborhood.

"Are we following them?" I asked, frantically starting the car.

"Nah," Elise said, nonchalant. "I'll meet up with them later."

"Oh." I slowed down.

"But I don't want to go home yet," she said as we came to a stoplight. "Let's go to your house."

"I don't know," I said, worried about my parents and what they might do. Then I remembered that Mom was away at a conference. "Yeah, okay."

At my house, Elise and I went straight to the pool. We stretched out on loungers, the weather-resistant fabric rough against my skin, and she lit up a cigarette for each of us.

"Why'd you call me? You didn't need me," I said. In the rush of the moment, I was only focused on what we were doing, but now that we were alone, I was curious.

"Yes, we did! You brought the peanut butter. It wouldn't have worked without the peanut butter," she said, shooting me a sleepy smile.

"Anyone else could've brought the peanut butter." I only kept pushing because I was secretly hoping that what she wanted wasn't the peanut butter but *me*.

"You were our lookout! You were crucial to the entire operation, and I won't let you minimize your importance," she said, sliding off of her lounger and scooting onto mine. "Also, I missed you."

Hearing those words thrilled me. "You did? Why didn't you just—" Text? Call? Sit with me at lunch?

She sighed. "You're always with Melody and it's obvious she doesn't like me."

"No, that's not true!" I said, but it was.

Elise rolled her eyes. "Yeah, okay."

"She just doesn't know you," I said, slinging an arm around her. It was so easy, slipping back into how we were that first night, like no time had passed. "I think you should give her another chance. You guys have a lot of things in common." I didn't want to lose Elise again, but I didn't want to hurt Melody either.

Elise raised an eyebrow. "We have a lot in common? I'd rather die than spend an evening baking stuff and then setting up a table in the cafeteria to sell crappy cookies."

"One, Melody's cookies are amazing. Two, she isn't like that all the time. She can be fun. And three, she thinks boys are stupid too, just like you do."

She sighed again, dramatically, then began to fiddle with her lighter, flipping it open and closed, sparking a flame and letting the wind blow it out.

"Fine, whatever. But if she tries to get me to bake something again, I'm out."

"Okay," I said, relieved. "I'll let her know."

Elise laughed lightly, resting her head against my shoulder and closing her eyes.

14.

I turned seventeen in Elise's pink convertible, the two of us in the front seat, my feet propped up on the dashboard, her legs hanging over the driver's-side door, our eyes staring up at the dark sky.

Melody had brought cake to school on Friday and we were going to have a sleepover at her house, as was our tradition. But when Elise asked if I was free, I canceled on her at the last minute, lying about a stomachache. I'd been doing that a lot lately, even though I wasn't *trying* to avoid Mel. Elise joined us for lunch more often but they remained cordial at best.

"I don't get her," Melody told me once, and I almost laughed because that was exactly how Elise felt about her.

"She's fun," I'd said, and left it at that.

It wasn't that I didn't want to spend time with Mel anymore. I just found myself saying yes to Elise more, gravitating toward her, spinning in her orbit.

We were on our second cigarette when midnight came for me. A new year, a new me.

"Happy birthday," Elise said, tapping her ashes over the car door. "Welcome to seventeen."

"I hate birthdays," I said, wrapping my jacket around me tighter. The wind chilled my fingers but I didn't want to pull the top over us and lose the stars.

"Why?" She turned to me, curious.

"Bad memories." When I turned five, my parents lost me inside a department store. When I turned nine, my dad had been gone for weeks and forgot to call. When I turned thirteen, no one remembered until early December.

But although most of my birthdays were forgettable at best and traumatizing at worst, not all were like that. One of my favorite memories was from my sixth birthday, when my parents got me a bike. Electric blue with a shiny bell and wire basket—it was love at first sight.

The day started off horribly. That morning, Dad said he had to go into the office even though it was the weekend, leaving Mom in charge of teaching me. But she didn't believe in training wheels, on bicycles or in life, which meant I quickly racked up an impressive array of scrapes on my knees and elbows, hands and shins.

"I don't understand," Mom said after I crashed for the fifth time. "Christian picked it up right away." I wanted to cry but I knew she'd only yell at me for it, and say something about how crying was a weakness. She believed that as a girl, I shouldn't cry *especially* because that was what people expected from me.

"I'm sorry" was all I said.

Things were no better when Dad emerged from the house in a crisp shirt and slacks, hair gelled back, his laptop bag over his shoulder.

"Christian practically taught himself," Mom said, helping me up yet again.

"Hey, come on," Dad said, walking over to us.

"Stay out of it, Stephen," she said, straightening the bike. "Don't you have to go?" She didn't bother glancing back at him. I looked between them, terrified another fight was about to erupt.

Dad didn't answer, just watched as Mom sent me down our driveway yet again. By then I'd learned to stay close to the lawn, and Dad saw me land on the grass a couple more times before he intervened again.

"Why don't I go to the store on my way home later and pick up some training wheels?" he offered. "We can try again tonight."

I would've liked that, but Mom said no. "I told you to stay out of it."

"You're not making this fun—it's her birthday. All she's doing is falling and hurting herself over and over."

"She has to learn on her own. She's got to toughen up. She's not always going to have the option of training wheels, then what?"

"She's six," he said, shaking his head. "She should be having fun."

I looked from one to the other, wishing I could just disappear. Or better yet, be like Christian. They never fought because of Christian. Mom was right: He was always fine on his own and he never needed training wheels.

"Fine, you want to do this, go right ahead." Then she went inside, leaving the two of us staring at each other in mild surprise. Mom didn't give in often, if ever. Maybe she felt bad for yelling at me on my birthday. Or maybe she was just tired. Of me.

Dad called in sick, bought a set of training wheels, and spent the day teaching me how to ride a bike.

"You're getting the hang of it," he told me in the afternoon when we were done, and I could tell that he meant it.

I felt so good, being out of Mom's ice storm and basking in the warmth of his praise.

"Did Christian really do this without training wheels?" I couldn't stop myself from asking. It was always there—*he* was always there, two steps ahead of me, and I was always chasing him.

"I don't remember," he said. "I really don't."

I didn't believe him. Christian was a prodigy, always faster, better.

"Your mom—" He broke off, sighing. "Listen to me, Remy. None of that matters. What Christian did or didn't do isn't important. And besides, this just means we get to spend more time together, right?"

I hadn't thought of it that way, hadn't thought he'd want to spend time with me.

"We'll do this every day until you win the Tour de France," he said, shooting me a wink.

"What's that?"

His laughter was infectious. "Just a silly joke. But we'll do this every day until you're the best bicyclist in the neighborhood," he promised.

"Better than Christian?" I asked, not believing him.

"The best." By the end of the week, the training wheels were off. I didn't need them anymore, but that didn't mean I didn't need my dad anymore.

"I love birthdays," Elise said, bringing me back to the Cadillac and the stars. "It always means one year closer to freedom." She stretched her arms overhead in an exaggerated yawn.

"True," I said. "I can't wait until I'm out of that house." Away from my parents and their path of destruction. I'd leave and never look back.

"What will you do? Where will you go?" Elise asked, flicking her cigarette away, a burning streak of orange against the night.

I released a stream of smoke, watched it mark the air. "I don't know. I just want to get out."

"Come on," she said, her eyes on me. "Use your imagination."

"I guess I'd be in college." I shrugged, tossing my cigarette as well. I watched it hit the pavement, its spark bursting, then dying.

"Really? That's it?" Elise said, shaking her head in disbelief, her dark hair brushing her face softly. "What about after?"

"Whatever people do after college. Get a job or something." Melody was always talking about which schools were on her list, how she was going to be a doctor. I'd never thought that far ahead. I didn't know what kind of life I'd have. I just knew there was another one out there waiting for me. A Remy Tsai I'd step into once I left home. Someone who'd know what to do, who'd never feel lost again.

"Get a job, get married, have kids, retire, wait to die," Elise said with a sigh, like she was disappointed in me. "Boring. Don't you want anything *more*?" She lit yet another cigarette and offered it to me. "More than what our parents have. More than an ordinary existence in an ordinary town like Lyndens Creek. More than a one-size-fits-all life. Just *more*." Her voice was threaded with confidence, her eyes wide.

A shiver slipped down my spine. Take me with you, I wanted to say. Don't leave me behind to live this ordinary life. Elise played with her lighter, flipping its heavy top open and shutting it, the metal gleaming even in low light. She sighed, turning away from me, eyes focused on the sky.

"Then what?" I asked, my voice a whisper, like she was telling me a fairy tale and I didn't want to break the spell.

"I know what I don't want more than what I want," she said, her eyes faraway. "I don't want my life to be a waste. I don't want to blindly follow some checklist. I don't want to be forgotten." She snapped the top of her lighter closed a final time, the strike of metal against metal ringing in my ear.

"No one could ever forget you," I said, my hand reaching for hers, tugging her back to earth. She turned from the stars to me and smiled.

"I want my life to mean something. I want to be remembered. Because why even bother being alive if you're not going to leave a mark, if you're not going to really *live*?" I'd never thought about it that way. If anything, I did everything I could to *not* leave a mark, to become invisible and avoid setting off my parents.

We were quiet on the drive back, her words echoing in my mind. "Want to go to my place?" she asked when we were close to my house. She was going to drop me off but she didn't want to say goodbye and neither did I. "My dad's not home," she added.

"Where is he?" I looked at her curiously.

"Oh, at his girlfriend's again." She shrugged.

Elise never talked about him, except to say if he was home or not. He reminded me of my parents, always absent. But instead of buried in work, he was always at his girlfriend's house.

I knew almost nothing about the girlfriend, just her name, Heidi, and that she worked as a real estate agent—Elise called her The Realtor. I'm not sure Elise knew much more.

When Elise's grandmother left her the Pink Mansion in the will, her dad had wanted to "unload it." That's what Elise said, complete with air quotes. They drove down from Chattanooga one weekend the summer before sophomore year to meet with real estate agents, and that's how her father met Heidi.

"Do you not like her?" I asked, wondering why he was always at her place and never the other way around.

"I've met her a few times. She's okay I guess," she said, like she hadn't ever given it much thought. "She's not trying to be my mom, so I don't hate her."

Elise didn't like talking about her family, barely ever mentioning her father and never talking about her mother. All I knew about her was what Elise had told me that first night. I couldn't tell if she never wanted to talk about her mom because she missed her or because she didn't.

It was almost one in the morning when we pulled into her driveway. She parked but didn't get out, staring off into the distance. Shivering from the cold, I grabbed the cigarettes and she lit two. The wind gently lifted her hair off her shoulders, and in the moonlight she looked ethereal—skin glowing, eyes sparkling, a hint of a smile on her lips. I wondered if she was imagining what the future held.

"Why are you here with me?" I asked. I realized I sounded insecure but I needed to know what she saw in me. "I mean, why do you even like me? I'm not . . ." I left the rest unsaid. I'm not pretty like you, not funny or brilliant like you. I'm not *interesting* like you.

"I make it a policy to have an opinion on everyone, and I have pretty good instincts," she said, turning toward me. "I'd noticed you around school before the night of homecoming. I thought you were a Hermione."

"A Hermione." I looked at her in confusion.

"You know: straight As, boring, *tame*. A little like Melody, no offense."

"Wow," I said. I was hurt but tried to pretend I wasn't. "Is that what you really thought when you first saw me?"

"Yes, but I was wrong," she said, draping an arm around my shoulders. "I've never been more wrong about someone in my life."

I shot her a skeptical look, but felt a little better.

"I'm serious. Your ex-boyfriend was an asshole, but in a way I'm glad. Because I got to meet you. The real you," she said, playing with my hair.

"Spoiler alert: I *am* pretty boring," I joked.

Elise shook her head. "No, you're not. You're just like me. You're tough, you've been through a lot, more than any of the losers at this school." She turned to face me, staring into my soul. "That makes you special. Surviving—*having to survive*—makes you stronger. Things have never been easy for people like us, Rem. I'm really, really glad I met you."

"Me too," I said, smiling, blushing. No one had ever called me special or said I was strong.

"I want you to have this," she said, pressing her lighter into my palm, closing my fingers around it with both of her hands. The warmth of her touch lingered after she let go. "Look at the bottom."

I angled it toward the scant moonlight. *Elise x Remy*, it said, inscribed in a simple script.

"Happy birthday." She had the softest smile.

"When did you get this done?" I stared at her in surprise. I couldn't believe she'd noticed me admiring it, or that she'd give me something that obviously meant a lot to her. Elise always had it on her, was always fiddling with it. My thumb traced over the silver filigree. It looked like an antique, like it held an important piece of her history, like it was a piece of *her*. I'd never gotten something so personal before. This was the kind of thing people only gave to *family*. And maybe that was what Elise was saying—that we could be family. I held it tightly in my hand like it was proof I was loved, and maybe that's exactly what it was. "Are you sure?"

"I'm sure," she said, still smiling. "Come on." We went inside, up to her room. As we got ready for bed, I set the gift on my pillow and stared at it. Soft light from the street filtered through the blinds and hit the metal like a spark. Maybe it really was a piece of her, I thought as I drifted to sleep.

Elise was electricity. I was the night. She banished the darkness, she lit me up.

15.

Every relationship has a pivotal moment that defines it. Ours was the night of Northside Hospital's annual Thanksgiving fundraiser, held at the Four Seasons downtown that year. We were friends before, maybe even best friends, but after that night, we were family.

Elise spent Thanksgiving break in Chattanooga with her father, packing up the rest of their things. She sent me pictures of weird stuff she found in her closet—a self-portrait done in macaroni from kindergarten, a half-used pack of hair extensions—and funny selfies of her sprawled on the floor exhausted. And then, late Saturday morning, she texted to say she was back and wanted to hang out.

> Me: Can't
>
> Me: I have to go to this black tie dinner the hospital's throwing to get money from rich old people and pretend I love my mom
>
> Elise: Okay, I'm in
>
> Elise: Just how black tie is this thing?

I stared at her message with surprise. Christian and I never,

ever brought anyone to these things for the same reason we almost never invited people over to our house.

Before I could come up with an excuse, she sent a picture of a deep red cocktail dress. "This okay?" she asked.

Fuck it, I thought, and sent her a thumbs-up emoji. They always had a few no-shows every year, and in public my parents liked to pretend everything was perfect—their marriage, their kids. It was always unsettling when my mom squeezed my shoulders and kissed the top of my head, or when my dad laughed at all of her jokes and looked at her as if he still loved her. But all of that just meant they'd be too preoccupied trying to convince everyone they had it all to cause any kind of scene.

The night started out as expected, a crowd of wealthy donors mingling in a large ballroom, waiters in crisp uniforms offering cocktail shrimp and mini crab cakes. Elise and I huddled together by one end of the bar, sipping sparkling apple cider, laughing as she made fun of what some of the donors were wearing: "Sequins should be banned." Mom chatted people up with Christian by her side, occasionally glancing at the door for Dad's arrival. He'd gone into the Coke office that morning, taking his tux with him. He was supposed to join us here but when it came time to sit, he still hadn't shown up. Watching Mom smile and make excuses for him to our tablemates, I could see the lines tighten around her eyes in anger.

Elise, not picking up on the tension, was peering at the person on the other side of my mom.

"I keep forgetting that Christian's your brother," she said, distracted.

I gave her a look. "We have the same last name."

"Yeah, but I didn't want to assume," she said, her eyes still on him. Christian was Riverside-famous. Everyone at school seemed to have a crush on him, from the captain of the volleyball team to the president of Speech and Debate. Even Melody, who considered boys a waste of time, was drawn to his good looks and stellar grades. But he was more than grades and academic extracurriculars. He'd been class president every year until he ascended to student council president his senior year. He played three varsity sports, was the captain of the basketball team, and was being recruited by coaches at Brown and Princeton.

Christian was like our mom, constantly working to surpass that Asian-American stereotype. Mom was always telling us that we were American just like everyone else. She liked to remind people that both she and Dad had been born stateside, and once, when drunk, she delivered a rambling speech at the dinner table on the Japanese internment even though we weren't of Japanese descent. "They locked up people who looked like us," she said, pointing to her face. "Did they round up Germans or throw Italians into internment camps? No, of course not. Two-thirds of those interned were born here, but that didn't matter. My grandmother wore a pin that said 'I'm Chinese, not Japanese' every day for years. Every single day. *For years*. Because she was afraid they'd take her store and ship her off by accident."

It was like she wanted to wear pins that said "I'm American, not Chinese," like it was still necessary to prove we belonged here.

All of this stuck with Christian but never quite affected me in the same way. Maybe because he *was* a stereotypical academic overachiever, he felt like he had to prove he wasn't *only* that. Just like Mom, who was a doctor—a brain surgeon. Maybe I never felt that kind of pressure because any success at school I experienced was owed to Melody.

But Christian. Everyone wanted to be him or be with him. He was golden, could do no wrong, but more important, he was respected. And *loved*. In our family, the lines had been drawn early—Christian and Mom, me and Dad. Mom never bothered to hide the fact she favored Christian, her perfect everything. "The flagship child," she called him once as a joke. He was going places and I was going nowhere. If he was the flagship child, I was an obscure and failing franchise, an eyesore they didn't want marring the family name.

No one ever thought we were related.

"Are you surprised?" I asked, startling Elise, who finally took her eyes off him.

"I just thought you were an only child, that's all," she said before changing the subject. "Where's your dad?"

"No idea," I said, a little worried. I didn't know where he was, if he'd even gone into the office that morning. Mom looked like she wanted to break something and I just wished he'd get here soon.

As Mom chatted with the donors at her table, her voice grew more and more strained. "Text your father," she whispered to Christian when there was the slightest lull. She shot me an annoyed look, like his absence was somehow my fault.

"I have," he said. "Five times."

She glanced at Dad's empty seat and then at the table two over from ours, where her assistant Greg sat. Elise's impromptu appearance had meant bumping him to a seat at a nearby table belonging to an attendee who was a no-show. I could see the gears turning in her mind. She was thinking about recalling Greg to fill the empty seat between us.

I wondered where Dad was, if he was going to show up at

all. He and I played hooky once, the second year after we began attending the annual Northside fundraiser, skipping it at the last minute without telling Mom.

"Come on," he'd told me, right before I was about to change into my dress. "I don't want to do boring grown-up things tonight." Mom and Christian had gone earlier in the day to help set up, and we were under instruction to arrive half an hour before the donors came.

"Does Mom know?" I asked, hopeful, but also dreading Mom's wrath.

He shot me a conspiratorial wink and shook his head. "Better to ask for forgiveness than permission."

I hesitated, afraid of what might happen after.

"Don't worry," he said, as if reading my mind. "She won't be mad at you."

We went to the movies and I remembered the thrill of defying Mom's orders. Dad's phone rang a couple times but he ignored it, so when she called me I didn't answer either. We both knew there'd be consequences later, a storm waiting on the horizon, but I also felt safe, because we were a team and I had someone in my corner.

After, we got ice cream, sitting outside sharing a large cup of mint chocolate chip as the stars appeared one by one. "Do you love Mom?" It was a question I'd been obsessed with for as long as I could remember, but I never felt brave enough to ask until now.

"It's complicated," he said after a lengthy pause.

I remembered feeling confused, almost angry. I was eleven and I thought it was simple: People should only be together if they loved each other.

"What I do know is that I love *you*." He kissed me on the head and I couldn't help but smile. Christian had Mom, and the grades, and everything I didn't, but Christian didn't have Dad or this moment.

Though now at the fundraiser, sitting next to Dad's empty seat, I wondered where he was, if I still had him.

Mom turned to me. "Call him," she said, her voice low. Maybe she was thinking of the same memory, wondering if we were still somehow conspiring to ruin things for her. I pulled out my phone, angled it so she'd see I was calling him, but two rings in he showed up, tie askew and hair windblown, just as the waiters were sweeping away the salad plates.

"Sorry, sorry," he said, plopping down between Mom and me. "Sorry, everyone."

Mom's smile was wide but lacking any warmth. "Where were you?" she whispered in a hiss.

"I got a flat, had to call a car."

"You couldn't have called me?" she said through her teeth.

He shrugged. "I'm here now, aren't I?"

Mom's eyes flashed with anger.

"And before that?"

"I was at the office," he said as he unfurled his napkin with a snap. "I told you."

"I called your office," she said, straining to keep her words controlled and steady.

"I must've set all calls to go to voicemail." That was his M.O.— plausible deniability. He waved down a waiter and ordered a vodka soda.

Glancing at them out of the corner of my eye, I tried to keep calm. They were in public, they wouldn't cause a scene. They wouldn't, they wouldn't. Being out of the house with them had always been a safe space.

They were supposed to put on a show. All smiles and bad jokes and fake laughs. I glanced at Elise, but she didn't seem to notice, or if she did, she was pointedly ignoring them. It was like she could feel my distress and didn't want to cause me any more by drawing attention to my parents.

When the main course arrived, Dad sighed heavily.

"What now?" Mom asked.

"They never do steak well here," he complained.

"I ordered for you because *you weren't here*," she said, careful to plaster a smile on her face this time.

"It's overcooked." He did this sometimes, going on the offensive when he fucked up. Land the first blow. Insult the food, make her defensive.

"Then send it back," she said.

"No, it's fine," he said, shaking his head. "You can order it bloody here and it'll still come out charred." Then he turned his attention to my plate. "And look at Remy's risotto. Watery."

"It looks fine. Right, Remy?" Mom asked, an edge in her voice.

Before I had a chance to come up with an answer that wouldn't anger anyone, Dad rolled his eyes and said, "When did the definition of *fine* become *mediocre*?"

Mom dropped her fork and let it clatter loudly, drawing the attention of those sitting near us. "I'll order you the salmon."

"No," he said, sighing heavily. "It's *fine*."

It went on like that for the rest of the night—whispered snipes and sarcasm. Elise tried to distract me with invented backstories for some of the guests at other tables, but all I could focus on was the storm that was brewing between my parents. When the dinner was finally, finally over, we went outside and waited for the valet to bring Mom's car around. Dad began to move toward the driver's door when Mom yanked him back, causing him to stumble on the curb.

"It's my car," she said. "Yours is in the shop, remember?" She refused to let go.

"It's not like I got a flat on purpose. The tires were old, and it's not my fault they couldn't get the tire off and had to tow it."

"It's never your fault, right?" she said bitterly. "Nothing's ever your fault."

Elise glanced at me. I was flooded with shame. Again. I should've made an excuse and told her she couldn't come. She reached for my hand and squeezed. Eventually, Dad relented and got into the passenger side, shutting the door with enough force to shake the whole car.

In the back, I sat between Christian and Elise, holding her hand the whole ride back. Our eyes locked in the dark, neither of us letting go.

Back at the house, Elise and I went down to the basement but we could still hear them above us, loud words and heavy pacing.

"It's late," I told her. "You should go." I didn't want to be alone but I didn't want her to witness more than she already had.

She shook her head. "I want to make sure you're okay."

"I'm fine," I said with a weak smile, and she gave me a look like she didn't believe me.

"My dad's home tonight," she said, and I understood what she meant. He was there, so we couldn't be, for reasons still unknown to me. I wished she'd just tell me, but despite seeing how messed up my family was, she still seemed to hold back.

We sat on the floor with our backs against the couch. I took out Elise's lighter, my birthday present, and ran my fingers over the inscription before flipping the heavy top open and closed like I'd seen her do.

"What the fuck is your problem?" Mom said upstairs.

"My problem?" Dad said. "Don't you know already? It's you."

"I asked you for *one thing* and you couldn't do it. You knew this was important to me, you *knew,* but you didn't care."

"I had a flat tire!"

"That doesn't explain where you were all day," she snapped.

"I want a divorce."

The house fell silent.

"Remy—" Elise whispered.

"Shh," I said, leaning toward the staircase, just straining to hear. This wasn't the first time, or the second, that I'd heard those words from him. It was terrifying each time—an end to the madness but an unknown future.

Mom finally broke the silence. "What?"

"I want a divorce," he repeated, keeping his voice in check.

She didn't say anything for a long time. And then she just *laughed.*

He lost it. "I *said,* I want a divorce!"

"It's late," she said. "I'm going to bed."

"Did you hear me?" he called out after her.

"Good night, Stephen," she said, and I could picture her walking away from him, flicking a dismissive hand in his direction.

"I'm serious this time. I've called a lawyer."

Her footsteps stopped. "Oh, really?" I could just see the expression on her face, the arched eyebrow—a challenge.

Elise squeezed my hands, pulling me back to reality. "Remy?" she said, her voice a soft whisper. "You're crying."

Surprised, I touched a hand to my face. "Oh."

She let go of me, pushed herself up.

"Don't go," I said.

"I'm just going to find some tissues."

"Don't go." I hated the way I sounded, so weak, so helpless.

She sat back down, facing me, and wrapped both of my hands in hers, her touch warm and comforting.

Above us, the war raged on. "So tell me, what did the lawyer say?" my mother asked, and I closed my eyes, imagining her expression with startling clarity: the contempt in her eyes, the frown, the downward twist of her lips.

"You don't believe me," Dad said.

She scoffed. "Of course I don't. It's childish, honestly. What, every time we have a fight you'll just announce you want a divorce? If you were going to do it, you would've done it already. I know what you really want. You just want me to beg for you to stay, but I won't, not today, not anymore."

"No," he protested, though he sounded deflated. "I mean it this time."

"Okay, so then tell me. How do you want to do it? Who's getting the house? Who's getting the cars? Who's getting the kids?"

"Remy?" Elise shook me lightly. "Let's get out of here." Her eyes flicked toward the basement door that led out to the backyard. "Let's go for a ride."

I was frozen, unable to move.

"I'll take Christian, you'll take Remy," Mom continued. She had to know I could hear, but maybe she just didn't care. I wondered if Christian was upstairs in his room, if he was listening to every word or if he'd managed to escape.

For one brief moment, hope flooded me. We were a team, Dad and me. Maybe this was it, what I'd been waiting for all these years—maybe this was when we'd leave.

Then my dad said, "That's hardly fair. Christian's going to college soon."

His words hit me like a knife to the heart. He wasn't going to take me.

He didn't want me.

A sob tore its way out of me, but it sounded far away. He was supposed to care, we were supposed to have each other. That's all I could think. We were the outcasts, the resistance. We were the remainders. Christian had Mom and I had Dad.

"Remy, let's *go*." Elise was tugging my hand. When I didn't budge, she kneeled down before me. "Breathe for me, just breathe." She slowed her own breathing down and I began to follow her pace, taking deeper breaths. "Repeat after me: My name is Remy. I am seventeen years old. This won't last forever."

I nodded.

My name is Remy.

I am seventeen years old.

This won't last forever.

Elise was right. Nothing lasts forever.

16.

The summer before high school, my dad popped into my room on a random Thursday and asked if I wanted to tag along on a work trip.

"It's in Chicago!" he said. "I'll be busy during the day but we could do fun things in the evenings, maybe go see a show?"

"Okay," I said, excited for something that was going to be just the two of us.

"Great," he said, and I remember being a little surprised at how happy he looked. For a moment, we just stared at each other with goofy grins. "What are you waiting for? Go pack."

"It's this weekend?" I asked, shocked.

"Yeah, we fly out in the afternoon. I'll call my assistant, get you a ticket," he said like it was no big deal, fingers tapping the door frame.

"But—" I didn't finish. *But what about Mom?* She'd say no, she always did.

"Don't worry, it'll be our secret," he said with a wink after seeing my expression. "You know my motto." *Better to ask for forgiveness than permission.*

"Yeah," I said, laughing. "Okay."

It was an accounting conference, and on the first day, when Dad was downstairs making a speech or running some workshop, I ordered movies and room service upstairs in our room, went up to the roof for a swim, and got a massage at the spa.

"Whatever you want," he'd told me. "Just charge it to the room."

He called me after and I met him in the lobby for dinner. "Remy," he said, smiling when he saw me. "This is Brenda."

I looked at the woman beside him and smiled politely.

"She works with me," he continued. "She's brilliant."

She waved him off. "You're brilliant."

I looked between the two of them in confusion.

"Brenda and I are the only ones from the team here, so I invited her out to dinner," he said casually, but his smile was tentative.

"Hope that's okay?" she asked.

"Yeah, sure." I shrugged. In the car on the way to dinner, Dad sat up front while I sat with Brenda in the back. White, middle-aged, and petite with pale skin and soft brown eyes, she was unassuming and unthreatening, always full of smiles and compliments for me. "I love your hair," she told me that night. "You have such great skin," she said later.

She went to dinner with us again the next day, and came to *Wicked*. And on the last morning, she skipped her meetings and took me out for mani-pedis, which was surprisingly fun.

"Do you like Brenda?" Dad asked on the flight back.

"Yeah," I said. "She's cool."

He had the biggest smile on his face and let me have a sip of his champagne when the flight attendants weren't looking.

"Remy, I have to tell you something," he said near the end of our flight, suddenly serious. "Can you keep a secret? I mean it, Remy. You can't tell anyone, okay? Not even Christian. Not yet."

I nodded, thrilled he'd trust me with something that sounded so important.

He took a deep breath as the captain announced the beginning of our descent. "Things between your mother and I have always been, well, you know," he said. "And well, things will probably never get better." Behind him, outside of the window, I could see highways coming into view, the cars like lines of ants. "So," he continued, his voice straining a bit, "how would you feel if we got a divorce?"

My heart plummeted and I wanted to throw up. In some ways, it was what I'd wanted to hear practically my whole life. But faced with the actuality, I was terrified. Did it mean he was leaving us—leaving me?

"You want me and Mom to be happy, don't you?" he asked.

"Of course," I answered immediately.

"Good." Then Dad took another deep breath. "How do you feel about coming to live with me afterward?"

"Really?" I asked, so happy at the thought of a fresh start, just the two of us.

"If you want," he said, his smile hesitant like he was afraid I'd say no.

"Yes!" I said, and we shared relieved laughs.

The plane hit the ground with a thud but I was still soaring.

"So here's the thing—I haven't been totally honest," he continued, clearing his throat. "Brenda, she's more than just a colleague. It's complicated."

Suddenly it all made sense. Why she was with us all the time, why she was so nice to me.

"Oh." It felt like a punch to the gut. He'd *lied* to me.

"I just wanted you to get to know her without any pressure," he rambled on as we taxied to the gate. "So you could be honest with me. And you said you like her, so it all worked out."

I gave him a small smile but I didn't feel like smiling.

When we deplaned and headed toward baggage claim, I was still in shock. A million questions flooded my mind. Had it all been Brenda's idea? When did Dad decide all of this? When did they even start seeing each other? And, oh God, Mom. Dad had asked me to keep a secret, but now I couldn't imagine facing her.

"It's going to be okay, Remy," Dad said on the way home. "We'll figure everything out—I'm just so happy that you're on my side. I feel like I can do anything, knowing I have you." And like magic, all of my doubts seemed to evaporate. We were a *team*, we were a family, just the two of us. I was his favorite, like Christian was Mom's favorite. Someone wanted me, someone loved me. Everything would be okay.

Elise listened quietly as I talked about that weekend in Chicago, a warm hand on my shoulder. We were in the Pink Caddy, passing her last cigarette back and forth between us.

"What happened?" she asked when I finished.

"I don't know. For a few weeks, my dad seemed euphoric. Then he left for another work trip, this time without me, and came back sad." I turned away, blew smoke out, and watched it disappear into the night. We sat with the top down, shivering in our coats, fingers shaking and clumsy with the cigarette. "He and Brenda must've broken up. I don't even think he asked Mom for a divorce that time." An errant tear slipped down my face.

"Unlike now," Elise said.

"Unlike now," I confirmed. I didn't understand what had changed in the intervening two and a half years, how he could go from acting like he cared about me to not wanting me at all.

"Come here," Elise said, pulling me in and tucking my head against her shoulder. I played with the lighter she'd given me, flipping the heavy top open and closed.

"No one ever wants me," I cried harder. "Not Cameron, not my mom, not even my dad."

"Shh," she said softly, letting me cry and cry, smoothing my hair away with a gentle hand. "Did I ever tell you about my mom?"

I looked up, lifting a wrist to wipe away my tears. It was

really a rhetorical question—we both knew she'd never told me about her mom.

"I mean, there isn't much to talk about. She left when I was six." I remained quiet, focused on her voice. "She left one day, walked out the door without a single glance behind her." Elise still sounded shocked after all these years. "It's been just me and my dad ever since, not that he's ever been father of the year."

I waited for her to continue, and when she didn't, I asked about him. "What do you mean?"

"Nothing," she said quickly. "I'm just saying, I know what it's like to have shitty parents who don't care about you."

I began crying again, feeling sorry for both of us.

"Come here," she said, squeezing me closer. "They're all assholes, forget about them. Look, let's just leave everyone behind and start over, just the two of us."

I looked up at her through wet eyes. "Just the two of us?"

She nodded. "You and me, we can be each other's family, okay?"

"Okay," I said, sniffing.

"We don't need anyone else, not when we have each other."

I'd never felt more loved than in that moment, Elise holding me as I cried.

17.

My dad left that Saturday night and was still gone two days later when we went back to school. Time slowed to a drip and I found myself checking my phone between every period, unsure of what I was even hoping for. Dad wasn't going to text me in the middle of the day, wasn't going to call to say he was there to pick me up and take me with him to his new life. He wasn't going to swoop in to save me.

He was gone, maybe for good this time. And of course Christian wasn't fazed. Sitting with friends in the senior section at lunch, he was too busy laughing and joking to care. Our eyes met briefly across the lunchroom when he caught me staring and his smile faltered for a second before he turned away from me.

After school, he stopped by my locker, which he never did. "What's your problem?" he asked, leaning against the wall, arms crossed.

"My problem?" I said.

"Yeah, at lunch."

88

Before I could answer, someone down the hall spotted Christian and called out to him. "Hey, Chris, you coming to practice?" It was Cory from the basketball team.

"Yeah, be there in a minute, just talking to my sister."

"Oh. I didn't you know had a sister," he said, glancing at me before returning to Christian. "See you on the court." And with a mock salute, he was gone.

"Do you just tell people you're an only child?" I said, yanking my chem book out and shoving it in my bag.

"What? No," he said.

"Whatever," I said, turning to go.

"Wait." He stopped me with a heavy hand on my arm. "Why are you acting so weird?"

I'd never loathed him more than in that moment. "What's wrong with *you*?" I shot back. "Dad's gone and you don't even care."

"Really? *That's* what this is about?" he said with a scoff. "It's not like this is the first time he's disappeared. And for the record, I care."

"No, you don't. Because you don't have to care. You've got Mom."

"What's that supposed to mean? *We* have Mom. Both of us. Dad's the one who left and he left all of us. I didn't make him go. He ran off. *Again*."

"He only left because of Mom." Christian was willfully distorting what happened. I didn't know why I was bothering. He'd been brainwashed by our mom. He'd never understand. "Were you even there Saturday night? Did you hear them?"

"I was there," he said. "I was going to get my keys and bounce but then they started arguing downstairs, so I couldn't leave."

89

"Did you hear the whole thing?" I could still hear the disdain in Mom's voice when Dad said he wanted a divorce: *Oh, really?*

"As a matter of fact, I did. It's basically the same fight they have all the time." He rolled his eyes. "Dad's flakey, Mom gets mad, Dad runs off for a few weeks, comes back all contrite. Things are okay for a while and then it starts up all over again. Rinse and repeat." His voice was devoid of emotion, like he'd been reading me the weather report. Cloudy with a 30 percent chance of divorce. "I don't know why you're so worked up. You know he's coming back."

That was the thing. I didn't, not this time.

"Hey." Elise seemed to materialize out of nowhere. Her eyes traveled between us a few times, curious, then she smiled at Christian. "What's up, guys?"

"Nothing, let's go," I said, pulling her along.

"What's wrong?" she asked as soon as we were out of earshot. I just shook my head. In the Pink Caddy, I drew my knees in, curling into myself.

"I hate him," I said.

"Your . . . dad?" she asked, passing a cigarette to me and lighting one for herself.

"Christian." I held my cigarette between my fingers, unlit, forgotten. "Dad left two days ago and he's just acting like nothing's happened."

Elise studied me but didn't say anything, releasing a stream of smoke to the side.

"How can he just—" I broke off. It wasn't that he didn't get what I was going through—he didn't *want* to. It was easier for him to live in his bubble where everything was perfect and *he* was perfect.

She took the cigarette from my hand and lit it for me before passing it back. "People react differently to things," she said, shrugging.

"Are you defending him?"

"No," she said, but I wasn't convinced. She didn't know Christian like I did. When she looked at him, she saw what everyone else saw—student council president, valedictorian, star athlete, loved by all for his sly smile and self-deprecating jokes, the future leader of men. She saw who he was to everyone who wasn't me.

"We were close when we were little. We used to hide in the closet together when things got bad. We used to—" We used to be a team, he and I. Before the lines were drawn, it was the two of us. At least until he began to believe Mom's bullshit about how special he was, how he was so much better than me. "Christian doesn't care about anyone but himself," I said. He never stood up to Mom for me, never looked for me after a fight to tell me she was wrong or that he was sorry.

"Yeah, but maybe he's sad and just doesn't want to show it. Maybe—"

"Stop defending him!" I said, cutting her off. "Not you too. I don't think I could stand it coming from you."

"What?" she said, looking startled. "I'm not defending him."

"I just want someone to be on *my* side," I said, beginning to tear up.

"Hey, I am on your side, come here." She pulled me in for a long hug. "I'll always be on your side." When Elise dropped me off at my house, she placed a light hand on my forearm. "I meant that. I'll always be on your side, okay?"

We shared a small smile, and I thought: It'll be all right as long as I have her.

18.

By the end of her first semester here, Elise had cemented her reputation around school as something of a badass. She didn't give a fuck what anyone thought of her, and she had this effortless beauty that drew other people toward her—long, glossy hair, thick lashes, startling blue eyes. The combination gave her a strange sort of invincibility, like she was untouchable, and she knew it.

But Elise only ever wielded her power for good, sticking up for people who needed it. She saw herself as a protector of the downtrodden, an everyday heroine.

There was a girl in math, Jane, who was frequently tortured because her mother was in prison for embezzlement.

"Hey, Jane," Ethan, an obnoxious meathead, would say. "If your parents got divorced, who'd you rather live with?"

"It's a tough choice," his friend George would join in. "I mean, on one hand, you've got boring old Lyndens Creek, and on the other, you've got prison. It's a tough call." They'd crack up, give each other self-congratulatory high fives.

Or the time they made a show of opening a copy of the school paper issued that day. "Look," George said innocently. "The school raised almost ten thousand dollars for the Red Cross. It's a record. Hey, Jane, didn't your mom used to organize that fundraiser?"

"No wonder they raised more this year," Ethan said, followed again by laughter.

Timid and soft-spoken, Jane mostly endured it quietly. Elise would occasionally shoot them dark looks or tell them to shut up, but one day they crossed the line and she silenced them for good.

"When was the last time you saw your mom, Jane?" Ethan asked, feigning concern. When she ignored him, he poked her in the shoulder with his pen. She continued to ignore him, which pissed him off. "It doesn't matter. I heard she got a ten-year sentence. Oh no, what if she *dies* in prison? Then you'll never see her again." Jane teared up almost immediately.

"Oh shit," George said, shaking his head appreciatively. "Harsh."

Elise swung around. "Hey, assholes, say another word and I'll fucking end you."

They were stunned into silence. It wasn't just the words. It was the way she delivered them, like she had power and they were nothing.

Maybe they heard she orchestrated the revenge prank against Jae's ex-girlfriend, Dana. Rumor was that her family had to hire exterminators to get rid of the mice and that she was too scared to sleep in the basement anymore.

Or maybe they could sense Elise Ferro was someone you didn't fuck with. Either way, they stopped torturing Jane, at least whenever she was around.

Then there was the Friday we had a substitute in World History, the only other class I had with Elise. When doing roll call, Mrs. Jones stumbled through all the names and then got to mine. "Katherine Te-say?" I always dreaded moments like this.

"It's just 'sigh,' or 'zai,' like the word 'tsar,'" I said. "And I go by my middle name, Remy."

"Sah-ay," she said, drawing it out, clearly annoyed at being corrected. "And Remy. What an odd name. Katherine is what your parents picked for you and it's a perfectly good name, so that's what I'll call you."

Sliding down in my chair to avoid drawing any more attention to myself, I caught Elise staring at me, anger flashing in her eyes. I shook my head slightly: *Please don't make it worse.* To my relief, she said nothing, but I could see that rage simmering right beneath the surface. She remained quiet the rest of class, but as soon as the bell rang, she strode up to Mrs. Jones. I thought Elise was about to say something that'd land her in detention when she turned the wattage up on her smile and began chatting with her, laughing even. Confused, I waited for her outside.

"Come on," she said, looping an arm around mine and steering us away from the crowd heading to the cafeteria for lunch.

"Where are we going?" I asked once we were outside.

Grinning, Elise pulled out a set of car keys from her pocket.

"Wait, is that—"

"—the rude woman's keys?" she finished. "Yep." So that's what she'd been doing. "They were just sitting on the desk." We wandered the teacher's parking lot using the key fob to locate her car.

"What are we going to do?" I said when we found it, now worried about what Elise might have in mind. I knew she liked pranks, but we'd never pulled something off at *school*, and definitely not on someone who could get us into real trouble.

"Nothing crazy," she said, getting into the driver's seat. "Come on."

"Are we *stealing* her car?" I asked, not moving.

"Nah, just borrowing it. Don't worry, it's not a big deal," she said, pulling the seat belt across her.

It was a sign of how much I trusted her that I finally got in. "Okay."

We didn't go far, just to the parking lot of a nearby strip mall. Elise pulled out her cigarettes. It'd become a little ritual of ours, Elise lighting two and passing one to me. "Don't worry," she said. "We'll drive back and drop the keys off in the lost and found. She'll look for them when she realizes they're missing, but she'll find them eventually."

"You didn't have to do this for me," I said quietly, feeling vaguely embarrassed but also secretly happy that she cared so much about me.

"I wanted to! People like her are the worst. What the fuck did she even mean, 'What an odd name'?" Elise scoffed, that sharp glint in her eye. "It's unfair that we couldn't say anything just because she has all the power." That kind of thing really bothered her. The world was unjust, and someone had to right those wrongs. She was that someone.

I looked at her in awe.

"What?" she asked. "Do I have something on my face?"

I laughed. "No, just—thanks. For caring."

95

She smiled.

After we finished our first cigarette, Melody texted me.

Melody: Where are you?

I'd begun to hang out with Elise and her friends at lunch most days, and the more I avoided or ignored Melody, the more she tried to pull me back.

Me: Getting lunch off campus

Melody: We're not supposed to do that!

"Is that Melody?" Elise asked, rolling her eyes. "Let me guess, you're in trouble."

"No," I said. "Maybe."

"Melody's mad at you, isn't she?" she said.

"Probably," I admitted. "But it's not a big deal."

"I wasn't going to tell you this but she cornered me the other day," she said like she was confessing a secret.

"What?"

"Yeah, we're both in sixth-period Spanish, right? So after the last bell, she followed me out and pulled me aside. She kind of threatened me."

"Um . . . What?" I repeated. I couldn't imagine tiny Melody Moon threatening *anyone*.

"Okay, maybe not threatened, but warned. She was all huffy about how much time you were spending with me, how you and her were friends first, blah blah blah." Then Elise laughed, like it was Melody who was being completely ridiculous.

"Wow," I said, feeling a little worried about Mel—that she would corner Elise like that. She was stubborn and loyal but she'd never seemed possessive. Maybe it was a misunderstanding. Maybe she wasn't trying to threaten Elise but was just venting.

Maybe she was even trying to get us all to hang out together more. Whatever it was, it backfired. "What'd you say?"

"I chose to be the bigger person. I just smiled sweetly and walked away." She let out a big sigh. "Sometimes I wish I didn't care about being nice. Sometimes I wish I always said what I wanted." This surprised me—*didn't* she always say what she wanted? What was she holding back?

"What'd you want to say?"

Elise grinned, a mischievous spark in her eye. "You and me, outside after school"—she raised her fists, shadowboxing in mock seriousness.

"Oh my God," I said, laughing, eyes wide.

She laughed too. "To the victor goes the spoils."

"What, I'm the spoils?" I said, pretending to be offended but secretly pleased.

"Yes," she said, slinging an arm around my shoulders. "You're the spoils, the prize." It was incredible how a few words from her could make me feel lighter than air.

I knew Elise was just joking around, but it made me feel special, to be fought over, to be liked. To be a prize to someone like Elise, so confident and warm, sparkling with life. Someone who could have her pick of friends but somehow chose me.

My phone buzzed with a new text but I ignored it.

"Melody again?"

I shrugged.

Elise sighed once more, like she was bored even by the idea of Melody. "She's such a rule-follower, someone without imagination. She's the kind of girl who's going to grow up to be a doctor or lawyer or engineer."

"She wants to be a doctor," I said. She sometimes spoke admiringly of my mom, which was infuriating, especially because I never felt like I could tell Melody the truth about my mom.

"See? Exactly. I know her entire life already. She'll paint her life by numbers. Graduate with straight As, go to Emory, become a 'productive member of society,'" she said, adding air quotes. "She'll get married to an equally boring guy, have boring kids who'll go on to start the miserable cycle all over again. Then she'll pass away peacefully in her sleep at the age of ninety-one and her family will cry and grieve for a while, but ultimately, history won't remember her. And when they too are gone, it'll be as if she never even existed. What's the point of life if you're not going to *exist*? If you're just going to be forgotten?"

She hadn't mentioned my parents but I couldn't help thinking of them, their obsession with image and perfection. What was it for? It was all meaningless in the end. They were living a lie, a life they thought they should want. But Elise didn't believe in any of that.

"*I'm* going to be remembered," she declared. "*I'm* going to leave a mark." She was wild and free, she was larger than life. She was going to really *exist*.

It's not that I'd never thought about wanting to be remarkable, but I'd never believed in it with such certainty and confidence. And even if I did, I couldn't say it out loud like she could. Elise didn't seem to hold back, ever.

"*We* are going to be remembered," she said, smiling at me. "Together."

"Okay." I smiled back.

"We're different, you and me," she continued. "Special. People like Melody Moon have had perfect lives with nice parents and nice clothes and nice everything. And I used to be so jealous of people like her." I knew that feeling all too well, could still feel echoes of that desperation of wanting to have different parents, a different life.

What Elise was saying: Our wounds made us special.

"But you know what, Rem? I'm glad things haven't been easy for me. I'm stronger than all of them and I know what I'm capable of. But whatever. Family is the people you love, not the people who gave birth to you or raised you. You don't owe anyone anything. The only allegiance you have is to yourself and the people you *choose* to have in your life. As soon as I graduate, I'm out of here."

"Take me with you," I said, only half joking, watching for her reaction.

"Of course," she said like it was a forgone conclusion. "You and me, we're family."

Elise liked that I needed protection, and I liked that she wanted to protect me. We needed each other, we *chose* each other, and there was power in that.

MONDAY // AUGUST 28 // DAY 353

19.

There was power in that choice, and I can still feel it almost a year later. And now I am faced with another.

Elise and I, we're family. I needed protection then and she gave me shelter. But now it's Elise who needs *me*.

"Why don't we start over," Detective Ward says, and we begin again on Sunday night. We run through it one more time.

"Why were you at Elise's house?" she asks.

"We wanted to be alone," I tell her.

"Because you were fighting?"

I nod.

"What were you fighting about?" She tugs gently at her sleeves to straighten them. She seems relaxed and calm, while I feel just seconds away from losing it.

"I don't even remember," I lie, watching her carefully for a reaction. "It was something stupid." She remains neutral in her expression and I can't tell what she's thinking.

"Then you called Jack," she says.

"I called Jack and he came over. I let him in but Elise was out on the balcony in the back." I can still picture it now: Jack at the door, me stepping out. "Let me talk to her alone," he said, kissing me on the forehead. "Go home, I'll call you later."

"Okay," I said, and walked down the steps and path to the driveway and my car. I was about to leave, my key in the ignition, when the gunshots rang out one after the other. I ran and ran and ran, but I was too late.

Caught up in the memory, I start to cry, the salt stinging my skin. I am the ocean, it seems. I'll never run out of tears.

Detective Ward pushes a tissue box toward me with one end of her pen, examining me closely.

"Elise was still on the balcony and then she came inside and saw him. It was dark, so dark, and—and—" I can't go on, the pain in my chest too much to bear. *Elise needs you*, my mind whispers. Somehow I dig deeper, draw on the last of my strength. "We couldn't see each other. I only knew it was Elise because it couldn't be anyone else. Jack was in front of me. I don't think she even saw me. She—" I am sobbing into my hands, drowning in my own tears. "Elise was scared. She shot him."

She hadn't meant to. It was dark, she couldn't have seen who it was. If I close my eyes, I can imagine it all unfolding. Elise must've been so terrified. I can imagine being in her shoes, re-entering the kitchen from the balcony. The house is quiet, too quiet. I'm on edge from the night before. Then I look up and someone's walking toward me in the dark.

Her fear is so palpable, it burns through me. I can see her reaching for the gun almost by instinct. And then—

It's too painful. I can't.

Detective Ward waits for me to stop crying. It feels like years before I'm able to compose myself. She leans forward again, elbows on the table, hands clasped.

"That's interesting," she says slowly, every syllable enunciated. "Because I spoke to her last night and she says you *weren't* there."

"What?" Vera and I say at the same time. Vera turns and looks at me sharply, a message: *Don't say a word.*

"One of you is lying," Detective Ward says. "And what I want to know is why."

20.

Elise loved action movies, especially the ones with heroes, super-powered or otherwise. Stories with a good guy and a bad guy. People on a mission to right wrongs. People so driven by their pursuit of justice that they have to step outside of the law on occasion to deliver it.

She loved big showdowns between hero and villain. Even though the endings were always the same—good defeats evil—she always seemed on the edge of her seat like she was worried the heroes wouldn't prevail.

Her favorite was *Kill Bill*. Uma Thurman stars as the hero who kills her way down a list of assassins who'd walked into a little chapel and shot up her wedding rehearsal, putting her in a coma. These assassins were supposed to be her friends, her family—she was one of them, or at least she had been. So once she wakes from her coma years later, she exacts her revenge.

The first time we watched it together, we were in my basement celebrating the New Year with a bottle of wine pilfered from my parents' cellar, reveling in having the whole house to ourselves.

"It's my favorite movie," Elise told me. "Of all time."

"I saw it once. It's . . . a little too bloody for me," I said.

"I'll warn you when it gets to the violent parts," she said, pouring out two more glasses from the stolen bottle of wine.

I could tell it was important to her even if I didn't know why, so I agreed to watch it, scooting closer to her on the couch and resting my head lightly on her shoulder.

During the movie, I caught Elise glancing at me a few times, and I realized she *really* wanted me to like it. At the end of *Vol. 1*, Elise didn't say anything, just looked at me, awaiting my verdict.

"It was good," I said, trying to be diplomatic.

"Good?" She sounded disappointed.

"Really good," I said. "Really, really good."

"Promise?"

"Yes," I said.

"What was your favorite part?" she asked. I hadn't sold her yet.

"All of it," I said, wanting to be loyal.

"No, really," she insisted.

"Okay," I said, stalling. "If I had to pick, it'd be all the Hattori Hanzo scenes? When she convinces him to make her a sword."

Elise nodded eagerly. "What else?"

"Um. The O-Ren Ishii fight in the snow. When she actually apologizes to the Bride." I really did like these scenes, but I wanted to impress her, too, and I didn't want to let her down.

She nodded again. "See, I knew you'd like it."

"Mm-hmm." I hoped that would be it, that the questions would end.

"It's just all so poetic," Elise continued, excited. "Here's this girl who's lost everything, who's been betrayed by her family,

104

and—and she's not a victim. She doesn't let herself wallow in it. She's a survivor. She doesn't give up. She doesn't wait around for justice to deliver itself." Elise sat up and began waving her hands around as she spoke faster and faster. "She doesn't have anyone but she doesn't need anyone anymore. She lives and breathes revenge. Don't you wish the world could be like that sometimes?"

"What, filled with indiscriminate murder by *katana*-wielding assassins?" I said, laughing a little.

"No, I mean, don't you wish there was a way to get even?" Her face was flushed, her voice excited, growing louder.

"I guess," I said, confused. "But it's not like we can just kill everyone we don't like." I was joking but there was a flash in Elise's eyes, something hard. "I mean, we can't all fly to Japan, get samurai swords made, and hunt down every asshole who wronged us. It's a movie." I shrugged.

"Right. It's just a movie," she said, collapsing back against the couch and sighing. "It's just—I know it's a movie but it's so much more than that. It's the code she lives by. It's not just about revenge. It's having respect for yourself. It's believing you don't deserve all the shitty things that people do to you. It's believing that even if you get knocked down, there will be a day of reckoning. There'll be a day you'll rise out of the ashes and destroy the people who tried to destroy you." Elise looked like she was going to cry, but she didn't. She blinked away the tears and took a deep breath. "You know, there's a reason she doesn't have a name in the first movie. She could be anyone. The Bride could be me or you."

"Where is this coming from?" I asked softly, alarmed by the anger in her voice. Maybe it was the wine, I thought.

Elise's breath hitched, like she was about to launch into

another soliloquy, but then she caught herself and sighed.

"I'm sorry, Remy," she said. "You're right. It's just a movie and real life doesn't work like that. There is no karmic justice for shitty people." A tear slid down her face. "I know it's just a movie. I *know*, okay? But sometimes I just need to believe that I'm not always going to feel so helpless. I just need to believe that I'm strong enough to make it, that one day, they'll regret ever underestimating me." She released a sharp sigh and turned away from me.

"What's going on?" I said, placing a soft hand on her wrist and she flinched, even though I'd just had my head on her shoulder only minutes ago. "Elise?"

She shook her head. "I don't really want to talk about it."

And just like that, the person I thought I knew better than myself turned into a puzzle. I was about to ask again but she cut me off before I could speak.

"I don't want to talk about it. Sorry for being so melodramatic." She sighed heavily and took the bottle, tipping it back to finish what was left. "You know, Remy," she said. "You're lucky."

I stared at her in confusion and remained quiet.

"Like, your parents suck, right?" she continued. "But they're not *that* bad."

"What?"

"And at least you have Christian," she added.

I scoffed. "Christian is worse than useless."

"He seems nice," she said, and I swore I heard a hint of infatuation in her voice.

"Yeah, but he isn't," I said. "It's all just a facade."

"What do you mean?" she asked.

"Never mind," I said. "And besides, I think he has a girlfriend."

"What? Who?"

"The captain of the field hockey team, Vanessa something, I think?"

"Oh," she said, an entire ocean of disappointment squeezed into one syllable.

"Why?" I asked. "Do you like him?" We both knew she did but I wanted her to just admit it. We were best friends, family, but she still couldn't trust me.

"What? No," she said. Our eyes locked and we stared at each other, neither of us giving in.

"What'd you mean earlier," I said finally, breaking eye contact. "When you said my parents weren't *that* bad?"

"Just—" She turned to look me in the eye. "There are, you know, gradations. And your parents suck but they could suck more. So much more." She was talking about her mother, how she'd been abandoned.

"All they do is argue with each other and throw the word *divorce* around once in a while," she continued, eyes closed and oblivious to the impact her words had on me. "You're lucky, in a lot of ways."

"What?" I pulled away from her, shrinking into myself. I couldn't believe she was comparing our childhoods to see who had it worse. She'd seen what they were like, knew what it was like for me. Just because my mom didn't leave when I was seven didn't mean I was lucky. In some ways, I wished she *had* left.

We're different, you and me, Elise had said. *Special. People like Melody Moon have had perfect lives with nice parents and nice clothes and nice everything.* We were different from everyone but we were different *together*, with our far-from-perfect lives. We knew pain and were stronger for it. That was the story Elise told. Our creation myth of sorts. It'd always been us versus everybody else, never her against me.

Her eyes fluttered open at my prolonged silence.

"I'm *lucky*?" I was devastated. "How can you say that?"

For a moment, she looked lost. "Wait—"

"And what exactly makes me so lucky? That my parents don't love me and never did?" I was crying, angry now. "That I have no one?"

"I'm sorry," she said, eyes wide at my tears. "I'm sorry, Remy. I didn't mean that." She pushed her wineglass away from her and sat up straight, shaking her head roughly. "I'm so sorry, I don't know why I'm acting like this. You're right, you're not lucky."

What shook me the most was seeing this side of her, knowing how easily she could hurt me. It had to be the wine, I thought, though I couldn't get rid of the feeling there was something she wasn't telling me.

"But where is all of this coming from?" I just wanted her to talk to me.

"I just—" She took a deep breath. "It's a weird time for me."

"Why?"

"This is around the time my mom died three years ago?" she said hesitantly, like it was a question. "And I had to go to her funeral even though I hadn't even spoken to her in almost ten years."

It was like plunging into cold water, a shock to the system. Elise was finally, *finally* opening up. I dried my tears, sitting straighter.

"My mom didn't like me much either," she said with a weak laugh. "And my dad, well." She shrugged, turning away. "And my grandparents. They hated us, thought their precious daughter had married trash. Pretended we didn't exist for the most part." Her voice had turned dull, almost monotone. "And now we live in their house and drink out of their glasses and sleep in their bedrooms." She shook her head in disbelief. "Maybe we should burn it down." She seemed lost in thought. "Can you imagine, the granddaughter they were ashamed of destroying what they spent their life building? The banished princess returning to burn their castle down?" She laughed. "It'd be poetic." It was the same word she'd said about *Kill Bill*—poetic.

I laughed too, but I didn't really think it was that funny. I was still upset about what she'd said, about how I was lucky that my shitty parents weren't shittier, but I also understood what she meant about gradations. And she was sad, so I let it go.

"Do you want to watch the second one?" I asked even though I didn't really want to, hoping it would cheer her up.

"You really want to watch *Volume Two*?" she asked with a wobbly smile.

I nodded. "I want to find out what happens."

It was almost seven in the morning when we finished. I was on the precipice of sleep, slumped over against Elise, just barely keeping my eyes open.

"Rem?" she whispered.

"Hmm?"

"I love you."

My eyes fluttered open and I smiled. "I love you too."

109

21.

For a couple weeks after the New Year, I watched Elise carefully, wondering if she'd bring up that night or snap at me like that again, but she didn't. It was easy to think the Elise I'd glimpsed on New Year's Eve was a weird, one-time thing. That wasn't the Elise I knew.

She began to spend more time at my house. Even though she never said why, I knew she wanted to be there for me, shield me from my parents' battles. I'd never had that before, someone who cared about me like that. And while Elise still had other friends, I was her *best* friend.

A few faces had changed, but Julie Adichie and Jae Park were always at Elise's lunch table, along with newcomers Madison Laurent, who was Julie's girlfriend, and Ben Torres, who was a midyear transfer from Florida.

Some nights, Elise would drag me out with them, and we'd go to McDonald's or Waffle House for breakfast at midnight, or go for an aimless drive. On our first nighttime adventure, we all went to the football field at school and sat on the Astroturf, smoking and talking. At some point, Jae took out his phone to play music and Julie took Madison's hand, the two of them dancing in the dark.

"Come on," Elise said, pulling me up too. She twirled me and I laughed, feeling exhilarated, the winter air sharp against my skin. Eventually we all collapsed onto the ground, breathless.

Melody would never approve, I thought. It wasn't a school night, but it was still late and we were technically trespassing on our own school property. Then again, Melody and I weren't talking much by that point.

The last time we spoke had been over two weeks ago. She'd cornered me after school one day. "I'm worried about you," she began, and I could already feel my defenses coming up.

"What do you mean?" I asked. I'm sure she really thought she was worried about me, but I couldn't help but think that she was just jealous.

"You seem different. It's like you just moved on from obsessing over Cameron to obsessing over Elise," she said with a frown.

I shrugged it off. "What do you want, Mel?"

"Nothing," she said, looking hurt. "You're my oldest friend. My *best* friend."

I stayed quiet but felt bad. "You say that like we're not friends anymore."

"Are we?" Melody asked. "I never see you and you don't even bother to text me back most of the time."

"I'm sorry." I meant it, but both of us knew I wasn't going to come back to the fold. I never felt like I fit in with Mel and her friends, and now I had Elise, someone who knew and loved the real me.

"Elise—I don't know," she said, and my guard was up again.

"What about Elise?" I said, immediately ready to defend her.

"She seems kind of selfish?" Melody said, sounding uncertain. "Wait—maybe that's not the right word."

"Elise is one of the most selfless people I've ever met," I said, remembering our first night together. How she caught me when I was reeling and patched me up. She always knew what I needed, she was always looking out for me.

"That's not what I meant," Melody tried again, but I was already walking away from her.

Elise said Melody and I had simply outgrown each other. "But don't worry," she told me. "*We* will never outgrow each other." And I believed her.

Lying on the Astroturf, we were all still laughing, Elise's hand loosely on top of my wrist. Our eyes met and even in the dark I could see that undercurrent of electricity behind hers. She gave my hand a short squeeze and let go.

"I'm bored," Jae announced when the laughter died down.

"Well, we can't have that. What do you want to do?" Elise asked.

"I don't know. But *something*. Anything."

"I have an idea," Julie said. "We could go trash Mr. Dawkins's classroom."

"What? Why?" Ben said.

"Ugh, he *is* gross," Elise said. Dawkins, one of the AP Lit teachers, had a certain reputation for being a creep. He never said anything reportable but I'd heard girls complain about the way he'd look at them, staring a little too long, or the way he kept asking some of the students to come by his room after school for a chat— almost always his female students. I stayed clear of him and his classroom. Had he done something awful to Julie?

"I don't know how or why, but he found out about me and Madi," Julie said. "And he pulled her aside to ask her about us."

We all sat up and looked at Madison expectantly. "Well, I mean, it wasn't that big of a deal, but yeah, not exactly great either. He was just 'curious,'" she said, using air quotes. "He wanted to know why I broke up with my boyfriend for Julie, which isn't even what happened!" I couldn't believe he took it upon himself to target them like that.

"He said he was *concerned* about her," Julie said, rolling her eyes. "He wanted to make sure she was making good life choices."

"What the hell?" Ben said, leaning forward, elbows against his knees.

"Actually, he didn't even say Julie's name, just 'that girl,'" Madison added before reaching for Julie's hand.

"Wonderful," Elise said.

"Let's do it," Jae said. "Let's go trash his room."

"No," Madison said. "Let's just forget about it. I mean, he's a jerk but he's harmless, you know? More annoying than anything else. And I'm graduating in a few months, anyway."

"I don't know," Elise said. "I feel like we should do *something*." It was moments like this that I was extra grateful for Elise. She could be counted on to take action, fix things.

Madison shook her head. "That was a couple weeks ago and he hasn't said anything since. Honestly, I feel sorry for him. He's just sad and pathetic and lonely."

"You're way too nice," Julie said, but ultimately she sided with Madison, and we dropped it.

"How do you even end up like that?" Ben asked, reaching for another cigarette.

"What?" Elise said.

"Like Dawkins. Pathetic and creepy."

"Maybe he was always pathetic and creepy," Julie said.

"I don't think so," I said. Everyone turned to stare at me, surprised that I'd interjected. With Elise and her friends, I'd always felt a little out of my depth and liked to stay under the radar.

"What do you mean?" Elise asked.

"Just—" I thought of my parents. They couldn't have always been what they were now. They had to have loved each other at *some* point. There were photographs around the house with genuine smiles, with affection in their eyes. "People change," I said. "They change and get weird and bitter, and I guess, creepy."

"God, I hope that doesn't happen to me," Madison said, flopping onto her back, pulling Julie down next to her.

"I wonder about that sometimes," Jae said softly, staring at the ground. "Do you like any of the adults you know? I mean, do you want to be like them—your parents, your teachers? Sometimes I think about that and I just want nothing to do with them."

"Yeah," Elise answered, voice quiet. "I know what you mean."

"My mom's okay," Julie said. "But I don't want her life. She just seems trapped. Stuck." Madison took her hand and squeezed it.

"Like, my parents thought it was a waste of time when I started doing magic," Jae said. "But when I started getting all this attention, they got excited and made me work at it constantly until I hated it. They still show people that stupid clip of me on *Good Morning America* even though I quit pretty much right after I went on the show." He also stretched back down onto the ground, closing his eyes. "Maybe that's what happens to people."

"What?" Madison asked.

"The universe takes the things they love and turns them into the things they hate," he said. I thought of my parents then, what they let the universe take from them. How they ended up trapped and unhappy, their misery compounded by their efforts to hide it.

"That's just your parents being assholes," Elise said. "There's no way I'm going to be anything like mine."

"How do you know?" Jae asked.

Elise simply smiled and said: "The universe only takes things from you if you let it. So don't."

Later that night, when it was just the two of us, we went to the Pink Mansion, where we could be alone, her father gone for the night. Out on the balcony, Elise sat on the bannister even though it made me nervous. The drop to the river below was steep, and in the dark it was hard to see anything and that made it seem even farther away.

"Get down," I told her.

"I'm fine," she said, smiling down at me. "I'm not going to fall."

"Elise," I said. "Please."

"Trust me," she said. "I'm not going to fall. Join me, it feels good."

I shook my head and she shrugged.

"You know what we should do?" she said, her voice excited.

"What?"

"We should prank Dawkins," she said, eyes bright. "He's a predator. Come on, it'll be like a present for Julie and Madi."

"But Madison said she didn't want to prank him."

"She did," Elise insisted. "She was just too scared to admit it."

"I don't know," I said.

"We won't do anything big." She hopped down. "No mice or

slashed tires. We'll just find out where he lives and set off fireworks outside his house, like we did with Cameron."

It took me a moment before I caved. "Okay, I guess," I said, following her into the house and up to the attic. We rifled through box after box, starting with the ones near where we'd found fireworks the first time, but there were no more to be found.

Instead, we found a gun.

A small revolver with bullets beside it, all nestled in a leather case. Elise pulled it out, the attic light hitting the metal barrel like a spark.

I instinctively backed away. "Oh my God, put that down!"

She fiddled with it, checking to see if it was loaded. "Don't worry. There aren't any bullets." Elise pointed it away from us and pulled the trigger. *Click.* "See? Nothing to worry about."

"Oh my God." Alarmed, I recoiled from her, scrambling away.

"What? It was unloaded!" she said, like it was no big deal.

It took a few breaths before I could speak again. "Still. And why was there a gun here anyway? Did you know?"

"I had no idea," she said. "It must've belonged to my grandparents."

"Let's put the gun down," I said, both hands raised.

Elise ignored me and got up, posing with it pointed up close to her chest like she was an action hero about to kick down a door, a spy with a license to kill. Her dark hair looked coppery, almost golden under the light, and when she swept it back to one side, she shot me a quick wink.

"Put the gun down," I said, slowly getting up. I couldn't believe how cavalier she was being. "Please."

Elise sighed. "Fine, fine. What's wrong?"

"I don't like guns," I said. "I just really don't like them."

"Okay." She put it back into the case and snapped it shut. "There, all gone. Feel better?"

I nodded.

"Let's go to your place, watch a movie." She dusted herself off. "I'm tired. Dawkins can wait."

"I'm tired too," I said, secretly relieved that the prank had been abandoned. "Let's just stay here."

She paused. For a moment I wondered again about all the time Elise spent over at my house. I'd thought she wanted to be there for me, protect me from the havoc my parents wrought, but wouldn't I be safer here at the Pink Mansion, away from all of them?

"The thing is," she began, choosing her words carefully, "my dad might come back tomorrow morning."

So that was it. Her father.

Elise took a deep breath. "Things are a little weird between us right now." She sounded pained, like she didn't want to have to admit that there was something wrong.

"Is everything okay?" I asked. Finally, I thought. Maybe she'd tell me what was going on with her dad.

"Yeah, of course," she said, a little too quickly. "Everything's fine. He's just being kind of an asshole." I wasn't convinced. When she saw the concern on my face, she added, "It's nothing I can't handle." She attempted a smile that ended up looking more like a grimace. She wasn't willing to talk, but I knew if I pushed now she'd only dig in harder. I was frustrated that she was still shutting me out but I tried to let it go.

"What are you in the mood for?" I asked once we were in my basement trying to pick a movie.

She took a moment to think about it. "Christian Bale?"

I laughed. "Okay."

We fell asleep on the couch in the early hours of the morning, *The Dark Knight Rises* still playing in front of us.

That was the night I realized Elise loved superheroes, because superheroes were powerful and the one thing she could never tolerate was feeling powerless. That was partly why she loved playing pranks, why she was always looking out for her friends—she didn't want anyone else to feel powerless either.

22.

"I'm going to give you a chance now, Remy," Detective Ward says. "I'm going to give you a chance to change your statement."

Vera cuts in. "I need a moment with Remy. Alone."

"No," I say. "It's okay. I don't want to change my statement. I was there, and Elise only said that I wasn't because she thinks she's protecting me." Elise is telling the truth—I *wasn't* there—but the only way I can save her now is if Ward believes that I *was* there.

"And what, exactly, is she protecting you from?" Detective Ward says, an edge to her voice now, her impatience showing again, that flash of teeth.

"Nothing," I say, voice strong all of a sudden, strong enough to surprise even me. "She *thinks* she's protecting me. She's worried I'll get into trouble, she's—" I break off. "She does this. A lot."

"Lie?" Detective Ward asks, lifting her pen to make a note.

"No!" I need her to see Elise like I do, but I don't know how to make her understand. We stare at each other, eyes locked. I feel like I'm in the fight of my life—no, the fight *for* my life. For Elise's life.

119

I've already lost Jack.

I can't lose her too.

Heart racing, I manage to hold her gaze until she breaks eye contact. My head is pounding, but this small victory gives me strength.

"Let's go over it again," Detective Ward says, scanning her notes. "One more time, from the top. What were you doing before you and Elise went to her house?"

The question surprises me. I haven't thought of anything but the moments surrounding Jack's death. "I think we had dinner."

"Where?"

"I'm not sure. Panera, maybe?" I say, and that's the truth. Everything about yesterday feels out of focus, my memories cloudy and fragmented. Where we ate dinner. The 9-1-1 call I made. But some moments are so clear I can close my eyes and I'm there again. Elise's comforting hand on my shoulder. Jack pressing a kiss to my forehead. The gunshots.

That gun, that fucking gun. Jack would still be alive if we'd never stumbled across it. Yes, Elise thought she saw her father, and yes, she and Jack were arguing over the pranks. But without the gun, none of this would be happening. The three of us, we'd be in school today. I'd be taking that physics test, but then I'd get to see Jack at lunch. And after, we'd go to the lake.

No matter how bad things got, we would've all survived if it weren't for that revolver.

"You're not sure?" Ward asks. Her voice jolts me back to reality, to the place where I've lost Jack. Where I might lose Elise too.

"No, I'm sorry," I say, and I can tell she believes me. I have no reason to lie about that. My memories are shards of a broken vase that I'm trying to piece back together.

"And before dinner?"

"I was with Jack that morning." He met me at the lake and we sat by the water, dipping our feet in. I was mad at Elise about the final prank we pulled the night before. If I close my eyes, I can still feel Jack's arm around my shoulders, heavy and warm. A safe harbor.

"Doing what?" she asks, leaning toward me, pen positioned over paper.

"Just hanging out." The tears fall quickly. I miss him so much that I shake with longing. My body still remembers his touch, still hears his voice, still misses him. I can't imagine feeling that way about anyone else again. I can't imagine anyone in his place.

I don't know what's worse—losing him entirely or this tortuous longing. I already fear the day I wake up unable to remember the sound of his voice, or the way we held hands, mine in front of his.

Detective Ward pauses her questioning about the timeline of that awful day. Instead she says, "Tell me about Jack."

23.

Elise's birthday fell on the Saturday after prom, and she spent the entire Friday afternoon before trying to convince me to crash a senior party with her.

"It'll be fun," she promised. "Madison and Julie are going, and so is Jae."

By then our circle of friends had come down to the five of us, with Ben leaving not long after he joined—Elise was not for the faint of heart.

"Madi said it wasn't seniors only," Elise added.

We were passing the last cigarette in her pack back and forth between us while lying on the lounge chairs by the pool in my backyard. It was almost warm enough to swim.

"Please, Remy? For my birthday?" She turned to face me.

"It's just going to be a bunch of drunk idiots hanging out. I'd rather stay in tonight, count down to midnight like we did for mine," I told her. It'd been the best birthday I had in years, maybe ever. "Or we could just watch both volumes of Kill Bill again and eat cake."

"Tempting," Elise said with a smile. "But no, come on. It'll be fun. It's an anti-prom party."

"The one Summer's throwing?" I asked. Summer Stevens was well known for her benevolent popularity and aggressive tennis serve, and for throwing the best parties. She'd gotten into Cornell early and was cruising through the rest of her senior year.

"Yeah, and everyone's going to be there."

I raised an eyebrow. "Everyone?" I just wanted her to admit that she liked Christian. For her to tell me things like I always did with her.

"Everyone," she confirmed.

"Like who?"

"Well, like I said, Julie and Madi. Jae too."

"Who else?" I asked, growing suspicious. "Christian?" She almost never brought him up, or even interacted with him directly, but after the Thanksgiving fundraiser I'd sometimes catch her staring at him with this look of curiosity. Of interest.

"What? No, Mr. Student Council President? He'll definitely be at prom," she said, her words measured yet casual, like she wanted to sound nonchalant. But she was right. Of course he'd be at the dance.

"Okay, we can go," I said reluctantly.

"We won't stay long, maybe an hour tops. Promise."

I'd ordered Elise's birthday present months ago, a vintage cigarette case like the ones in old movies, with an inscription mirroring the one on my lighter: *Remy x Elise*. It'd been hard not to give it to her as soon as it arrived. I put it in my bag, nestled in a box with pale pink tissue paper. In my mind, we'd go to the party, Elise would get bored after an hour, and then we'd leave with plenty of time until midnight.

I was only half-right.

Elise did get bored after an hour, but she didn't want to leave. The kitchen ran out of drinks almost immediately, so the five of us were hanging out on Summer's deck sipping sugary mixer. Elise lit two cigarettes and passed one to me.

"I'd do everything so differently," she said, nodding toward the house, the party. "This is just sad."

"So do it," Julie said, like issuing a challenge.

Elise's smile grew. "Okay." She began to outline plans with more and more excitement. They'd use the football field. Julie's sister had a stereo and mixing equipment. And then it was just a matter of doing a little shopping and getting the word out.

I pulled her aside before we all left. "It's ten," I said, trying not to whine.

"Oh. I hadn't noticed."

"It's okay," I said. "But let's just go."

"What? No, we have a anti-anti-prom party to throw," she said, laughing lightly.

"But you promised," I said, hating the way I sounded, like a petulant child.

"Soon," she said. "Two more hours, okay?" She lit another cigarette, releasing a stream of smoke into the night.

Her present was still in my bag. I'd planned to give it to her right at midnight when we were alone. I wanted to see her face light up. To hear her tell me how much she loved it, and how much she loved me.

"Okay?" Elise repeated, looking at me expectantly.

"I—" Opening my bag, I pulled it out. "I wanted to wait until midnight, but here." I handed it to her. "Happy birthday."

"Oh," she said, surprised. Dropping her cigarette and snuffing it out with her shoe, Elise reached for the box. She tugged on the intricately tied ribbon, unraveling an hour of my work in less than a second. "I love it," she said, a smile forming as she saw the cigarette case. "It's beautiful."

"Look at the bottom," I said, feeling a little nervous. I wanted her to like it as much as I liked the lighter. I wanted her to treasure it.

Remy x Elise.

"I love it so much." She reached for her pack and began to fill the case. "I really love it," she said again, fingers brushing the filigree.

"Really?" I said, happiness surging through me. I thought we'd leave then, spend the rest of the night just the two of us. I was hoping she'd abandon her idea of throwing a party to rival Summer's. That she'd see the cigarette case and be reminded of how special our friendship was. That she'd ditch the party to be with me.

"Really," she said, eyes soft as she pulled me in for a hug.

"Come on," I said, tugging on her wrist when we broke apart. "Let's go."

"Oh." She stepped back. "Um, Remy, no."

"What?"

"I already said I'd do it, and Julie and Jae are already getting the word out. I can't just abandon everyone." It was true that leaving now might disappoint the others, but I knew Elise and she always did what she wanted. If she wanted to skip the party and spend the rest of the night with me, then she'd just do it. Which meant she *didn't* want to go with me, or at least that she wanted something else

125

more than she wanted me. She was fast becoming my whole world. I didn't even talk to Melody anymore because I'd chosen her. Elise was my person but it didn't always seem like I was hers.

"How are you even going to get the alcohol?" I asked, thinking she was going to ask us to raid our parents' liquor cabinets.

She gave me a weird look. "I have a fake."

"You do?" I'd never seen her use it before, and maybe it was unfair because I never asked her about it, but I couldn't help but think this was yet another thing she kept from me.

"How do you think I buy us cigarettes, Remy?"

"I—" I began. "I don't know, you always go to the same gas station. I thought maybe the guy there didn't card?" It sounded dumb as soon as I'd said it.

"Oh. Um, no." She stuck the cigarette case in her bag and pulled out her wallet. "Here." It was a Tennessee license that said she was twenty-two. "I never told you?"

I shook my head. "Aren't you afraid we'll get into trouble?"

"Look," she said, sighing. "This isn't really your kind of thing."

"What do you mean?"

"Don't take this the wrong way, but you're a little uptight. No, that's not the right word, sorry. Inflexible, that's better. You like schedules. 'It's ten, let's go home now,' that kind of thing."

I was too shocked to speak. It took only a few words from Elise to make me feel special, but it took only a few words from her to make me feel like shit.

"Why don't you go home? I'll join you later. Take my keys. I'll catch a ride with Jae or something, okay?" She pressed the keys to the Pink Caddy into my hands and gave me a quick hug before running to catch up with the others.

126

"Okay?" I said, but she was already gone. I couldn't believe how easy it'd been for her to leave me behind without a backward glance.

Not feeling like going home, I sat on the front steps staring off into the darkness. I felt betrayed. I thought about driving to the football field where they were heading, and joining up with them again. I could be spontaneous, I could be fun.

The things she said about me were devastating, and the way she said them was like she was talking about someone like Melody—completely dismissive. But that wasn't the most heartbreaking thing about what she'd said. What hurt the most was knowing that she was enough for me, but I wasn't enough for her.

Then the door opened behind me, startling me out of my thoughts. I turned around to see a guy standing there in jeans and a worn Superman tee, towering over me with his own look of surprise.

"Shitty night?" he said, plopping down.

"Do I know you?" I asked, hoping to make him go away.

"Don't think so," he said. "Hi, I'm Jack."

24.

My heart didn't skip a beat when our eyes first made contact. Sparks didn't fly, the earth didn't shake. If I couldn't be with Elise, I wanted to be alone.

"I hate these things," Jack said, cocking his head back at the door and the party beyond it.

I glanced over, trying to place his face. I might've seen him inside but couldn't remember where. With his imposing height, square jaw, and dark hair, he looked like he could actually tie on a red cape and fly off as Superman. He looked like a jock, not like someone who'd hate parties.

"Then why are you here?" I said, wishing he hadn't sat down. I just wanted to be left alone to despair in peace.

"Mistakes were made," he said, the corners of his mouth lifting. Then he grew more serious and added, "Let's just say I was trying to be someone I used to be."

I raised an eyebrow.

He ran a hand through his hair and sighed. "A year ago, I would've loved this. I would've been the one turning the music all the way up. I would've been the one showing up with tequila and making everyone take shots. But now it all just seems—I don't know." He sighed. "Pointless, I guess. Now it's like I don't even understand any of them anymore, like we exist on different planets. I've moved on."

That was how I felt too. Everyone pretending to be somebody else, everyone trying to lose themselves. What Elise and I had was different, I thought. What we had was real. I couldn't understand why she'd choose anything over me.

"But it's easier, sometimes," Jack continued. "To try and be the guy you were. Everyone liked that guy, everyone thought he was fun to be around." He didn't sound angry, only sad.

I looked at him more closely this time, really trying to place him, but still couldn't. His eyes were dark and soulful, betraying what had to be a deliberately crafted appearance of someone carefree, maybe the person he used to be. Maybe he wasn't like them after all, maybe he understood.

He turned toward me, and when our eyes made contact for the second time, my heart did skip a beat.

"Hey, do you want to get out of here?" Jack said. I hesitated and glanced at the Pink Caddy. Elise really wasn't coming back for me.

"You okay?" he asked.

"Yeah," I said, shaking my head a little to clear it. "Yeah, let's get out of here." I thought briefly about going to the football field again, but even if I did go, Elise would just give me a quick hug and spend the rest of the night making sure everyone else had a good time.

Inflexible, that's what she'd called me.

Jack stood up, offering a hand.

A little uptight.

"Let's go," I said.

Jack had a motorcycle. He saw the apprehension on my face when he passed me a spare helmet.

"This your first time? Don't worry, I'll go slow and steady. Just hold on to me." At first, I held on to his sides gingerly, my fingers barely touching his Superman tee, which made Jack laugh. "You can also hold the bar behind you, but it's less comfortable." I placed my hands, then arms, around him, and it hit me—I was really doing this. I'd never been on a motorcycle. I'd never left with someone I'd just met.

"Where are we going?" I asked.

"Have you ever been to Morgan Falls?"

"No."

"It's basically my favorite place."

We passed by the school, then merged onto the highway. For twenty minutes we rode in silence, the bright overhead lights of 400 flying past us. His body was warm, hot even, despite the chill from the wind all around us. I wondered if he could feel my heart pounding against his back. I didn't dare breathe too much, afraid I'd somehow cause us to tip over.

"What'd you think?" he said when we got off at the park.

I pretended to check my limbs and count my fingers and toes. "Looks like everything's all there."

He laughed. "It's not that bad."

"It's only terrifying," I shot back, but I was smiling too. See, I thought. Not uptight.

Morgan Falls Overlook Park lived up to its name with trails, a dock, and a beautiful area with swinging benches that opened up into a huge reservoir below.

We leaned against the safety railing together, looking out at the water, its calm surface glistening faintly under the moonlight.

"Come on," Jack said, getting up. I followed him down to the dock, which was just a plastic floating platform that extended out into the water. "I love it here at night, when no one's around." He took off his shoes and rolled up his pants to dip his feet in the water.

I slipped out of my flip-flops before swinging my legs into the water too. Jack lay down, arms overhead, hands under his head. I joined him and we looked at the stars as we swayed softly with the water. It felt like all the times Elise and I hung out in the Pink Caddy at night, our eyes on the sky, but also different. Brand new and thrilling, yet quieter, more pensive.

"Do you ever get hit by a weird sense of longing?" Jack said.

"What do you mean?"

"Like a sharp and sudden pang. It's almost like feeling homesick, but homesick isn't the right word for it," Jack said. "You might not be far from home, or you might even *be* at home and still get hit by it, this—this yearning. The feeling of being incomplete, like you're missing something." Then he turned to me and laughed. "You think I'm crazy, don't you?"

"No, I—" I was surprised by his sudden admission, but even more surprised that he had put into words a feeling that, for my whole life, I had known so well but could never describe. "I think I know that feeling you're talking about." It was more like a yearning for an alternate past, an alternate life. "I think it *is* a kind of homesickness," I said. "But not for home. It's like a piece of you is missing. Maybe you lost it, or maybe you never had it, but something is just not there and you don't know where to even begin looking for it. A homesickness not for a place but for another life entirely. Another *you*."

"Yes!" Jack said, springing up to sit. "Exactly. It feels almost like I veered off course somewhere and ended up in the wrong timeline of my life. The wrong version of myself. And now I don't know where to go."

"But you can't go back," I said.

Our eyes locked and I found a spark of recognition in him. A small smile appeared on his face and I knew he was thinking the same thing.

That feeling, it wasn't loneliness. It was a mix of hopelessness and despair, fear and longing. The need to reach, grasp for something in the dark without knowing what it was that you even wanted. It was being lost, wanting to want something, wanting to know what to want. An exhausting aimlessness.

I hadn't experienced that in a while, ever since I met Elise. I never felt lost after she found me. As long as I had her, I had nothing to fear. Only now I wasn't sure I'd always have her.

Pulling out my lighter—Elise's lighter—I stared at the moonlight reflecting off the metal. Elise was wild, Elise did what she wanted. She burned brightly, and I wanted to be like her. Unpredictable, maybe even a little dangerous.

I didn't want to be jealous of her, of what she might be doing at her anti-anti-prom party. I wanted *her* to be jealous of *me* and what I might be doing without her.

Pushing myself up on the floating dock, I turned to Jack with a smile before slipping out of my jeans and pulling off my top. "Come on, don't be so serious," I said, more to myself than to him, and then jumped into the water.

"Wait," he said. "We shouldn't. It's dark and the lake bed has uneven drops."

I emerged and swept my wet hair back.

"It's dark."

"We won't go far," I said. "We'll stay by the dock."

"I don't know."

"Wait, can you swim?" I asked.

He laughed. "Yes, I can swim." And then he joined me in the water.

We stayed by the dock and shoreline, our feet slipping against the lake bed. We chased each other back and forth with splashes and then Jack dove under. I looked all around me at the inky water and called his name. Suddenly he burst above surface right in front of me, laughing. Before I could slip away, his hand found mine.

"Hi," he said, his voice soft.

"Hi," I said, and everything seemed to fall away.

It was April, but without the sun I was shivering. Gently, he pulled me closer until I could feel his breath on my skin. Then, with eyes closed, our lips touched and I was no longer cold.

When we got back to his motorcycle, we were soaking wet. We'd stayed as long as we could in the water, only getting out when I began to sneeze. "Here," he said, offering me his Superman tee once we were out.

"I'm okay," I said, even though I was shivering in my tank top. I wanted to seem tough, like I could take care of myself—like Elise.

He stood there in a thin black tee, hand outstretched. "Come on, you're freezing."

"I'm fine," I said, embarrassed when I promptly sneezed.

Jack laughed, offering it to me again. He was so thoughtful—first at the lake when he was worried about swimming in the dark, and now trying to keep me warm. More thoughtful than any of the other boys I'd known.

"All right." I slipped into it. It was soft and smelled like him, a faint hint of peppermint. We made a quick stop at a gas station for coffee, and on the ride back, I relaxed against his body, resting my cheek on his shoulder and closing my eyes.

I wondered where Elise was, if she was having fun.

Pushing her out of my mind, I focused on Jack, how warm and strong he was in my arms. How kissing him had felt, our bodies brushing gently in the water, his skin like silk against mine.

We must've been gone for at least a couple hours, but when we got back to Summer's house, the Pink Caddy was still sitting by the mailbox in a long string of cars.

I wasn't ready to say goodbye and he didn't look like he was either. He took my hand and we walked to the swings on the playground by the tennis courts.

"I haven't done this in forever," I said, kicking hard to go higher. "Did you ever jump off as a kid? I was always too scared."

"Oh yeah," Jack said, laughing beside me, keeping pace. "I sprained an ankle that way."

"Really?" I turned to look at him, half laughing, half impressed. He nodded, his smile mesmerizing.

We kept going for a while until we got bored and climbed up the jungle gym to lie on the highest platform and look at the sky, our knees touching. He asked me if I thought there was anyone out there in the vast expanse of the universe, if I ever felt small, and I told him that his life mattered, that *he* mattered.

Then Jack kissed me under the stars, and my heart felt like bursting. I closed my eyes and curled onto his body.

"We smell like lake," I said.

He laughed, then sniffed my hair. "You're right."

"Hey!" I elbowed him.

"But in a good way. Very earthy."

"Earthy? You mean like dirt?"

"Shhh," he said, kissing me again. Then in a mock sexy voice, he whispered in my ear, "I've never met anyone like you before—so beautiful and so . . . aromatic?"

I laughed and he kissed my forehead. I closed my eyes again and we fell into a lovely silence. I was almost asleep when he nudged me. "Remy."

"Yeah?" I said, rubbing my eyes.

"Tonight's been magical," he said softly. "I haven't felt like myself in so long." His words reminded me of what he'd said earlier that night, about how he wasn't the same person he used to be.

"What do you mean?" I rested a light hand on his cheek, fingers brushing his hair.

He hesitated, looked unsure.

"You can tell me," I said.

"I don't want to make things weird." He turned away from me to stare at the sky. "People don't know how to deal with me when I—"

My hand slipped down his arm to find his. "Tell me."

He kept his eyes on the stars as he began. "My grandfather passed away last year," he said quietly. "We were really close."

"I'm so sorry," I said. Christian and I rarely saw our grandparents, even over the holidays, and we'd never been close, but the pain in Jack's voice was so raw, it cut right through me.

Jack really *was* different from all the guys at school, all the guys I'd ever met. He seemed older, even though he was the same age as Christian. He seemed *real*, like maybe he also had a wound that needed attention. The damaged parts of myself could see that he carried the shards of his broken heart with him everywhere he went, and I thought it was tragic, romantic even.

"Growing up, my mom was around but she was working all the time," Jack said. "She's a flight attendant, gone for days at a time. Grandpa was kind of the one who raised me. He was the one person I could count on."

I wanted to hold him tight, comfort him.

"I never thought he would ever *lie* to me. That was the worst part—he didn't tell me until the start of senior year—" He broke off, looked away.

"What happened?" I asked gently.

"My grandfather hadn't been feeling well all last summer, nothing serious, just getting colds all the time and headaches and random pain all over. He insisted it was just him getting old." Jack sighed and turned away, blinking fast like he was on the verge of tears. "I ended up taking the year off school to spend more time with him, and he was so angry, telling me not to waste such an important year of my life."

"I'm so sorry." Unsure what else I could say to ease his pain, I shifted closer and pressed a kiss against his forehead.

We remained like that for a while, me leaning on my elbow watching over him, a soft hand resting on his chest, a finger tracing small circles against his black tee.

Jack was so vulnerable, and he reminded me of myself before I met Elise, alone and in need of protection. In that moment, I knew I could be the person to give it to him.

"Remy?" he said. "Tell me something true."

I looked into his eyes. "I'm really glad I met you."

His smile could light up the world.

"Tell me something true?" I asked.

"You're the first person I felt like I could talk to in a long time," he said, and under the moonlight, he was beautiful.

25.

I texted Elise as soon as I got home, so excited to tell her about Jack, my anger from our fight largely dissipated in the rush of the last few hours. Maybe it'd been an off night for her, I thought. Maybe I'd misunderstood her. I thought she'd want to celebrate her birthday the same way we celebrated mine, but maybe what she really wanted was a party.

Whatever it was, I could never stay angry at her for long, and I thought that things would just go back to normal.

Me: Where are you?

Me: I have to tell you something omg

She didn't respond. I was so tired I fell asleep waiting for her.

The call came at three in the morning. "What? Hello?" I answered, barely awake.

"Remy?" Elise sounded like she'd been crying. Elise never cried. Ever.

"*Elise?*" I rubbed my eyes and swept my hair back, sitting up.

"Can you come get me?" she asked, voice small.

137

"Just tell me where to go," I said, already getting out of bed.

"I'm in that strip mall near school," she said. "Hurry."

The streets were empty that time of night, giving the town an eerily abandoned feel. Standing in front of the CVS with her arms wrapped around herself, Elise was alone, shivering. I pulled up alongside the curb.

"What happened?" I asked, waiting for her to get in. I didn't understand where the others had gone, or how she'd ended up there. "Are you hurt?" She looked awful, hair in disarray, eyeliner smeared from crying. It was terrifying seeing her like that.

"I'm fine. But I don't want to talk about it." She buckled her seat belt and stared stubbornly forward. "Where's my car?" She sounded tired but also irritated. Was she upset that I didn't show up any sooner? It took me a moment to wake up before I sneaked out. Why wouldn't she just tell me what'd happened?

"It's parked in front of my house."

"Okay," she said, softer this time, and that was when I noticed it.

"You're drunk." It was less an accusation and more of a statement.

"Maybe," she said, closing her eyes. "Please, Rem, let's just *go*."

We remained silent on the drive back. I wished she would just *talk* to me. I was her best friend. In the ten minutes we spent on the road, I spun through all the things that could've happened. She said she wasn't hurt but she didn't clarify what that actually meant.

When we arrived at my house, she stumbled inside with me through the basement, careful not to wake anyone.

"Come on," I said, heading for the stairs, one of her arms slung over my shoulders, half of her weight on me.

"No, can we just stay here?" She collapsed on the sectional, burying her face into a pillow.

"E—"

"Shhh," she mumbled. "Sleep now. Talk later." I was worried but I was afraid of upsetting her, so I just filled a glass with water and left it on the coffee table next to her.

I turned off the lights and lay down, dragging a quilt over me. When I was about to fall asleep, she reached out and touched my shoulder.

"Remy?"

My eyes flew open. "Yeah."

"Nothing, never mind," she said, falling silent again.

"What is it?" I flipped over to face her. "You know you can tell me anything." *Please*, I thought. Please just talk to me.

She swallowed slowly and turned, our eyes meeting in the dark. "You and me, we're family," she said. "Right?"

I nodded, though I couldn't help thinking about earlier that night, when she'd left me behind for her other friends, when she made me feel like I was a burden.

"That's all that matters. You and me, just the two of us," she said, and I decided then that all was forgiven.

"You and me," I said in agreement, like it was a promise.

26.

When I woke up again, it was almost noon and Elise was sitting cross-legged on the couch watching *Kill Bill: Vol. 2* with the TV muted.

"Hey," she said, smiling at me.

"Hey," I said, rubbing my eyes and sitting up next to her. "Why are you watching this without sound?"

She shrugged. "I didn't want to wake you. And I know pretty much every word anyway." Nudging me over, she shifted to rest her head on my shoulder.

"What happened last night?" I asked quietly. I couldn't wait to tell Elise about Jack, about us swimming in the dark, kissing under the stars. But I pushed all of that aside for now. "Did someone hurt you?"

"No, nothing like that." She sighed. "So we went to the football field. Then word got out and everyone showed up. I mean *everyone*. It was less an anti-anti-prom party and more a prom after-party."

"That sounds fun?" I said, unsure of where this was going.

"It was, for a while at least."

The movie continued playing in front of us in silence—the Bride showing up at the residence of her next target, Bill's brother Budd. She geared up, *katana* drawn and ready, but before she could even get close, Budd hit her in the chest with a shotgun blast of rock salt. I winced even though it was still on mute.

"Christian came," Elise said, her voice tensing. "We—"

"What?" I was shocked.

She'd said that he *wouldn't* be there. But she was only talking about Summer's anti-prom party—she hadn't said anything about the party she was throwing on the football field. Had she known he'd be there? Was that why she ditched me?

"What happened?" I asked, wondering if he was back at the house too, if that was why she'd insisted on staying in the basement the night before.

She looked miserable. "I have to tell you something first," Elise said. "About Christian. And me." She looked away. "Last night wasn't the first time we hung out."

I didn't immediately understand what she was saying. "Wait, *what?*"

"I was sleeping over one night, and I went downstairs for a glass of water. He was there too, and at first we just talked. But then—"

I could picture it: she and him in the kitchen, chatting and laughing. Flirting. Maybe even talking about me. What would Christian have said about me? What would *Elise?*

I knew she had feelings for him. She didn't acknowledge them after the fundraiser, refusing to admit she liked him when I asked, but she defended him unprompted. And now I was almost certain she wanted to throw that party on the football field because she thought he might come. Maybe she hadn't wanted to talk to me about it because he was my brother or because she knew I hated him.

But this was worse, so much worse. She'd *lied* to me. A lie of omission, but still a lie.

"Then what?" I turned to fully face her. She finally looked up, meeting my eyes.

"He told me that he and his girlfriend had been fighting. And we talked about, I don't even know, and I—" She stared at her hands on her lap. "Then he kissed me," she said.

Her words sent me reeling. I couldn't believe what I was hearing. I couldn't believe she'd hidden something like this from me. The betrayal stung. We were best friends, we were *family*. She clasped my wrists, holding on to me tightly. "I'm sorry I didn't tell you earlier, okay? I'm sorry."

Maybe it wasn't fair, but all I could think was that Elise was *mine*, the only thing that was mine in a world where Christian

141

almost always got everything, even if he didn't want it—didn't want her. She was the only person in the world who had chosen me. We'd chosen each other. And now it felt like everything we'd been was a lie, even though I knew that wasn't true.

"When?" I whispered, the only question I could manage.

"A couple weeks ago." She was still squeezing my wrists, not letting me turn away. "It was stupid. *I* was stupid. And last night, I saw him and he was with his ex and he wouldn't even talk to me, wouldn't even acknowledge me standing in front of him. When I tried to talk to him, he turned and walked away without a single word."

"Let go," I told her, looking down at our hands. "You're hurting me."

"Sorry," she said, releasing me immediately.

I pulled into myself, drawing my knees up and hugging them with my arms.

"It was humiliating," she went on. "You were right—he's an asshole."

Even angry, I could sense something off about Elise's story. All of this over a kiss. Maybe there was something she wasn't telling me. Maybe it'd been more than a kiss.

"I should've listened to you," she said. "I—"

Out of the corner of my eye, I could see the Bride being bound up and dragged to a pine box.

"Say something?" Elise said, eyes pleading.

I didn't know what to say. I could tell how upset she was, but how could she not have seen that this would affect me too? She'd kissed Christian and intentionally kept it from me even though she knew how I felt about him. Or more important, how I felt about the two of *us*. I told her *everything*. And now I was supposed to just forget about this betrayal because it'd all blown up in her face? Now she told me that I was right about Christian all along, that he was an asshole, and I was just supposed to commiserate with her? Fuck that.

I turned to face the screen and watched the Bride get buried alive. "I know she's supposed to be this hero or something, but she spends most of the movie getting beaten up."

"What? No," Elise said. "I mean, she does get beaten up a lot, but she comes back stronger than ever every single time." She could tell I was unconvinced, so she continued, "Every superhero needs a villain that is their equal. The stronger the villain, the stronger the hero. Every one of these stories has the hero failing again and again and again but getting stronger each time so that they're ready for a final showdown at the end."

I stared at her.

"That's why you have to be strong," she said. "That's why you have to get up every time you're knocked down. That's why I love all of these movies so much. That's why I love *this* movie so much."

I turned back to the screen, watched a flashback of a younger Bride training under the cruel tutelage of Pai Mei—suffering but growing stronger. Then, as if drawing on that strength, the present-day Bride punched through her coffin and clawed her way up. I understood what Elise was saying. What doesn't kill us makes us stronger.

"Look, I'm sorry I didn't tell you about Christian, okay? Are you going to be mad at me all day?"

"No, it's whatever," I lied. I *was* still mad at her, but I knew it'd be hard to stay mad at her for long. She said she was sorry, and she seemed sincere. She acknowledged it'd been a mistake but now she knew what Christian was really like.

"Good," she said. "Because you've just given me an idea and I need your help."

27.

Elise's plan was simple. She'd go to the hardware store and buy liquid chalk markers, the ones that car dealerships used to write prices on the windshield. That night, after everyone had gone to bed, she'd strike.

"It's just chalk," Elise said with a shrug. "It'll wash off."

She wanted to call Christian out on all the things he'd said to her, how he'd led her on. She planned to mark up his Mercedes, take a picture, and post it on the school's Facebook page, tagging all the right people. She wanted to humiliate him like he'd humiliated her. She wanted to destroy him. Her other plans had been brilliant but this one seemed to have evolved. This was much more personal, designed specifically for Christian. The golden boy. The flagship child. Student council president, popular at school, going places. It had to be as public as possible.

"It's what the Bride would do," Elise said, the excitement in her voice rising. "Actually, no. I'm going easy on him. The Bride's justice wouldn't be this nice."

I questioned her. "Nice?"

She nodded. "This is nothing."

I was so glad I hadn't gone with her to the football field then, glad I hadn't witnessed whatever it was that made her so determined to do this.

"Don't worry, Remy, I know what I'm doing," she said. "It'll be a birthday present to myself."

"But—" What she was about to do just didn't feel right. Her plan, while genius, felt particularly vindictive. The price didn't seem to fit the crime. Cameron and I had been together for a year and he was an asshole when he broke up with me at homecoming. Jae's girlfriend Dana had cheated on him with his best friend. Christian had kissed Elise once and led her on for a few weeks. It just seemed extreme.

"Oh, I forgot about your text," she said suddenly. "What'd you want to tell me?"

Jack. I didn't know how to tell her about him. Our nights had sharply diverged when she left me at Summer's house. She seemed so devastated by what happened at the party that I felt bad telling her what an amazing time I'd had with Jack.

"Nothing," I said, deciding to fill her in later. I told myself I was sparing her feelings, but maybe I was just scared to tell her about him, unsure of how she'd react when she was angry like this, if it would only anger her more.

I kept hoping she'd change her mind about the prank on Christian. We spent the day watching movies, going for a drive, and smoking in the car—all the things I'd wanted to do with her the night before. I didn't mention Christian at all until the drive back to my house late Saturday night when she brought up the plan again, clearly still intent on going through with it.

"Are you sure you want to do this?" I asked her when we pulled into my neighborhood. "I mean, will it really make you feel better?"

She turned to me sharply. "Of course it'll make me feel better. That's the whole point. Remember when we pranked your ex?"

"Yeah, but—" I wanted to tell her it wasn't the same. That Christian was my brother. That we couldn't just do this, drive away, and never look back.

As much as I hated him, I still had to live with him. And I could get into serious trouble with my parents.

"Why is this so important to you?" I said, growing frustrated. Things were bad enough at home for me, and I couldn't afford to make it worse.

"It just is," she snapped.

"But *why*?" I asked. Christian had been right—Dad was gone for ten days but ultimately returned. The house had recently settled back into a tense quiet, with Mom and Dad avoiding each other, sleeping in separate rooms. One of them leaving early for work, the other coming home late.

I hated that Christian had been right, that they ran on such an awful but predictable loop, but I was also just relieved that Dad had come back.

She parked down the street from my house but left the car running. "Look. I can't always do something about every single injustice, but when I can, I will."

"What are you *talking* about?" I said.

"You wouldn't understand." The sudden sadness in her voice startled me.

"Wouldn't understand what?" Elise never hesitated. She was fearless, especially when she saw an injustice.

"Nothing, never mind," she said coldly, turning firmly away from me.

"Don't do this," I said. "No one else is here. It's just you and me. You know you can tell me anything. Don't shut me out." When she didn't respond, I pulled out her cigarettes and lit two for us, and she finally turned around to face me when accepting one.

"There's nothing to tell," she finally said, but she seemed torn, avoiding eye contact and taking frequent sips from her cigarette.

She was constantly circling *something* she wouldn't tell me, and I couldn't take it anymore. "What did you mean when you said you can't always do something about every single injustice?" I asked. I couldn't ask her about it directly, so I just wanted to keep her talking with the hope that she would tell me once and for all.

"Let's just forget it," she said. "We don't have to do the prank." She sounded pained.

"What?" I was relieved, but more worried than ever. Elise was not one to change her mind, just like that. Elise was not one to back down, ever.

"Let's just go to my house," she said. "My dad probably won't be back until late tomorrow."

"But it's your birthday," I said, saddened by the thought that her father wasn't home, like he had forgotten.

She glanced at me like she could read my mind. "Trust me, him not being home is the best birthday present he could give me." Then without another word, she started the car. Elise never wanted to talk about her father, never wanted me to run into him, but I *still* didn't know why.

"Is everything okay?" I asked, knowing that it clearly wasn't.

"Yeah, it's fine," she said in a tone that ended the conversation, pointedly looking away.

That night, we went down to the river behind her house. It'd been dry the last few months and the water was low, quiet and soothing. We smoked one cigarette, then two, as the dark sky opened up and revealed a scattering of stars.

"I'm sorry Christian was such an asshole," I said, breaking the silence.

"It's not your fault," she said, sighing. "It's just bad luck." At my questioning glance, she shrugged. "Everyone likes to pretend they have control over their lives, but none of us really do. Sometimes shit just happens, sometimes there's nothing you can do about it." That didn't sound like the Elise I knew. The Elise I knew didn't back down, didn't throw her hands up in surrender, not ever.

"What's wrong?" I asked again.

"Nothing," she said, getting up. "Come on, it's getting cold."

I followed her back inside and up to her room, where we climbed into bed, neither of us falling asleep.

"I'm so tired," Elise said, sitting up. "Not sleepy. Tired."

I pulled myself up too, propping myself on one arm and tucking my feet beneath me.

"I'm tired of everything." She was staring straight ahead to the opposite wall, back against the headboard, chin resting on her knees, arms hugging herself.

I didn't speak, didn't ask questions. The second I said anything, I risked her shutting down. It'd been like that all day: start-stop conversations, me asking her what was wrong only for her to fall silent.

"How are you not exhausted too?" she asked softly. "How are you not sick of the bullshit? Is life just one long line of wanting something you can never have?" She was talking about Christian again, I thought. "Of being forever trapped?"

The sadness in her voice shocked me. She'd always been so

strong and in control, so sure of herself and of her future. I drew confidence from her by just being near her, drew inspiration from her every moment of every day. The night before, with Jack, jumping into the dark water and kissing under the moonlight—I never would've done that before I met her.

"Sometimes I don't know if I'm going to make it," she said with so much sincerity it scared me.

"What do you mean, if you're going to make it?" I said. I'd never heard Elise say anything like that before.

"Out of here," she said. "Out of this town, this state, this life."

"Oh," I said, relieved.

"Don't you ever worry that this is it? That this is the one shitty life you're going to have and there's nothing you can do about it?" This didn't sound like her at all. The Elise I knew was determined to make her mark on the world. She wasn't worried about having a shitty life.

"Is this because of Christian?" I asked. "Because he's not worth it. And you don't have a shitty life."

"It's not because of him," she said. "Well, it's not *just* because of him."

"What happened?" I crossed my legs so I could sit up straight, and she finally met my eyes.

"I know I always act like I know what I'm doing, but—" She took a deep breath. "But I don't." She held my gaze, and it was like I could see into her soul. "Don't tell the others, but most of the time I have no idea what I'm doing. I just think about the person I wish I were and try to act like her. Fake it till you make it, you know?" she finished with a sad laugh.

I didn't want to believe her. Maybe this was just a bad day, an aberration. All her confidence and swagger—that was the real Elise. But then I thought of the times Elise invoked the Bride. She wanted to be just as badass, just as tough. Just as impossible to defeat. *It's what the Bride would do.* When she didn't know what to do, the Bride was the one she turned to, the source of her courage.

"You know you never have to fake it around me, right?" I said. "You know that I love you, right? You never have to pretend to be anyone but yourself with me. Never."

"Remy, I—" She burst into tears.

I didn't know what to say so I scooted closer, put both hands on her shoulders and squeezed.

She pulled away, wincing.

"Sorry—" I said, worried I'd hurt her somehow.

"Do you ever feel like we're stuck in the part of a movie where we're getting beaten and it feels like we'll never succeed?" she asked. "I mean, I know we're not in a movie, but you know what I'm talking about, right? The part where the odds feel insurmountable and you're exhausted and running out of hope and"—she hiccuped—"and somehow you've got to go on?"

"I do," I said, but I didn't understand what this had to do with Elise.

"If I tell you something will you promise not to tell anyone else?"

I nodded. This was it, I thought. The moment she'd finally, *finally* tell me the thing she'd been alluding to for months.

"Promise," she insisted.

"I promise," I said. She'd been there for me and I didn't want to let her down.

Elise took a deep breath, like she might lose her nerve. Then she pulled her shirt off and turned on the bedside lamp. Sweeping her long hair aside, she angled herself and shrugged off one of her bra straps so I could see it: a patch of sickly green skin—a healing bruise.

"What happened?" I asked, completely shocked. I didn't know what she was going to tell me but never in a million years would I have thought that this was it.

She let her hair fall and pulled her strap up before slipping back into her shirt. "What always happens. My father."

28.

It all came back to me then, what she'd said New Year's Eve.

Your parents suck. But they're not that bad.

There are gradations. All they do is argue with each other and throw the word divorce around once in a while.

You're lucky, in a lot of ways.

All this time, she'd built a wall of silence around her father, a barricade to protect herself, but once she chipped away the smallest opening, it all crumbled, the dam breaking.

"This is nothing," she said, slipping back into her shirt. "A few days ago, he shoved me. I lost my balance and caught my shoulder against the corner of one of the kitchen counters."

"Oh my God."

She pulled back into herself against the headboard, and staring off at the other wall, she began to name some of the things that her dad had done to her over the years.

"When I was eleven or twelve, he picked me up from a sleepover and slammed my head into the window—twice—for wearing red lipstick. Told me I looked like trash."

She spoke softly, almost monotonously, like she was listing off items on a menu.

"When I was eight or nine, he shoved me so hard my face slammed into the leg of a chair when I fell. It's how I got this scar," she said, touching the scar above her left eye. I'd always wondered about that scar and assumed it was from a childhood accident. And then I thought, with growing horror: Had there been other things I overlooked?

"Whenever he gets angry and can't reach me right that second, he'll grab whatever's nearby. A coffee mug. A frying pan. He once pulled the biggest, thickest hardcover book off our shelves and flung it at me over and over again, then when he got tired, he picked it up and beat the shit out of me with it."

It was scary, hearing her recount such violence in a muted voice, like she was talking about someone else. Like it was too painful to talk about herself.

"And what's worse, he always tells me after that it hurts him more than it hurt me, that he only hits me because he loves me."

Silently, her tears fell one after the other as the sobs wracked her body. I'd never seen her cry like this before and it terrified me, even though I didn't want to admit it. Elise was the strong one, Elise always knew what to do.

I wasn't the strong one.

I didn't know what to do.

"Sprained wrist, dislocated shoulder, more bruises than I can count over the years. One time it got so bad that I went to stay at a friend's house for a week until he came and literally dragged me out kicking and screaming." I began to cry and soon I was sobbing too. "He threw me into the car and fought with her parents out on their lawn. They called the cops. And I thought maybe I was saved. But the police came, took one look at me—healthy and unhurt because I got to have a whole week away from him—and let him take me home. Said something about referring the issue to social services. But they didn't. Because no one ever showed up. And that was when I realized if the cops weren't going to do anything about it, no one was going to do anything about it," she said.

"Why didn't they?" I cried, shocked. They were police officers— they were supposed to do something, protect her.

She tried to wipe her tears away but they kept coming. "The cops believed my dad because of course they did. Who were they going to believe?" she said as more tears fell from her face.

"How could they?" My heart broke for her, for the girl who didn't get the help she needed.

"TV shows and movies almost always show the police as these heroes, but sometimes they're not. I've read that a lot of cops hit their own partners and children. And they're the ones who're supposed to protect people," she said, shaking her head. "It's been a long time since I've pinned my hopes on being saved by someone else."

We stayed like that for a while, crying together on her bed. Overwhelmed, I found myself pulling away from Elise, afraid to touch her. It was too much to process, the ground beneath us fracturing. Everything we had before seemed like an illusion now broken by the awful truth.

I felt guilty, angry at myself for all the things I'd said before, things that had seemed harmless at the time but now were insensitive at best. I should've been listening when she was talking about how there were gradations of horrible. I should've known it'd come from a dark, dark place. My childhood, with all the fighting and neglect, could never compare with what she'd gone through—what she was still going through.

Elise wiped away her tears with the back of her wrist and sniffed. "For the longest time I thought it was my fault. He *told* me it was my fault, every time. I was useless, I didn't appreciate how hard he worked to feed me, how my mom had left him with this—this *burden*. He said I was stupid and would never amount to anything, just like her. She came from this fancy family, she'd been a fucking debutante, he said. Never worked a day in her life. He told me I had to toughen up if I wanted to survive. That he was trying to make sure I didn't end up useless like her." She began to sob then, covering her face with both hands.

"But the thing is," she continued, breath hitching, "it had nothing to do with me. It never did. It didn't matter if I was the perfect daughter or not, because nothing was ever going to be enough for him."

"Oh God, Elise," I whispered, the panic rising, threatening to pull me under. The room felt too small all of a sudden. I wanted to get out. I just wanted to escape this entire conversation. I didn't know how to comfort her. I didn't know what to do.

"When I got older, I saw the pattern," she said. "If he was having a bad day, he'd make sure I'd have one too."

Elise needed me. I had to snap out of it, be strong like she was, do what she would've done for me. Instead I was paralyzed.

She cried harder. "Sometimes I think he's right."

That jolted me out of it. "What? No!"

"You know how in movies you just *know* things will be okay? That the good guy will win the day, that the setbacks, as awful and insurmountable as they seem, are just that: setbacks."

She looked at me expectantly and I nodded slowly.

"I wish I had that certainty," she said, turning away from me, shoulders shaking. "I wish I knew I was going to be okay." She looked up at me like I had the answer to her question, like I could tell her definitively that she was going to be all right, that she'd triumph over any and all obstacles, that she was unstoppable. No one had ever looked at me like that before. Had ever needed me like that.

She trusted me, I realized, and I wanted to be worthy of it.

"I think you do know," I said quietly.

"I do?"

"Yeah," I said with more confidence than I felt. *Fake it till you make it*, that was what Elise had said. "And maybe *we* know that the hero will win the day, but *they* don't. You don't know how things will turn out now, but *I* do." I scooted closer and laid a gentle hand on hers. "I'm watching the movie of your life right now and I'm telling you that these are just setbacks. I know nothing can stand in your way." It's what she would've told me, but more than that, it's what she needed to hear.

She stared at me for a moment before nodding slightly. "You're right. We're the heroes in this story, born of tragic circumstances, yes, but also strong enough to overcome them. We'll win the day," she said, like ultimate triumph was in the stars for us. She dried her eyes and managed a watery smile, laughing a little at herself.

"Feel better?" I asked, taking both of her hands in mine and giving them a small squeeze.

She nodded. "They'll be shouting our names one day," she promised, like we'd be conquerors marching through the streets. "You and me."

I laughed too, relieved she seemed to be feeling better. "Okay."

"It'll always be you and me," she said, and I nodded.

We believed our wounds made us special. We believed what didn't kill us made us stronger. We believed our tragedies were romantic.

At least that was what we told ourselves. But that night, it was beginning to sound less like an inspirational motto to live by and more like something we *had* to tell ourselves to survive.

I told Elise I knew how things would turn out, that I knew she'd triumph, but the truth was that I had no idea. It'd shaken me to the core, hearing her talk about her father. I had wanted so desperately to know what was going on with her, but now that I did, I only felt more helpless. I wanted to be strong enough for both of us, but I didn't know if I *could*.

29.

"He hasn't always been awful," Elise told me later that same night. I was lying next to her in bed, halfway asleep.

"Hmm?" I said, my eyes still closed.

"I've always wanted a dog but my dad's allergic," she continued, voice barely above a whisper. "For my birthday one year, he took me to an animal shelter and spent the day with me playing with the dogs there. He was so puffy and red when we left." I could hear a smile in her voice.

"We were never allowed to have a pet," I said. "Too messy, too much work."

"It's the first thing I'm going to do when I turn eighteen," she said. "I'm heading to the nearest shelter for a dog."

"That sounds awesome."

"It can be ours," she said, shifting toward me.

"Yeah?" I said, blinking sleepily in the dark.

"Yeah," she promised, and I fell asleep dreaming of the life we could have one day.

In the middle of the night, I woke from the cold, turning to find Elise missing. Wrapping the blanket around me, I slipped out of bed to look for her.

"Elise?" I called out in a whisper that seemed to echo through that big house. In the dark, everything looked haunted as I wandered the hall. She was in the master bedroom, both doors to the smaller balcony wide open. "What are you doing out here?"

She turned around, cigarette in hand, hair fluttering in the wind.

"I left something out earlier," she said. "About my dad."

"What?" I asked, confused.

"My dad." She took a big breath before continuing. "He always says he's sorry, every time. And the weird thing is most of the time, I believe him."

"You do?" I joined her, leaning over the ledge on my elbows.

"He cries and begs for forgiveness. It's hard to explain. He promises me he'll never do it again, and even though he's broken it a million times, I still believe him when he swears it'll be different. Is that fucked up?"

I lit a cigarette and released a stream of smoke, trying to clear my mind.

"It's like, I *know* it's not true, but I can't help but hope. And sometimes it is true, at least for a while. Before this"—she lifted the bruised shoulder a little—"it'd been almost two months. It's gotten better since we moved here. All the money my grandparents left me helped, dating The Realtor's helped." That's what she still called her father's girlfriend.

"There are gradations," she said. "And it could be worse. It could always be worse."

"I don't know," I said.

"You know my mom left when I was a kid. She just packed up her things and never looked back." She flicked her cigarette over the ledge, watched as it spun out of view. "She never hit me or anything, but sometimes I can't decide what's worse."

"What do you mean?" The stars were out in full force that night, the sky clear, the moon dark.

"I don't know. In the end my dad stayed. Maybe that counts for something." She sounded lost in thought. "That has to count for something, right?" It was shocking to hear her talk about her father like that. Why was she trying to redeem him?

"You're defending him?" I said, so confused. I pulled back, rewrapping the blanket around me.

"No," she said carefully. "I'm not *defending* him, I'm just saying—forget it."

"What?"

"It's easier, isn't it, to just run away? Like my mom did, like your dad's always doing." Elise was completely still, her eyes piercing. She was saying that her father wasn't a complete monster and that was hard for me to comprehend. What he did was unforgivable. She'd been so clear about it the night before but now she sounded uncertain.

I pulled her lighter out and began flipping the top up and down absently, letting the swoosh and clicks comfort me. I still thought of it as hers, then.

"My mom didn't have to leave me behind. She could've just left my dad," Elise pushed on. "She didn't have to, but she left me anyway."

I struggled to understand how her mom's actions could excuse her dad's violence, but she seemed so sure of her conclusions that I didn't push back. The silence and smoke surrounded us, the cold night numbing my fingers as I held on to my cigarette, unsure of what to say, how to help her.

"You know what I learned, Rem? Love isn't enough. Love doesn't make people stay." Her voice was rising, her words growing rushed and uneven. "Do you know what makes people stay? Need. My mother left me behind because she didn't need me."

"What's the difference?" I shook my head. "Love, need, it's all the same. You love someone, you need them," I said, but doubt crept in, my heart faltering.

"You could say it means the same thing. Or you could say that true love is pure need." Elise sounded so wise beyond her years, like she had all the answers.

I remained quiet, confused.

"I need you, Remy," she said softly. What she was saying: I love you.

After a moment I said, "I need you too." What we were saying, together: love is to need and to be needed. Love is truest, strongest when you need each other, when you can't live without each other. Anything less is ephemeral. Anything less risks heartbreak.

We *needed* each other. What we had was true love.

We were misfit toys who didn't belong anywhere. And then, for the first time in our lives, we belonged somewhere. We belonged to someone, to each other. Home wasn't a house. It wasn't on a map. Home was a person and for me, that person was Elise. We were a little family of our own making, and I thought nothing could stand in the way of that. Back then, I never thought I'd want anything else.

30.

As I piece our history together bit by bit, Detective Ward stares at me with piercing eyes. We are sharks trapped in a tank together, circling and circling. She listens to me talk about how I met Jack, about Elise's anti-anti-prom party.

It's so surreal, sharing all of it with a stranger. There are moments when I'm so lost in my memories that I almost forget where I am and why I'm here.

I almost forget that these memories of Jack are the only pieces of him I have left.

I almost forget that there won't be any new memories with him because he is gone forever.

I almost forget that hours ago, I held him in my arms for the last time.

Almost.

I could live inside of our first memory at the lake forever. When the stars smiled down at us and everything was possible.

I linger on these memories with Detective Ward and she

doesn't cut me off or urge me on. If anything, she seems to soften the more she hears me talk about him.

But eventually I arrive at Elise's call in the middle of the night, and everything that followed.

Tell me something true. I hear Jack's voice in my head.

It grounds me. Give me something true, something real to hold on to.

The truth is I failed Elise. I shrank away from her when she needed me most.

Detective Ward twists her wedding band around her finger as she watches me. Behind her, the camera blinks, slow and steady. Vera sits quietly beside me, jotting down notes.

I relay every detail, every word from that night. Describe the bruise on Elise's shoulder, the tears on her face. I sound tired, almost like the way Elise sounded when reciting some of the things her father had done to her over the years. Like I'm talking about someone else.

I desperately wish I was someone else, that none of this was happening.

It's strange, talking about that night with someone. Acknowledging the truth. Saying the words out loud. Especially when I promised Elise I'd never, ever tell anyone.

Detective Ward picks up a folder and opens it up on her lap, but I can still read the label on the side: *Elise Ferro.* I know what she's looking at. The things I'm sharing with her are details of a larger story she's already aware of. It's not a betrayal if she knew, is it?

As she skims the file, I brace myself for the question she doesn't ask: Why didn't I tell anyone then?

I've failed Elise so many times, in so many ways. There's so much I have to atone for.

162

Maybe Ward can see the devastation on my face because she closes the folder and sets it facedown on the table so I can't see Elise's name on it, but I catch it anyway.

"It's not your fault, you know," she says quietly. The words mean nothing to me—I know the truth—so I don't bother responding.

"It's not," she says again, and all I can think is—*isn't it?*

This is a question I've found myself circling in the three weeks since that night. If I'd said something when she first told me, then maybe Elise would've been safe. If I'd done something, then maybe we wouldn't even be here today, if only, if only—

My mind comes up with a million reasons. Elise didn't want anyone else to know. Elise had already tried getting help once. Elise had just turned seventeen and had only one year left.

I was scared. I didn't know what to do. It wasn't my story to tell. I have a million reasons and none of them are good enough.

Lurking behind all the excuses is the truth: Maybe it was just easier to do nothing. To think that Elise had it all under control. It was bad, but maybe it wasn't *that* bad—bad enough to go to the police and risk everything. Risk no one believing her and angering her father further. Or the flip side, risk people believing her and then losing her to the foster system.

Maybe it was easier to imagine us as heroes-in-training, to tell myself that these were merely setbacks for Elise. This was the part of the movie where the hero got beaten up, where all hope was lost, the dark before the dawn. She'd take all of this pain and suffering and use it to get stronger, to get so strong she could take on the world.

Detective Ward looks like she's about to say something else when there's a soft knock on the door.

"Sorry to interrupt," an officer says, waving a notepad at Detective Ward. "You told me to get you."

"I'll be right back," Ward says to us. She leaves the door ajar and I can see the two of them talking on the other side of the hall. He's pointing to something in his notes and she's nodding along.

Vera takes the opportunity to see how I'm doing. I tell her I'm fine and tune her out, straining to hear what they're saying in the hall. A million thoughts flood my mind. Is it Elise? Is she okay? Is it Jack's mother? His cousin Evan? Are they here? My heart is beating so fast it's going to explode. It feels like all of the air is being sucked out of the room. My hands fly to my throat as I gasp and choke.

"Remy!" Vera's voice sounds so incredibly far away and all I can hear is my pounding heart.

Finally, Detective Ward steps away for a few minutes before returning to the room. Her expression is carefully neutral.

"We need to talk about last night."

My eyes remain on the door. Still open, it provides a limited view of the hall. It's not a particularly busy station and I glimpse only a couple people walking by. I wonder where Elise is. I have a feeling: She's here, I know it.

"Remy's answered your questions about last night already. Twice," Vera says as Detective Ward checks the camera again.

"I have an update. We have a warrant for your phone and took a look at your call and text history. I just want to make sure everything lines up," she says, sitting down to the same notepad the police officer had.

Vera yanks it from her and begins to skim. "We need time to go over this; we've never seen this."

Detective Ward considers it and reluctantly says, "Fine. Fifteen minutes." When Vera looks like she's going to balk, Ward adds, "It's only the last few I want to talk about," and Vera finally acquiesces.

After Ward leaves, I look over Vera's shoulder as she reads it, then answer her questions about which number belongs to Jack and Elise. I don't have them memorized, but I can recognize Elise's by her Tennessee area code and Jack's by the frequency of our texts.

"*Oh,*" Vera says like she's realized something awful just as Detective Ward knocks on the door and sits down across from us. I look up at Vera, desperate to know what she's found.

"We've confirmed these texts and calls against what's on the victim's cell phone found at the scene," Ward says. "His cousin helpfully provided the passcode, so we took a look there and of course we'll confirm with the phone records once we get them, but we don't expect to see any surprises. So here we have you calling him at 11:02 p.m.. Then at 11:18 p.m., he sends you a text saying he's there. And then, fourteen minutes later, at 11:32 p.m. precisely, you call 9-1-1. You say that you let him in, then said goodbye, that he startled Elise, causing her to shoot him, but fourteen minutes is an awful lot of time for something you'd expect to happen quickly."

I pull the handwritten notes toward me, confused, panic rising. It takes me a moment to find the information she's referencing. Vera, on the other hand, dives right in.

"This means nothing," she says.

"I think it's suggestive," Ward counters.

"Yeah, suggestive of nothing," Vera says. "Fourteen minutes isn't a lot of time. Say he texts her from the driveway and she doesn't see it right away, there's two minutes. Then, like Remy said, they talk for a bit, easily six or seven minutes there. And then finally she's at her car and hears the shots, running back inside. And a few minutes with the body, in shock. Fourteen minutes is nothing."

As she talks, though, my heart is pounding because Detective Ward is right: Where did those fourteen minutes go? All the things Vera says are possibilities, but I was there, and I can account for maybe seven of those minutes.

He arrives, we exchange a few words, I leave, and then as soon as I start the car, I hear the gunshots. Maybe Vera's right, that I didn't call 9-1-1 right away, that maybe I was in too much shock to pull myself away from his body long enough to call 9-1-1.

Still, it bothers me. Something about it feels off but I can't quite explain why.

I run through the night one more time in my mind, try to snap the fragments of my memories together into a coherent whole. Elise and me fighting, then separating. Jack showing up at the door, telling me he'd talk to Elise. I'm in my car, the keys in the ignition, about to leave.

Nothing's making any sense. I try to follow what Vera's saying, but no matter how I divide the time, there's always a few minutes left over. I didn't miss his text, and I opened the door as soon as Jack arrived. We talked for a bit but it wasn't that long. Then I went to my car, ready to go home and let Elise and Jack work it out themselves, so we could put the fight behind us.

That's where they found my keys, still in the ignition. Everything is still hazy but I remember running up those steps.

Maybe Jack didn't find Elise right away. Maybe he waited for her to come back inside from the balcony, and when she did, he startled her.

And maybe, when I went to my car, I dozed off for a few minutes before being jolted awake by the sound of gunshots. It can all be explained. That's what matters in the end.

Fourteen minutes isn't a lot of time, I tell myself over and over. It doesn't mean anything.

I'm not sure who I'm trying to convince, Ward or myself.

31.

We break for lunch. My parents have gone out and bought me a turkey sandwich but I can't think about eating. Instead, I hide out in the bathroom for as long as I can.

I splash cold water on my face, trying to wake myself up. I'm so tired that I'm teetering a little. I'm running on empty, but I can still feel the spikes of nausea-inducing adrenaline. My stomach twists, and all I can do is focus on not throwing up. My body thinks I'm about to die. It thinks I'm in the fight of my life, and maybe it's right.

Every second I'm locked in that room with Detective Ward feels like life or death.

I hold myself up with both arms against the counter. I look in the mirror and a stranger stares back out at me, but I can't quite look away.

This *is* life or death, I think, but it's not only our lives on the line. It's our friendship that's endangered.

From the moment she crashed into my life, it's always been just the two of us, Elise and I. She was a shooting star, a devastating asteroid that shattered my world upon impact. And in its ashes, I was reborn—*we* were reborn—whole, complete.

I can't lose her. I can't let her down again. I can't let one tragic mistake consume us.

I won't let it destroy us.

32.

Elise didn't just love heroes—she wanted to be one. And not just an everyday hero who occasionally spoke up for bullied classmates. She wanted to be the real thing.

"You know what we should do?" Elise said the day after her birthday. I watched her carefully, almost hyperaware of her every move. I was worried about her, but I was also scared, not just of saying or doing something wrong, but of the entire situation. She acted like she had it under control, but how do you control something like that?

"What?" I said, distracted, flicking a cigarette over the balcony ledge, staring at the river below. It was late morning, the sun's heat growing oppressive.

"We should help people," she said, eyes lighting up.

"With what?" I asked, confused.

"Anything," she said, grabbing my shoulder in excitement. "Like what we've been doing, with the pranks, but more."

"More?"

She nodded, taking a quick inhale from her cigarette. "Like we should get organized, take cases."

"*What?*"

"Yeah, like the Deadly Vipers," she said. "Or the Justice League or Avengers."

I laughed, thinking she was joking.

"I mean it!" she said, but she was laughing too. "I know it sounds a little ridiculous, but don't you think we could help a lot of people?"

"Sure," I said, not taking any of it seriously. "Who'd you be—Superman?" In some ways, Elise had always seemed superhuman to me.

I thought of Jack then, and wanted to tell Elise about him. But I still held back. We were in the middle of a conversation and there was always time later.

"No way, Superman's boring. Batman," she said, and I thought, *Of course.* An orphan who overcame terrible tragedy and personal demons to become bigger than life. "A hero no one wants but everyone needs."

I nodded.

"I am vengeance. I am the night. I am Batman!" she finished with a grand sweep of an arm, and I swore she was electric.

"What about me?" I asked, playing along. "Don't tell me I'm Robin."

Elise tapped her cigarette over the balcony, considering. "Wonder Woman," she said. "Too pure for this sinful Earth." She smiled and reached out with a hand to brush a stray hair from my face.

When we went back inside, I checked my phone and saw a couple messages from Jack waiting for me.

> Jack: So I thought about waiting a couple of days to text you so I could seem really cool and detached but screw that because I'm low key dying to see you again

> Jack: Are you free for dinner tonight?

I loved that he didn't care about playing it cool and I couldn't keep the goofy grin off my face as I wrote back yes.

Elise noticed. "Did something happen? You seem different."

"Different how?"

"Happy? Keyed-up?"

"Oh. Um, I forgot to tell you. I met a guy," I said, dreading this moment. "At the party. After you left."

"You did? Why didn't you say something sooner?" she asked, looking slightly betrayed. "Wait, is this the thing you texted me about but wouldn't tell me?"

"I wanted to," I said. "But—"

But you needed me, and you were devastated, and—

Instead, I said, "There just wasn't a good time and it wasn't important." That was sort of true, but at the heart of it, I was a little scared of her—scared that she'd be angry that I'd had such a good time when she'd had such a shitty one.

Maybe what I was really scared of was how it might change things between us. Elise was always the one who made decisions for us, where to go, what to do—who to hang out with. And bringing Jack into my life, *our* lives, hadn't been sanctioned.

It hit me then how paranoid I was being. Elise was my best friend! She'd be happy for me.

Wouldn't she?

"Who is it?" she asked.

"Jack. I don't know his last name yet, actually," I said with a small laugh, trying to sound extra cheerful. "I can't wait for you to meet him, though. I think you'll like him." I watched carefully for her reaction.

Her expression was unreadable and I grew uncomfortable at the silence stretching between us. Oh no, I thought. She *was* angry.

But then she smiled. "Can't wait to meet him," she said.

"Really?"

She nodded, still smiling. "Anything for you."

33.

Back at home I took a shower and washed Jack's Superman tee. The whole house was quiet—Mom in her study, Christian gone, and Dad at the office or on a golf course. Exhausted from the night before, I fell asleep and only woke when my phone buzzed on my chest.

Jack: Lola's helping me pick out a shirt for tonight

I sat up and rubbed my eyes, confused.

Me: Lola?

Then Jack sent a photo of him and his golden retriever, both of them adorable with wide grins, looking carefree under sunlight. Sitting up, I stared down at it, smiling as I saved it as his contact picture.

Jack: Just to let you know, I am not above using my cute dog to flirt with you.

I couldn't stop grinning, so busy rereading his words over and over again that I almost forgot to respond.

    Me: Of course not.

    Jack: Is it working?

    Me: Send me more Lola pics

He sent three more: Lola and him at the lake, both of them soaked; Lola alone chasing a toy; a selfie of Jack kissing her head.

How was he so cute? It wasn't humanly possible. I flopped back onto my bed and wanted to die from happiness.

    Me: Careful

    Jack: ?

    Me: I think I'm falling for your dog

    Jack: I should've known this would happen

    Me: It's okay, I think I like her human too

    Jack: Whew

A few minutes later, I was still thinking of what to say when he sent another message.

    Jack: Tell me something true?

I stretched my hands overhead before turning to my side to cradle my phone.

    Me: I've always wanted a dog

    Jack: Are you allergic or something? :(

    Me: No, my parents have a strict no pets policy

    Jack: That sucks, wow

He sent me two more pictures of Lola, one at bath time and another after as she snoozed away on his bed, wrapped in a towel.

    Me: She's so adorable it should be illegal

    Jack: She tries

    Me: But where is the lie?

Jack: You're right, let me call the cops

Me: Officer, my dog is too cute, send help

Jack: Lol

After a few moments, I shot his question back at him.

Me: Tell me something true?

Jack: I can't wait to see you tonight

He answered every message almost immediately, and after seeing his words, I clutched my phone to my chest, breathless. Then I reread our entire exchange, smiling the whole time.

I was trying on dresses when Elise called.

"Is Christian home?" she asked.

I glanced out the window to see if his car was in the driveway. "No, why?"

"Okay, I'll be there in fifteen," she said.

"Wait, what?" I put down a purple cocktail dress, deciding it was too formal.

"All of us are going to meet up tonight. You and I can get dinner before." I could hear the jingle of her keys in the background, the sound of the front door swinging closed.

"I can't," I said, feeling a little guilty but too excited to see Jack to let it change my mind. And even though I didn't want to admit it, I needed a break from being with Elise after the revelations of the night before.

"You can't? Why?" she asked.

"I'm having dinner with that guy I was telling you about— Jack?"

"Oh," she said, followed by a long silence.

"Go out and have fun, I'll see you tomorrow at school," I said, feeling awkward and uncomfortable. Elise had done the same thing, hadn't she? Friday night, when I wanted to hang out, just the two of us, she pressed her keys into my hands and left me behind.

"Can you cancel?" she asked.

"Why?" I said, surprised.

"We're planning to figure out how we're going to help people," she said. "I want you to be there. It's important."

"You're actually doing that?" I asked, sitting down to pay better attention to what she was saying. "I thought that was—I thought you weren't serious about it." She'd talked about it earlier but I was hoping she'd let it go.

"Why wouldn't I be serious about it?" she said. "I meant every word I said. There's so much injustice in the world and we could be *doing* something about it. Don't you want that, Rem? Don't you want to make a difference?" She sounded like she actually believed we had superpowers, like we had a responsibility to fight evil.

"Just go without me," I said. The truth was I wouldn't have wanted to go even if Jack and I didn't have plans. Part of me was still afraid she'd change her mind on pranking Christian, get the others worked up and make it hard for me to say no.

"We need you," she said. "I mean, how can we have a Justice League without Wonder Woman?"

I smiled, shaking my head at her ridiculousness. "I'm sure you'll figure something out. You can tell me all about it after."

Another pause.

"When are you leaving?" she asked.

I looked at the time. "I don't know, half an hour?"

"I'll drive you," she said. "I'm on my way over anyway."

"You don't have to do that," I said, but she'd already hung up. I tried to text her but she didn't respond.

Elise showed up twenty minutes later, parking right in the driveway, taking Christian's spot.

"What happened to avoiding Christian?" I asked.

She shrugged. "Fuck him. Why should I be the one who has to suffer because he's the asshole?" And just like that, she was over him, or at least she seemed like it.

"I guess." I glanced out onto the street, hoping Christian would stay wherever he was, not wanting to deal with a potentially explosive fight.

She changed the subject. "Is that what you're wearing?" I'd decided to go with jeans and a black top, red heels and matching wristlet.

I nodded. "Why?"

"Nothing. You look nice," she said with a soft smile.

"Thanks," I said, smiling back, my excitement growing.

"Where are you guys going?" she asked, flopping down on my bed on top the clothes I'd rejected.

"The Good Place." It was a diner with an old-fashioned jukebox, red leather booths, and a vintage Coke refrigerator with a clicking handle.

"So, fancy Waffle House," she said with a laugh.

"Breakfast *is* the most important meal of the day," I said, grinning.

"Come on," she said. "Let's go before you're late."

"You really don't have to," I said, still confused about why she wanted to drive me and worried what Jack would think. Would it look like I already wanted him to meet my friends? Or worse, that Elise was there to give her approval?

"I have nothing else to do, and besides, you'll be able to leave

175

with Jack after without dealing with your car." She looped my arm with hers. "And I'll get to meet him."

"I guess." She was so insistent that I gave in. I decided to tell Jack I'd needed a ride and that was why Elise drove me.

We arrived a little early and were sitting on top of the Pink Caddy's trunk when Jack showed up.

"Cute," Elise whispered to me when he pulled off his helmet, and I bumped her with my shoulder.

Jack walked up to us, smiling, but I could see he was confused. "Hey," he said, keeping some distance between us, a little shy.

"Hey," I said, giving him a hug. "This is my friend Elise. She drove me."

"I'm Jack," he said with a wave. "Cool car." He'd seen it two nights ago at the party, but not up close.

"Thanks," Elise said. Then she gave me a quick hug. "See you later."

We went inside and slid into a booth across from each other. "So," he said, taking one of the oversize menus.

"So," I said, nervous. Our eyes met and we laughed at our own awkwardness, at the *newness* of whatever was happening between us.

Then something outside caught Jack's attention and he turned slightly, leaning toward the windows. "Isn't that your friend?"

"What?" Startled, I looked up to see Elise still sitting cross-legged on the back of her car. "Yeah, it is," I said in complete surprise. I pulled out my phone.

> Me: You're still here?
>
> Elise: Sorry, I got hungry and breakfast for dinner
> sounded really good
>
> Elise: I just ordered takeout and I'll be out of here
> soon

Through the glass, she held up a hand in a small wave.

"What's up?" Jack asked.

"Oh, um, she's hungry so she ordered takeout," I said. I shook my head in disbelief.

> **Me:** You couldn't have gotten takeout anywhere else??
>
> **Elise:** Omg, I didn't think about that
>
> **Elise:** I can leave right now, I'm sorry!

"Oh, why don't you just tell her to join us?" Jack said with a warm smile.

"Well, she has a thing later, and—"

"It's fine." He reached for my hand and held it, the light brush of his touch making me blush. "I want to meet your friends anyway." He was being really kind, but I was annoyed that all I got was five minutes with him alone. I couldn't believe Elise was crashing our date.

I took a deep breath. "Okay."

> **Me:** Do you just want to eat with us?
>
> **Elise:** No, I don't want to interrupt your thing
>
> **Me:** It's fine
>
> **Me:** I mean, you're already here, you might as well
>
> **Elise:** Only if you're really okay with it
>
> **Me:** I'm okay, just come inside and stop being a weirdo stalker staring at us
>
> **Elise:** Lol, okay, coming

She hopped off the trunk and grabbed her shoulder bag from the back seat before walking toward us. "Sorry," she said when she came to our table, sitting with me, opposite Jack. "I didn't mean to crash your date."

"Don't worry about it," he said with an easy smile.

"Rem?" she asked me, like she was double-checking.

"It's fine." But it wasn't. I kept glancing at her, trying to figure out what she was doing, if this was all part of some plan she'd hatched. Then I felt guilty, thinking of what she'd told me the night before, remembering the bruise on her shoulder. She didn't want to be at the Pink Mansion. She didn't want to be alone, that was all. Or maybe she really was just craving eggs and pancakes.

"Have you already ordered?" Jack asked, handing her a menu.

Elise shook her head. "I was just about to call it in," she said, flagging down a waiter. After she ordered, she turned back to us. "Are you also a sophomore?" she asked Jack.

He shook his head. "I'm a senior but I took the year off."

"Oh," she said, and I was grateful when she didn't pry. We talked a little about the party Elise threw on the football field on Friday night, about how tedious some of the teachers were at school, about any summer plans we might have.

"I want to get back into swimming," Jack said. "I'm so out of shape."

"You look fine," Elise said.

He smiled. "Thanks, but I'm probably slow as hell in the water right now. What about you guys, any plans?"

I shook my head. "My parents are probably going to make me study for the SATs. I'm already behind, according to my mom. Christian, my brother, started studying for it as a fetus, so."

Jack laughed. "Wait, is your brother Christian Tsai?"

"Yep." They were in the same grade, I realized. Even if Jack had taken the year off school, they would have been juniors together, and sophomores before that.

"I didn't know he had a sister," he said.

"No one does," I said. "I would've been surprised if you said you *had* known."

"Are you guys friends?" Elise was trying not to sound strained, but I could hear it in her voice. I looked at Jack, silently praying he didn't know Christian.

"Not really?" he said like a question. "I think we were on the swim team together freshman year, but we don't exactly know the same people." He was clearly being polite, and I was relieved that they weren't friends.

"It's okay," Elise said, grinning. "You can tell us what you really think of him. I mean, both of us think he's kind of an asshole." I elbowed her. "What? It's the truth."

"I don't know him well enough," Jack said, remaining neutral. "He seems kind of intense, I guess." I liked that he didn't just follow Elise's lead, that he wasn't tempted to shit-talk Christian just because she was.

As soon as Elise finished eating, she checked the time on her phone. "We have to go soon, Rem," she said without looking up.

"What?" I asked. Jack looked surprised too.

"That thing tonight?" she asked, eyes meeting mine. "Remember?" It had all been part of her plan, I thought. Unbelievable.

"You said you were going to go without me, *remember*?" I shot her a look.

"Can we talk?" She took me by the wrist, pulling me out of the booth toward the bathroom before I could answer. I looked over my shoulder, trying to tell Jack sorry.

As soon as the door shut behind us, Elise checked the stalls quickly to make sure we were alone. "I really need you there tonight."

"Why?" I demanded. I knew she didn't. Maybe I'd been right to be worried when I didn't want to tell her about Jack, but even then I couldn't have imagined she'd do this. "Please don't tell me it's because you want me there to talk about the Justice League or whatever it is you're calling it, because I honestly don't even care about it, okay?" I regretted my words immediately.

That left her quiet, the silence heavy between us.

"I'm sorry," I said. "I didn't mean that."

"Yes, you did." She turned away from me, looked at herself in the mirror. "I'm sorry I'm such a burden." Her voice was flat, her spark gone.

"That's not what I meant," I said. "I'm sorry."

"I just—" She took a deep breath, exhaled slowly. "I just don't want to be alone right now. And I know I won't be alone, but the others there, they don't know me, not like you do." Our eyes met in the mirror. "No one does. The things I told you last night—I've never told anyone. Ever." She seemed to shrink into herself, arms crossed, shoulders hunched. "I need you, Remy," she said. "Please."

"Of course," I said, hugging her tight.

"I'm sorry."

It scared me, seeing someone so strong on the edge of tears, on the verge of breaking down.

"I need you, I need you," she said, but the words that had once made me feel loved now filled me with apprehension.

34.

"I'm sorry I have to go," I told Jack. "And I'm sorry we didn't get to spend any time alone together." We were out in the parking lot, standing by his motorcycle, his fingers gently trailing along my arms, Elise a few spots away, already starting the Pink Caddy. I turned my back to her to steal a moment for myself.

"Hey, don't worry about it. I'll see you later, and I think your friend just wanted to make sure you were okay," he said. Even that sounded like he was making an excuse for her, and I liked him even more—he was so generous and understanding.

"I'm sorry," I said again. "And I forgot your shirt." After washing it, I'd left it in the dryer.

"Oh, the Superman one?" he said. "Keep it. I like the way you look in it."

"Are you sure?" I asked, but I was secretly pleased.

He leaned in and left the lightest kiss on my lips, sending me soaring. I pulled him in tighter, arms wrapped around him, hands slipping into his hair.

"Okay." I lingered, not wanting to leave.

The ride to the football field was mostly quiet. The sky had darkened while we ate, leaving only faint brushes of pink and purple. We were the first ones there, sitting together on the bleachers, smoking while we waited.

"Are we going to do anything tonight?" I asked.

"What do you mean?"

"You know, a prank," I said.

"Oh, like if we already have a target or something? No," she said. "We're just here to figure it out."

"Why do you want to do this again?" I asked, turning to lie down on the bench.

"Because." She dropped her cigarette, stamped it out. "I know what it's like to feel helpless. You do too. It's awful. No one should ever, ever feel like that. And we can't do anything about our parents, but—"

"Okay, okay," I cut her off. I knew her entire speech already.

"I knew you'd understand," she said. "Look, I think Julie and Madi are here. Jae too."

I took one last look at the stars, remembering me and Jack lying under the same night sky, before I swung my legs around, got up, and stretched as Elise waved them over. Jae brought drinks left over from the party Friday night. Once we were in the middle of the field, I scanned the place, looking for signs of the party—errant plastic cups, trash—but found nothing.

"We cleaned up," Elise said, as if reading my mind. "Can't get caught if we want to do it again."

"Do it again?" I asked in a whisper, but she pretended not to hear me.

"So, what's the plan?" Jae asked, pouring out a screwdriver for himself and passing the vodka and OJ to Elise. "Who are we going to fuck up?" he joked, taking a sip.

"No one," she answered.

"What'd you want to talk about?" Julie asked, and as Elise began to describe her vision of a ragtag group of vigilantes, my phone buzzed.

Jack: Meet me after your thing?

I glanced up to see Elise still preoccupied and quickly typed back a response.

Me: I don't think I can

Jack: If you need a ride, I could pick you up?

Then he sent a picture of him and Lola making puppy dog eyes, and I couldn't help but smile.

"Remy?" Elise said.

"Sorry, what?" I looked at them blankly.

"I was saying this could be a way to help people," she said, a little annoyed.

"Yeah," I said, confused by what she wanted me to say.

"Like what we pulled off with Jae's ex and your ex, but on a bigger scale," she continued. It annoyed me, the way she'd trot out our first prank every once in a while, like it was one of her signature achievements. That night was supposed to be special, but the way she brought it up cheapened the memory.

"There *are* a lot of assholes out there," Julie said.

"And it wouldn't be limited to exes," Elise added quickly when she saw the reluctance on Madison's face. "And it wouldn't really be about revenge."

> Me: I don't think I can
>
> Me: I'm sorry
>
> Jack: It's okay, thought I'd ask.
>
> Me: I'm sorry
>
> Jack: Don't be
>
> Jack: Me and Lola will be here :)

Then he sent another sweet photo of Lola. I saved all the pictures he sent me in a new album, *Jack & Lola*. When I caught Elise looking at me, I put my phone away, sad I was here talking about pranks when I could've been with Jack.

"I'm in," Jae said, with Julie agreeing soon after that.

But Madison hesitated. "I don't know. How will this even work?"

"We'll be like vigilantes," Elise said. "Like with Mr. Dawkins. We'll look for people who *deserve* to be brought down." She set her cup down. "We'll be like secret heroes, helping people who need us." It was the conviction in her voice that cut through me, that raw pain. Any lingering resentment from earlier that night evaporated.

"Okay," Madison said. "I'm in."

Elise glanced over at me, and it felt like there was no space between us, like looking at her alone was enough to feel electric. *Are you with me?* she was asking.

There was a time I would've run into battle for her without hesitation, but now I wasn't so sure. It used to feel like she was the only one who really knew me, the only one who could ever know me, but now I wondered if that was true. Finally I tilted my head down ever so slightly in acknowledgment, and she smiled at me.

It was pitch-black when Elise and I went back to the Pink Mansion. We put blankets down on the balcony and lay there, smoking and watching the dark, dark sky, the moon and stars hidden behind a thick cover of clouds.

"Promise me something," she said, eyes vulnerable, all her usual confidence gone.

"What?" I looked at her with concern. It was scary, seeing her like this.

"Promise me that you'll never leave me." She sounded unusually despondent, almost like I'd already left. "I need you."

"Don't be silly," I said, tapping my cigarette against a mug beside me.

"I'm not. People are always leaving me." She was talking about her mom. "Sometimes I think I'm just this black hole of *need*. That I just need and need and need. That I'm too much for anyone to handle. And that's why they always leave."

"I won't leave," I said fiercely, wrapping an arm around her shoulder. "And I need you, too." I remembered everything she'd done for me, how she'd been there for me. I had to be here for her.

"You'll never choose someone over me?" she said.

"Never," I promised, even though it felt like she was only asking this question now that I had someone else in my life.

"You won't get all wrapped up with Jack and forget about me?" she asked.

"You're being ridiculous."

"Promise me you won't ever choose him over me," she insisted.

"I promise," I said. "There, happy?" I couldn't believe she'd felt so threatened by Jack so soon, but maybe it was just because of the weekend and how awful it'd been for her.

Elise answered with a smile and rested her head on my shoulder. The weekend had been a roller coaster, but as we lay there, I had every reason to think we were back on solid ground.

FRIDAY // APRIL 7

35.

The next time I saw Jack, I turned off my phone and didn't tell Elise where I was going. It was the first night of spring break and I knew she'd want to spend it staying out late, the five of us, maybe go to the football field, but all I wanted was to see Jack again. I felt a little bad, but I just wanted to avoid a repeat of last time. She couldn't crash our date if she didn't know where I was.

He picked me up at seven and seemed almost nervous, making awkward conversation and insisting on paying for dinner.

"Everything okay?" I asked. It'd been so easy to talk to him the night of Summer's party only a week ago.

"Of course," he said. "Why? Are you not having a good time?"

"No, that's not it," I said as I watched him from across the table of the sushi restaurant he'd picked. He wanted to impress me, I realized. The nervousness, the insistence on paying. It was endearing, how much he wanted me to like him. When I reached for his hand, he looked startled for a moment before he relaxed into a smile.

I looked right at him. "We don't have to do this—the dinner and a movie thing. I don't care what we do, I just want to spend time with you," I said. The night was mine to give away and I wanted to give it to him.

For a moment, he looked caught off guard, then he smiled, eyes shy. "Okay."

"Tell me something true," I said softly.

Playing with my hand, intertwining our fingers together and letting go, he considered what to say. "I used to be a nationally ranked swimmer."

"Really?" I asked, impressed.

Jack nodded. "I think I still hold the under-eighteen national record for the two-hundred-meter butterfly."

"Wow," I said. "I can't believe I asked you if you could swim the night we met."

He laughed. "It's okay, you were just worried about my safety."

"Of course." I smiled. "So, are you captain of the Riverside swim team?"

"Um, I was. But I quit the team even before I took this year off." Then he quickly changed the subject, turning the attention back onto me: "Tell me something true."

I didn't know what to say for a long time. My life was boring—nothing had happened to me yet. The misfit child in a family of overachievers, I was the definition of unremarkable. I wasn't like Elise, charming and funny. Electric.

"I really want to meet Lola," I said, which was both something true and something that deflected attention.

Jack's smile lit up the entire restaurant. "Okay." We skipped the movie and went to Jack's house to pick her up. "I'm staying with

187

my cousin Evan right now. It's a long story," he said. "Wait here."
He disappeared into the house and came out with Lola a couple
minutes later.

"Whoa," he said when she jumped on me.

"It's okay." I bent over to greet her, rubbing her head and neck,
scratching behind her ears.

"She likes you," Jack said. "And Lola is a good judge of charac-
ter." I laughed as she licked my arm.

Jack packed a thermos of coffee and we walked a mile to a
dog park. With the sky almost dark, we had the whole place to
ourselves. Jack held my hand and tossed an old tennis ball for Lola
until she tired herself out. Eventually she settled down in the grass
near where Jack and I sat sharing one of the old wooden benches.

"Why'd you quit?" I asked, drawing up my legs and sitting
cross-legged.

"I was in a car accident almost two years ago." He lifted his
left hand, showing me a scar. I brushed my thumb over the glossy,
stretched skin. "I have a pin in my wrist, and some hardware in
my left shoulder."

"Wow." I touched the scar gingerly before wrapping both my
hands around his wrist.

"To be honest," he said, "I'm not sure I would've continued
even if I didn't get into an accident. I started swimming around
eight, and I was really good. Great, even."

Jack had a swimmer's body—broad shoulders, long legs and
torso, an arm span big enough it seemed like he could hug me twice
over. I could picture him cutting through the water quickly.

"I won a lot. More than a lot, actually," he said, opening his
thermos to take a sip.

"Don't be so modest." I laughed. "Tell me more about how you won everything."

He laughed too. "Sorry, that isn't what I meant."

"I know," I said, smiling.

"Okay, you're going to laugh again, but I kind of wish I hadn't won so much?"

"Oh my God." I bumped him with my shoulder and rolled my eyes. "You know that this is the very definition of humble-bragging?" He was so adorable.

"I know, I know, I'm terrible," he said, and I laughed. "But hear me out. When you're a kid and you find out you're really good at something, it becomes kind of addicting, the trophies and medals, even if they're just made of plastic. After a few years of this, it starts taking over your life. I lived to swim, I lived to win, and I didn't know what I was without it. And then it became less about winning and more about not losing." He shook his head, a rueful smile on his face. "I know, I know, first-world problems."

"No," I said, taking his hand. "I get it, actually. My parents, my brother—that's exactly what it's like for them. I'm kind of the family disappointment," I quipped in an attempt at a joke.

"That sucks, I'm sorry," he said, and I could tell he was sincere. "If your parents are like the grown-up version of Christian, then yeah, I can see how they're like that."

"They're all kind of intense and I'm just not." I reached over to pet Lola, who'd taken to sitting by Jack's feet and resting her chin on the seat of the bench between us. "And it's like life is a race that's theirs to lose."

"Exactly." He looked at me and my heart skipped a beat. There it was again, that rare kind of connection I felt from the night we met, when you see a piece of yourself in someone else and you feel less alone. "It becomes all about how to stay on top, how to be faster than anyone else and *stay* faster. But at some point you just can't. It happens to everyone, and even if I'd never gotten into an accident, I was getting burned out. It was bound to happen." He shrugged. "But honestly, it doesn't matter, because I *did* get into an accident."

I remembered what he said that first night we met, about that homesickness for another life, that feeling of being in the wrong timeline of your life, the wrong version of yourself. And even though he said he probably would've quit, I wondered if he thought of the accident as the thing that derailed his plans, that took the choice from him.

"What happened?" I asked.

"It was stupid, one of the stupidest decisions I've ever made. I was at a party and this guy I was friends with was pretty wasted and wanted to drive home. I offered to drive him, but we ended up in a crash anyway. Another car clipped us and we slammed into a telephone pole. We were lucky enough to walk away, but his car was totaled."

"Wow, what are the odds?" I said. "I'm sorry."

"Shit happens. I've long given up on the idea that there's such a thing as fairness." He was so different from Elise, who railed against the world, who couldn't tolerate any injustice, no matter how small.

"Did you quit right after?" I asked.

"Yes and no. Even after months of PT, it just wasn't the same. Maybe it was the surgery, the metal pins, the scar tissue, but I have a lot less range of motion on my left side." He demonstrated by stretching each arm back. "And you need a lot of upper-body flexibility to be a fast swimmer."

"Do you think you'll ever go back?" It was too sad, the idea that one night took so much from him.

"Maybe? My grandpa really wanted me to, thought I could maybe get a scholarship for college even if I'd never make the national team, and I promised him I would, but I don't know."

Lightning flashed in the distance, burning up part of the sky, and Lola perked up at the sound of faraway thunder just as it began to rain.

"Come on," Jack said, grabbing my hand and making a run for it. We laughed as the sudden deluge soaked us to the bone, Lola barking as we ducked under a canopy. We looked up at the same time and shared a breathy laugh. Then he leaned in, resting his forehead on mine, tangling our fingers together.

"Hi," he said softly.

"Hi."

When he kissed me, I held on tight, not wanting to let go.

SATURDAY // APRIL 8

36.

"Where were you?" Elise demanded the next morning when I finally answered one of her calls. "I drove by your house but you weren't home."

"Sorry, I was out with Jack and my phone died." The lie was innocent enough. I didn't owe her an explanation, but it was strange, intentionally lying to her for the first time. Then again, she was the one who lied first. "We got caught out in the rain and by the time I got home, all I could manage was a quick shower before I fell asleep."

"You missed everything," she said, clearly annoyed. "How soon can you get dressed? I'm coming to pick you up." Before I could even protest, she added, "Never mind, just get ready, I'll be there in fifteen," and promptly hung up. This was classic Elise. She made the decisions, dictated the terms, and I'd been more than happy to let her take the lead. It'd been such a relief to have someone to follow, but now it was beginning to grate on me.

Ten minutes later, she was already waiting for me downstairs. I hadn't even had time for a shower or to grab a bite to eat.

"You look terrible," she said when she saw me.

"Good morning to you too."

"And what are you wearing?" She stared at my shirt.

"Oh, it's Jack's," I said, and when she shot me a droll look, I added, "You didn't exactly give me enough time to get ready!" The truth was that I liked wearing his Superman tee, the cotton soft from years of use, and even though I'd washed it since he gave it to me, sometimes I could still catch a hint of peppermint.

"Okay, whatever," she said. "Get in."

"Where are we going?"

"You'll see."

"Can we at least get something to eat on the way?" I complained. "I'm starving."

"Fine, fine."

"What am I looking at here?" I asked when she pulled up to the school. They'd chained together the metal bar gates at the entrance and we had to go on foot.

"You'll see, come on!" she said, pulling me along by the wrist. It was strange, being on campus during break. It was completely deserted, the parking lots empty, the silence almost oppressive.

"What are we doing here?" I asked as we went around to the back doors, the entrance to the gym.

"You'll see," she repeated before pulling out a set of keys.

"Where'd you get those?" I asked, alarmed.

She shrugged. "On Friday. Don't worry, I'll make copies and make sure Ms. Corkern gets them back." Corkern taught sophomore chem. I didn't have her but Elise probably did. I remembered how she'd swiped that substitute teacher's car keys with no one noticing, not even me. Ms. Corkern also coached softball, which meant she'd have a key to the gym for early or late practices. So that was how they got in.

"What about—" Inside, I looked up at where the cameras were positioned.

"Don't worry, we took care of them last night. It was dark and we were wearing all black, our faces covered."

I squinted, looking at the cameras closer. "You—"

"—are awesome?" she finished for me with a laugh. "A genius? I'm aware." She'd cut the power supply line behind each one of them. "Come on." She took me by the hand, dragging me along as I gaped at all the disabled security cameras along the way. She finally stopped at a classroom in the language arts hall. "Ready?" she said, hand positioned over the doorknob.

I nodded, confused, until we entered and I saw Mr. Dawkins's nameplate on the teacher's desk.

"Ta-da!" Elise said with a wide sweep of her arm, smiling at her grand destruction.

"Oh my God." She'd outdone herself, they all had. All the student desks had been stacked into four towers that reached the ceiling. *His* desk had been egged. Silly string coated the walls, along with what looked like some kind of slime. And then there was what they'd written on the whiteboard. It was a satirical take on kindergarten rules, complete with cutesy decorations. Stay in your seat, raise your hand, walk, don't run, say please and thank you—the usual suspects. Then there was the last one, which was simply, "Don't be a perv."

Elise laughed, looking at it again. "The best part is that everything was written with dry erase markers *except* that last one, so when he goes to wipe the board, he'll clear everything and realize the last line's in Sharpie. Julie came up with that."

"Wow," I said, surveying the disaster.

"I can't believe you weren't there," she said. "Our first mission and you were MIA." She shook her head in mock disappointment until I looked sufficiently chastised, even if I didn't feel it. "So, what do you think? Pretty awesome, right?"

"Yeah," I said, mostly still taking it all in—the destruction of the classroom, the security cameras, the clever key theft. This was also classic Elise: brilliant plans, even better execution. But I didn't feel the thrill I used to, though it was clear she did.

"He's so gross," she said. "An obvious first target." That was true. I hated walking by his classroom, especially if he was standing by the door looking out onto the hallway.

"I wish you were there," she said, not letting it go. I knew what she wanted me to feel—left out, jealous even. But I had no regrets over spending my night with Jack, and if I had the choice, I'd choose to be with him again.

"When did you guys plan this anyway?" I asked out of curiosity.

"Just last night," she said. "That's why you should always come hang out with us."

"But you said you got the keys—"

"Yeah, earlier that day, but I hadn't tried them, wasn't even sure I'd gotten the right ones. Then we got bored and it kind of just snowballed from there."

Elise remained jubilant all day, thrilled with what they'd accomplished in just one night. She replayed every moment with excruciating detail, how she'd swiped the keys, how they parked at Jae's house, the closest one to school, and walked the whole way. How they basically strolled in, cut the cameras, and destroyed Dawkins's room.

"The only thing we haven't figured out is what to call ourselves," she said at the end.

"Why not just use Deadly Vipers?" I asked, surprised she hadn't thought of it already. "It's catchy and seems dangerous."

"See, this is why we need you, Rem," she said. "You have all the good ideas."

"Ha, ha," I said, nudging her with an elbow.

"I'm serious," she said. "You should've been there. You should've seen us." She was so proud, and I was impressed. But the message was clear: You should've been with me, not Jack. I didn't tell her that I was happy with the choice I made.

But it wasn't just Jack or the prank. The truth was I hadn't wanted to see *her*. But I couldn't really explain why. All I knew was that I had begun to experience a sense of guilt around her since the night she told me about her father.

She was my favorite person in the whole world and this was the first time I'd purposely avoided her since we met.

37.

They were arguing again, my parents. I was supposed to meet Jack, but in order to get to my car, I would have to go downstairs, where they were currently screaming at each other.

> Me: Sorry, I'm going to be late
>
> Jack: Everything okay?
>
> Me: Tell you later

I sat in my closet to wait it out, the small, dark space always a comfort, but I could still hear them. Dad was yelling about some work thing he needed Mom to go to.

"I told you," she said. "I can't. I have back-to-back surgeries that day."

"It's three weeks away. You can't possibly know what surgeries you have yet."

"I don't have to know which surgeries I'm going to have to know that I'm *going* to have back-to-back surgeries because I always do. I'm the head of neuro. I always have surgeries."

"It's just a two-hour lunch thing. You can't take a few hours off? Or use a personal day?" he said through gritted teeth.

"No." Her voice was deadly calm, her answer final.

"Let me get this straight. So when you need me to spend a night sucking up to donors and board members, it's nonnegotiable, but when I need you for *two fucking hours* you can't make it." He was exasperation, she was anger. These were roles they'd played for years.

"I don't know how many times I have to explain to you that

while you're off crunching numbers or whatever it is that you do all day, I'm off saving lives." These were all words she'd flung at him before. This was an old argument.

"Fuck you," he said, and I flinched, curling more into myself.

My name is Remy Tsai.

I am seventeen years old.

This won't last forever.

It worked, a little.

"Fuck you and your bullshit," he said. "I'm sick of your self-righteous posturing."

They went at it some more. He called her cold, she called him unsupportive. He accused her of lying, she accused him of adultery. Finally, they wound down, with him driving off, her going to the downstairs office.

They didn't want each other anymore but they couldn't let each other go.

    Me: Leaving now, be there soon

Jack sent me a picture of him and Lola with big smiles, and I felt a little better. He was already outside with Lola, talking to a woman who had to be his aunt.

"Hey," he said when I pulled up. He walked over and greeted me with a kiss to the cheek before finding my hand with his.

His aunt waved us over. "Call me Diane."

"Hi, I'm Remy," I said.

"Oh, she's so pretty," she said to Jack, and I blushed.

"I know." He smiled.

Then his aunt laughed warmly and patted him on the shoulder. "Have fun."

"Sorry about that," Jack said when he was in my car, though

he seemed at ease. He reached back to clip a doggy seat belt to Lola's harness and gave me directions to an access point to the Chattahoochee that had hiking trails.

"You okay?" he asked after we parked and got out to pick a trail off the large welcome map. "You've been pretty quiet."

I shrugged. "I'm fine. Sorry I was so late, by the way," I said, but he sensed something was off.

"Come here," he said, leading me to one of the picnic tables by the parking lot. "What's wrong?"

"Nothing, it's fine. Let's just go." I didn't want to talk about it. The only person outside of the family who knew was Elise and that was bad enough.

Jack finally acquiesced, but as we walked through the woods, I couldn't concentrate on anything he was saying.

"Seriously, are you okay?" he said when we finished the loop.

"It's dumb."

"I promise, whatever it is, I won't think it's dumb," he said, and we sat in my car watching the sky darken as I told him about my parents.

"They're fucked up." I told him about the fights, the multiple divorce announcements, the time my dad took me on a business trip to Chicago, the fundraising dinner from a few months ago and what'd happened after. I told him about the weird, fucked-up dynamic we had, my mom's favoritism, my dad's absences, Christian's coldness.

He listened patiently, only occasionally interrupting to ask a question or two.

"I just wish they'd do it already," I said. "Put us all out of our misery and just leave each other."

Jack nodded. "My parents split when I was two, and honestly, it's for the better."

"Really?" I didn't know much about Jack's family, but there had to have been a reason he was living with his aunt and uncle.

"Yeah. My dad moved across the country, and for a few years I'd see him at Christmas or for a few weeks in the summer, but now I don't even bother. Good riddance."

"And your mom?" I asked.

He sighed. "We're not really speaking right now. Mostly because of how she handled everything that happened with my grandpa."

"I'm sorry."

"Don't be, it's okay. We all have different reactions to tragedy—or lack of reaction," he said, tensing. "Besides, she's hardly ever home anyway, and my grandpa was really the one who raised me, so it's whatever. My aunt and uncle are all right, though." Behind us, Lola had fallen asleep and was now snoring. Jack and I laughed.

"Hey," he said. "I'm sorry this is happening to you." It was so simple, but so powerful. I couldn't help but think about how different he and Elise were.

Elise cared about me, I knew that. But where she was all about taking action and vanquishing your enemies, he didn't offer simple answers or any answers at all. He acknowledged my pain but he didn't try to fix it. They both talked about the ugliness within their families, but Jack didn't place our experiences side by side for comparison.

We drove back to Jack's place in a comfortable quiet. When I pulled up to his house, he didn't leave right away. "There was this thing my grandpa said to me all the time, and I never really got it until after he passed away."

"What was it?" I asked.

"Life's hard, shit happens, but what's the point if you don't try anyway?" he said.

"I like that."

"Me too. I always thought it was just a pithy line, but lately I've been thinking about it more and more. Maybe because I miss him, but also maybe because it helps."

Long after I said good night to Jack and Lola, what he said lingered in my mind. It reminded me of what Elise said: What's the point of living if you're not going to *exist*?

Elise was a striver, a crusader. She wanted to be remembered and she wanted life to be fair. She seemed to be waging a never-ending war against the injustices dealt to her, while Jack was just trying to make the best of it and move on. It'd been thrilling at first, being caught up in Elise's rebellion, but what about the things we couldn't do anything about? Her father, my parents. She wanted to rage, but I didn't want the capacity for endless anger.

Like Elise, Jack knew life wasn't fair, but he knew there was nothing he could do about it. And what he seemed to be saying—what his grandfather was saying—was that there could be power in acceptance. In knowing life was unfair and trying anyway.

SATURDAY // APRIL 15

38.

The first time Jack and Elise clashed was at the end of spring break. Even though I still saw her almost every day and kept my phone on when I was with Jack so Elise could reach me, she complained that I was ditching her, so on Saturday, Jack brought Evan and the four of us went out for dinner together. I couldn't be ditching her if I brought her with me, and now that I'd had some time alone with Jack, I wanted them to get to know each other, become friends.

We went to the Good Place again to have breakfast for dinner. It started off okay but devolved quickly after we all ordered.

When I said I couldn't decide if I wanted something sweet or savory, Jack stepped in and said, "We could get both and share? You get sweet and I'll order savory."

"Okay!" I said, excited that we were ordering as a couple. Elise, on the other hand, seemed less thrilled.

"So," Elise said, turning to Jack. "What do you do all day?"

"What do you mean?" he asked.

"Since you're not in school." The question itself wasn't rude, it was the way she'd said it that was oddly dismissive.

Jack ignored her tone and answered politely. "I work at a gym. I read. I sometimes go on a run with Lola, my dog."

"That's a cute name," she said, but her smile didn't quite reach her eyes.

"Everything okay?" I whispered to her while Jack and Evan were in a side conversation.

"Yeah, why wouldn't it be?" She seemed confused, but I knew she understood what I was asking. I hadn't brought it up since the night she told me about her father, afraid of what she might've said, but it was still there, following us. Most moments with her felt like they had before, like we could almost forget she ever told me. Almost.

"Elise—" I began.

"I'm *fine*," she said, shooting me a look that shut me up.

Halfway through dinner, Evan got a call from his girlfriend, Lara, and had to step outside.

"Those two break up like every other week," Jack said, shaking his head.

Elise glanced out with interest at the parking lot where Evan was sitting on the curb hunched over his phone, clearly anxious.

When he came back inside, he sat back down next to Jack, looking distressed.

"Everything okay?" Jack asked like he already knew the answer.

"It's over. Like really over this time," Evan said.

"I'm sorry," Jack said with a sigh. "But you say that every time—maybe it's not really over?"

Evan shook his head. "She's already with some other guy. Apparently for a few weeks now."

"What?" Jack looked genuinely shocked.

"I think I'm going to head home early," Evan said, avoiding all of our gazes.

"Yeah, of course," Jack said. "Remy can give me a ride back later."

"Wait," Elise said, reaching across the table to catch his wrist. "Don't go. I know just what you need."

Not all of the Deadly Vipers were available on such short notice, but there were more than enough people for Elise's idea.

"I don't know," Evan said after she pitched it to him. "It seems like a lot."

"I mean, she just did that to you—cheated on you and then humiliated you. Doesn't *that* seem like a lot to you? What'd she say exactly?"

"She said she was bored of walking all over me," Evan said, flushed with embarrassment.

Elise shook her head sadly. "You have to have some respect for yourself. You have to stand up for yourself when no one else will."

Her words took me back to the night we watched *Kill Bill* for the first time. *It's not just about revenge. It's having respect for yourself. It's believing you don't deserve all the shitty things that people do to you. It's believing that even if you get knocked down, there will be a day of reckoning. There'll be a day you'll rise out of the ashes and destroy the people who tried to destroy you.*

"People are always saying you have to let it go, you have to move on, you have to focus on yourself, forget about them. Because success is the best revenge," Elise said. "But that's total bullshit. You know what's the best revenge? Actual revenge."

Evan paused to think, then nodded. "Okay."

Jack shot me a confused look. "What's Elise planning?"

"I don't know," I said, a little worried about what she had in mind. Her plans were so unpredictable, anywhere from completely benign to destructive. Whatever it was, I hoped it stayed on the tame side.

First, we stopped by Publix to buy five large cans of tuna.

"Salted or unsalted?" Evan asked.

"Doesn't matter," she answered. "As long as it's in oil."

"I don't think this is a good idea," Jack said when Evan and Elise were ahead of us in the checkout line. "Have you guys done this before?" He frowned.

"Not this specific prank, but pranks in general. Small stuff," I said, even though that wasn't quite true—what we'd done to Dana, Jae's ex-girlfriend, wasn't small.

"What are we doing?" I asked her in the car.

"You'll see," she said with a sly smile. Elise had a flair for the dramatic and liked saving her plans for a big last-minute reveal.

Back at the Pink Mansion, we met up with Julie and opened the large cans of tuna suspended in oil, cautiously draining them into Tupperware, tossing out the fish before we left again. A little before midnight, we arrived at Lara's house, parking near her car. We went up to Lara's car, a black Corolla. Everyone stood still in anticipation, staring at Elise for direction.

"When you turn on the heat or AC, when you have the fan on and even when you don't, air from the outside comes into the car through tiny vents located underneath the windshield wipers," Elise explained. "We're going to pour the tuna oil into those vents." Jack looked at me in sharp surprise, but Evan seemed excited.

"Are you serious?" Jack asked. I was shocked too, by both the genius and simplicity of it. She always knew how to accomplish a lot with very little—a ruined car with a can of tuna fish. But Jack didn't seem to be balking at her genius, and underneath my awe, I was worried, too. We'd never destroyed someone's car. We'd never done anything so permanent.

Elise tilted her head slightly, as if pausing to consider an answer. "Yes," she said. "I'm dead serious." Then she turned to Evan. "You should do the honors."

"Don't do this," Jack said.

"Why not?" Evan said. He was getting keyed up, bouncing a little on the balls of his feet.

"Come on, it's not worth it," he said. "Let's just go home."

"Go ahead," Elise encouraged him, ignoring Jack.

Evan looked between them but nodded at Elise. Then he carefully popped open the Tupperware and began to pour slowly. From now until the day the car would be flattened at a junkyard, the pervasive smell of rotting fish would haunt Lara. She'd have to take the entire car apart to clean it but even then, the scent of bad tuna would linger. "The scent of justice," Elise called it.

"Where'd you get the idea?" I asked her.

She shrugged. "I considered it for Christian but then realized your parents might just get him a new car."

"Oh." I didn't know how to respond. Maybe she *had* considered it for Christian, or at least thought of it then, but she never told me, never seriously entertained the idea. I couldn't see her doing something so extreme then, but now here she was, charging ahead with it.

"Okay, that's it," Evan said, tapping the container empty against the windshield. Elise and Evan stood there for a while admiring their work as Jack shifted his weight between his feet in obvious discomfort. I turned away, trying hard to not think too much about what we'd just done.

We went back to Jack and Evan's house and ordered pizza. Evan and Elise were in a good mood, talking and laughing about the prank we'd just pulled, but Jack remained quiet, watching them intently. I reached for him and he let me take his hand. This was a mistake, I thought. The dinner, the attempt to spend time with both of them. I caught Elise glancing over at us. Her smile was sweet, but I couldn't help but wonder which victory she was thinking of: the mission, or the night itself. She saw an opening when she learned of Evan's breakup and she wasted no time taking it.

"God, I wish I could be there," Evan said. "See the look on her face."

The next morning, Lara would wake up, get dressed, and on the drive to work or school, the smell of tuna would hit her. She might roll down a window, maybe think it was something from outside when the stink didn't dissipate. But it'd only stay, grow stronger, work its way through her entire ventilation system.

Elise called it a prank but it wasn't, not really. What we did permanently ruined Lara's car. But Elise didn't care about the damage, the fallout, or what would happen after. And drunk off revenge and his newfound power, Evan didn't care either.

At the end of the night, when Jack took me home on his motorcycle, he lingered after he dropped me off. "We shouldn't have done that," he said with a shake of his head.

"It'll be okay," I said. It was done and there was no undoing it, though I was uneasy too.

"I don't know," Jack said. "I'll be the first to tell you that Lara was a shitty person, but I'm not sure she deserved that. I'm not sure *anyone* deserves that." He sighed. "I should've said something."

"You did," I told him. "Right before Evan poured the fish oil down the vents."

"I should've stopped it. That's what my grandpa would've done," he said before sliding his helmet back on.

Elise said it wasn't revenge, that this was about justice. But what we did that night wasn't about righting a wrong. It was about payback. Maybe I didn't have a right to complain—the very first prank we ever pulled was on *my* ex-boyfriend. And back then, it had seemed thrilling, had made me feel powerful when I was at my most powerless. Maybe it's what Evan needed. Though I couldn't help but think that when Elise was encouraging Evan to pour the oil down the vent, she wasn't thinking about him at all.

Elise felt powerless, and in some ways, she'd always felt that way. The pranks, the Deadly Vipers, the "justice" she wanted to deliver—it was all just a means to wrest control when she had none.

It scared me, watching her. The pranks were escalating. At the beginning, it'd been setting off firecrackers outside someone's dorm window, and now it was destroying someone's car.

That night, as I lay in bed struggling to fall asleep, I just wanted to figure out a way to help Elise, to get her to put an end to the pranks. But the more I thought about it, the more I wondered if there was anything that would make her stop.

39.

Elise loved playing judge, jury, executioner. I watched from the side-lines as the Deadly Vipers—Elise, Julie, Madi, Jae, and now Evan—spent our lunch hours debating who their next target should be. I was technically a Viper, but I stopped giving any input for the most part.

There were times I didn't know how to talk to her anymore. "Hey, how are you?" I'd asked, the first day back from spring break.

"What do you mean?" She gave me a weird look. "Things are fine," she said. "*I'm* fine." She hated being asked how she was, but every time I did, she acted like she didn't know what I was talking about. It almost felt like she regretted telling me in the first place. She never brought it up again, refused to even acknowledge anything was wrong. But it was always there—this tension between us.

Things only got worse as the pranks took off. At first the targets ranged from teachers with a history of misconduct to the better-known bullies at school, like Ethan and George from math, the assholes who taunted weaker students for sport—at least when Elise wasn't around.

The administration and school security investigated the Vipers's spring break prank on Mr. Dawkins. But the investigation didn't result in discovery, the exact opposite—Dawkins quietly resigned. What was once an open secret had been fully exposed through a single trashed classroom and Riverside had to take action. The school never contacted the police and seemed to end the investigation the moment he left. They probably didn't want to draw even more attention to the matter.

Emboldened, Elise charged full speed ahead with her plans. There were more mice in bedrooms, tuna oil in the ventilation. They slashed tires, egged cars, filled balloons with vinegar and food coloring, then ambushed targets. She was always devising new ways to fuck with people. She wanted to push the limit, or maybe she wanted to find out if there was one, and she grew bolder and bolder each time they escaped capture. After Dawkins, the Vipers were always careful to take action off school grounds to avoid drawing too much attention to themselves.

I went to the first few missions but soon began making excuses every time they had another. The pranks had been thrilling at the beginning but they'd lost their appeal. On some level, I really did understand that Elise needed to take control, deliver her brand of justice, but it was also exhausting always raging against the world.

When I wasn't with Elise, I was with Jack. As I started to spend more and more time with him, I had less time for her. We went on hikes with Lola, to the lake, for rides on his motorcycle, my arms wrapped around him tight. I told myself I was running toward him and not away from her, but maybe that was just a convenient lie.

"I don't understand," she complained to me after I skipped the third prank in a row. "You never had a problem before." We were at my house after school, just the two of us like always. "What's different?"

I shrugged. "I just don't want to anymore."

"It's Jack, isn't it?" she asked.

"No." Though maybe it was, at least partly.

"He's just trying to steal you away from me," she concluded, stretching out on one of the lounge chairs by the pool.

I laughed, thinking it was a joke.

"I'm being serious! He was a competitive swimmer, wasn't he? And now he can't compete, so this is what he does instead." Elise scoffed.

"That's ridiculous." I lit us two cigarettes and passed her one. It was four in the afternoon, and we had the whole place to ourselves. Mom and Dad were at work, and Christian was probably with his girlfriend.

"Then come back," she said, tipping her sunglasses down to look at me.

"Finals are next week," I protested.

"Fuck finals," she said. "This is more important."

I didn't answer, snuffing out my cigarette and staring at the water. Finally I turned to her. "How are things?"

"*How are things?* Really, Rem?" she asked.

Ever since she showed me that bruise on her shoulder, she never brought up her father again.

"They're fine," she said. "God, I wish I'd never told you, honestly. It's not a big deal. I can handle myself, stop asking!" She paused. "You haven't told anyone, have you?"

"No." I shook my head. "I would never do that." It hurt to think she didn't trust me. She wished she'd never confided in me, and now she thought I might've told someone when I promised I wouldn't.

"Good." Her eyes were so piercing that I almost flinched. "And don't change the subject. We're talking about you."

In the days after the prank on Lara, Jack had told me, "It's not about fairness. It's just revenge. There's already so much awful shit out there, why add more?"

I heard that even after Lara's parents paid thousands of dollars to clean out the ventilation system in her car, the stink of tuna lingered. When Elise found out, she laughed.

It just seemed cruel.

"Come out with us tonight," she said, lighting a second cigarette. "We're getting Mr. V."

"The *principal*?" I used to think Elise was an everyday heroine, a protector of the downtrodden. That she only ever wielded her power for good, sticking up for people who needed it. But what had Mr. Voss done?

"Yeah—"

Before she could launch into a speech about why we had to get mild-mannered Mr. Voss, I cut her off. "I already have plans," I lied.

"With Jack?" she said. "I thought he worked Wednesday nights?"

I shrugged. "He swapped shifts." It was so strange and awful, how easy it'd been to lie to her. We were best friends, soulmates. It was us against the world. Only, it was starting to feel different.

She examined me, taking a long drag and exhaling the smoke. Her expression was unreadable. "Fine, whatever," she said. "But tell him to watch out. I won't let him win so easily." She meant it as a joke and I laughed, but it didn't feel very funny. I used to love the idea of being fought over, being a prize, but now I wasn't so sure.

40.

They were arguing again, my parents. They were below, in the kitchen, and I was in my room upstairs, trapped again. My phone began to buzz but I ignored Elise's call. Then she texted me.

> Elise: **Where are you**
>
> Elise: **Pick up**

Things between us were still tense enough that I didn't feel as comfortable talking to her about this like I used to. Ever since Elise told me about her father, I'd felt like I *couldn't* talk to her about my parents anymore. That even though she didn't explicitly compare my parents to her father, it was always there, this distance between us. The things she said to me over six months ago on New Year's Eve haunted me, about gradations, about how I was lucky.

I tossed my phone aside and shut myself in the closet again, but who was I kidding? I could still hear them. If I'd really wanted to shut them out, I'd wear headphones, turn the volume all the way up. But I didn't know what I was afraid of more—the storm itself or not knowing what was happening.

"You're lying, I know you're lying!" Mom screamed, and I could hear angry tears in her voice. "Just admit it and stop playing games. Stop trying to make me feel crazy."

"The only one who's making you feel crazy is *you*," Dad snapped.

"Bullshit. You always do this, gaslighting me," she said. "But you can't say I'm making it up this time. You can't say I'm paranoid or I'm reading too much into things. This time I have the fucking receipts. Literally."

"That's it," my dad said. "I can't take it anymore."

"Don't run away from this!" she shouted after him, and for a breath or two, all I heard was the sound of two sets of footsteps, one chasing the other. "Can't we just talk for once?"

"What's there to talk about?" he said, lowering his voice. "You don't believe a word I say. You just want me to stand here and let you scream at me all day. No thanks. I'm out of here and I'm not coming back." Like so many of their fights, this one ended up here.

Throughout the years I felt at turns desperate and hopeful when my dad said he was leaving and never coming back, depending on how sure I was that he would take me with him.

With a deep breath, I waited for my mother's laughter, the slam of the garage door, and the disappearance of my father. He'd be gone a few days at least, maybe a week. Though maybe this time he'd take me with him. I didn't allow myself too much hope, having been down that road before, many times, but a tiny part of me wouldn't completely give up on him just yet.

"I'm serious," he said.

Mom laughed and I braced for impact. *Here we go*, I thought.

"Sure, whatever, go," she said. "Have a nice little vacation. I'll see you in a few days. Can you take the recycling on your way out?"

The silence was heavy and cold. I shivered, pulled a coat over me, and lay down on the closet floor.

"I'm serious," he said again, his voice drained of anger. "I can't do this anymore."

I became very, very still.

"Don't make me laugh," Mom said with a scoff. "You'll never leave me. You need me. You *need* to be married to me. You need a villain in your story. You like making other people fall in love with this tragic hero you so love to play." She projected strength at the beginning of her short speech, but now her voice shook with anger. "What do you tell them? Do you say we're only staying together for the kids? You must sound so noble, so self-sacrificing. You love it. You love having a villain in your story, you *need* it. What would you be without me? A lonely, pathetic middle-aged divorcé," she finished, leaving the house in an eerie silence. No angry footsteps or slamming doors. I didn't hear Dad leave. For the first time after one of their fights, I didn't hear anything at all, and that was somehow scarier.

I met Jack at the lake just as the park emptied for the evening. "Come here," he said when he saw me, folding me into a hug. "What happened?" I'd told him I needed to see him, but not why.

"My parents," I said. "It's nothing new, it's—" I couldn't finish.

"Hey, it's okay." He took my hand, leading me to one of the swinging benches that overlooked the entire reservoir. "It's okay to be upset." We swung slightly with the breeze and I leaned into his embrace, resting my head on his shoulder. "Just tell me what happened."

"My parents—I think my dad might really be leaving this time." I told him some of the things my mom had said, how she'd laughed at him. They had a pattern, but this time they broke it.

"Jesus." Jack ran his free hand through his hair in shock.

"It seems worse this time, but then again it feels worse *every* time. I don't know why I even care anymore."

"Of course you care." He pulled me closer, kissed the top of my head softly.

"I wish I were stronger. Like Elise." She almost never cried. She always seemed to know what to do. She was made of steel, unbreakable.

"You're wrong," Jack said. "You *are* strong."

"No," I began to protest.

"Let me finish."

"Okay."

"I wasn't going to tell you just yet, but I went to the pool for the first time last week in almost a year, and that was because of you," he said, pulling away to look at me. "I was in such a dark place when we met, but you inspired me, Remy."

Wow. No one had ever said something like that to me before. "When were you going to tell me?"

"I wanted to make sure it wasn't a fluke. But I've been back a few times since. And it was because of you." He sat back to face me, one leg crossed. "I still have bad days, but I'm having good ones too. Ones where I can remember all the good memories of my grandpa and smile."

I didn't know what to say. I'd always felt like the one who needed someone to swoop into my life and save me. Powerless, weak. But being with Jack felt like the opposite.

For a moment, the whole world seemed to spin around us, and we were the center of the universe, just the two of us. He touched a hand to my cheek, thumb smooth against my skin, and I leaned into him, into that feeling.

"Elise seems like this strong person, but just because she can hurt people doesn't make her strong. If anything, it makes her weak, always lashing out, always needing to prove how strong she is. And I know it seems like doing nothing is like admitting weakness, but it's not. My grandpa used to say survival is a talent. You're still here, you've survived so far, and you'll survive this too, and whatever else comes your way." He lifted my chin, cupped my face. And when we kissed, the breeze picked up and it felt like we were flying.

The house was silent when I came back, no one in the kitchen or living room, the office dark. But both cars were still in the garage, so I treaded lightly.

In the shower, I smiled, my eyes closed at the memory of us alone in the park, of us kissing on the bench, the feeling of his body beneath mine, of us in the water with no clothes on, nothing between us.

That night, I decided to move downstairs into the basement. I didn't want to be trapped in my room anymore. I took my pillow and my charger, planning to sleep on the sectional and go back for the rest of my things later.

But I wasn't alone down there. I saw him after I turned out the lights, in the backyard by the pool on one of the loungers, staring blankly at the water—my dad.

Surprised he was still here and buoyed by my talk with Jack, I wrapped a blanket around myself and walked over to him, sitting down in the chair beside his.

"Remy, hi," he said, looking up.

We both turned back to the water, peaceful and still.

"Why don't you just leave?" I asked, not looking at him. "Really leave." It wasn't exactly a question the way I said it. I'd been scared of the answer for as long as I could remember, but I didn't care what it was anymore, as long as there *was* one.

Dad didn't answer right away and I wondered if he'd heard me, but he finally sighed, acknowledging what I said.

"I . . . I don't know," he said.

"You and Mom don't love each other," I said, and it was the truth. "Maybe you guys did once, but whatever you have now isn't love." Another statement he didn't contest. "You always say you're going to leave her, but you always come back. Do you even mean it anymore?" There was no accusation in my voice, only sadness.

I thought Dad and I were the outsiders, that together we formed the resistance to Mom's tyranny, but now I wasn't so sure. I thought we were on the same side, looking out for each other, but maybe no one was ever looking out for me, and I was angry.

"Do you know what it's like watching the two of you destroy each other over and over and over again? What it's been like all these years? You're both miserable and you make everyone around you miserable." I took a deep breath. "What you and Mom have isn't love. It's just misery."

His silence was heavy, oppressive.

"Did you ever love each other?" I asked. I wanted to believe that love was real, that maybe before Christian and me they had starred in their own love story. That maybe once upon a time, things were good.

"I don't know," he said, unable to face me. He stared at the ground, hanging his head.

"Then why'd you get married?" I wasn't angry anymore, I just wanted to know.

"I guess I thought it'd make me happy, make us happy."

"Were you? Happy?"

"I think so. For a while at least." He still wouldn't meet my eyes.

"Why do you stay?"

"A lot of reasons."

"What's the main one? And don't say it's me and Christian." I wasn't giving him any outs.

Finally he looked at me, attempting a smile that ended up in a grimace. "What can I say, I'm a romantic," he joked weakly.

I stared at him blankly.

"It's terrifying," he said. The truth at last.

"Leaving her?"

"Being alone."

This moment between us was so strange and awful. I'd loved my dad, I'd resented him. I'd been surprised by him and disappointed by him, but I'd never felt what I felt then—pity.

It was depressing, growing up thinking your parents had all the answers, thinking age was the same as wisdom, all to realize one day that no one had the answers. That your parents were not gods or monsters but human, fallible. That in a way, they're children just like you. That all of us are just children, lost and scared, trying to find our way.

I thought of what Jack said, about how survival was a talent. We were all just trying to survive.

41.

Diane and Dale Novak, Jack's aunt and uncle and Evan's parents, were both educators—Mr. Novak taught second grade and Mrs. Novak was the vice principal of the middle school. On the second week of summer vacation, they invited me over for dinner. Their house smelled like cinnamon snickerdoodles and was filled with knickknacks from their travels.

"All from the pre-Evan days," Mr. Novak said with a laugh.

"Not all. Some of these are from when Evan was old enough to travel," Mrs. Novak said. "The best part of being teachers is having two months to travel every year."

It was my first time over for dinner and I mostly stayed quiet, sitting with Jack and Lola on one end of the table, Evan on my other side. After spring break, Evan, a junior like Jae, joined our lunch table, becoming a fixture soon after. After the fish caper, as the night came to be called, he seemed taken with Elise. It bothered me, not because I felt threatened but because he reminded me of myself when I thought Elise had all the answers, when I was sure

Elise was my soulmate, more sure than I'd been sure of anything my whole life. He looked at her like she was his savior, and I wondered if I had done the same.

I wondered if I was still the same Remy who desperately needed her. And if I wasn't, what did that mean for us? I couldn't bear the thought of not having her in my life, of losing *Elise x Remy*, but as I glanced at Jack, I knew we'd never be able to go back to the way things were—when Elise was the world and I was an ever-present satellite.

"So, Remy," Jack's aunt said. "Did you know Jack from school? The swim team maybe?"

"Um, no actually," I said. "I don't swim and we've never had any classes together." Riverside was also huge, with a student body of almost 2,500 kids.

"We met at a friend's house in March," Jack said. "We kind of started talking because neither of us wanted to be there." His aunt and uncle laughed at that.

"In any case," his aunt continued. "It's been good to see Jack so happy lately."

He and I shared a soft smile. I'd been happier lately too.

"Hey, Remy," his uncle said. "Did you know that Jack was an Olympic hopeful?"

"Really?"

"Oh my God, Uncle Dale, stop," he said.

"We have pictures of him and Evan going back to their days in floaties."

"Mom, ugh," Evan said. "Stop."

"I wouldn't mind seeing these pictures," I said with a sly smile.

"Do not encourage them, Remy," Evan said. "Do not."

"Ignore them, Remy. We'll show you *all* the embarrassing photos," his uncle said.

"Why are you like this?" Jack groaned, but he was smiling.

"We're bored! It's summer for us too," his aunt said, laughing.

We spent the rest of the meal talking about school, and their plans for the rest of summer. The dinner itself wasn't that remarkable, but that feeling stayed with me—that warmth and camaraderie from being around family who cared about you.

Even in public, my parents' forced closeness was unconvincing, at least to me. Melody's parents were nice, but they mostly kept to themselves and often spoke to Mel in Korean.

I didn't want to think about Elise and her father. She'd been texting me throughout the night but I hadn't had a chance to get back to her.

I couldn't avoid her forever, though. After dinner, Evan pulled me aside when Jack was helping clear the table. "Hey, Remy, Elise is really worried. Are you avoiding her?"

"No," I said, surprised she'd talked to Evan about me. "What'd she say?"

"Not much, just that she hasn't seen you in over a week."

"Oh. I guess I've been busy," I said. "I'll talk to her, sorry."

I called her when I got home and she picked up on the first ring.

"Remy?" Her voice sounded so heartbreakingly hopeful.

"Hey," I said, wracked with guilt. It wasn't like I was actively ignoring her. I always texted her back, just not right away. We saw each other a week ago, on the last day of school, but I hadn't seen her since, and it was the longest stretch we'd gone without seeing each other since we met. I used to spend all my time with her—I used to *want* to spend all my time with her, but I hadn't wanted to hear her complain about how I was ditching her for Jack anymore.

"Are you home?" she asked. "I'll pick you up. Let's go for a drive."

42.

We drove around in silence for a while, cigarettes in hand, with the top down. It unnerved me, how quiet she was.

"Hey, what's wrong?" I asked, even though I already knew the answer. I used to pick up all her calls right away and respond to her texts as soon as I saw them. And now I let her calls go to voicemail and forgot to text her back half the time. I used to spend every free minute with her, and even though it was summer now, I hadn't seen her since the end of school.

I knew she thought it was all Jack's fault, but it was more than just him. It was hard to admit, but part of me started pulling away from her the night she told me about her father, showed me that bruise on her shoulder. It was hard to accept that I was simply afraid—afraid of what I didn't understand, afraid of Elise, afraid *for* Elise. Afraid of her father. Afraid of the Deadly Vipers and what they were up to, afraid of her endless well of anger.

The day after the Vipers took Mr. Voss down, she told me the reason they went after him was because he'd known Dawkins was a creep but did nothing about it, or worse, tried to cover it up.

"How do you know?" I'd asked.

"Come on." She leveled a look at me. "He *had* to have known." Maybe that was true, maybe it wasn't.

"But—" I began to protest.

"God, you sound just like Madi. Okay, we broke into his office, forced the locks on his filing cabinets to find the personnel folders. We had proof. It was in Dawkins's file. He'd been let off with warnings in the past. Voss knew and just let him off the hook."

"What'd you guys do?" I said, unease growing.

"Nothing much, actually," she said with an innocent smile. "We just sent a letter to the local news channel with a copy of the evidence we found. It took only two days for them to run a story. After that, he agreed to retire quietly."

"He did? Was there an announcement?" I couldn't believe I'd missed it, but then again, I was doing my best to avoid the Vipers and their operations.

"No, not to the whole school. The board probably didn't want to draw more attention to it."

I stared at her in awe, but I shouldn't have been surprised. The power Elise possessed seemed limitless.

"Anyway," she said now. "I heard from Evan that you were at dinner." She sounded casual, but I could tell she cared, just not if she was angry.

"Yeah."

"That must've been boring." Stopping for a red light, she took a long drag from her cigarette.

"What?"

"Eating bland food and pretending to be someone else to impress Jack's aunt and uncle." She glanced at me for confirmation before the light turned green. "Bet you couldn't wait to get away."

"No, it was nice, actually," I said, shaking my head. "It was really . . ." I searched for the right word. "Normal."

She made a face. "Normal? Ugh."

"I don't know, I want that," I said. "A family like that." Even though Jack had shitty parents, he still had his aunt and uncle, family who loved him.

Elise pulled over into a gas station. "You *have* a family already—me. We'll always be family, you and me." I smiled faintly at the familiar words, often spoken by Elise like it was a promise. An unbreakable vow.

Elise wanted a remarkable life. She wanted to be remembered. Or maybe she was afraid of being forgotten. What she said about Melody, about how choosing to live a quiet life was the same as *not existing.* I had loved that. *Take me with you,* I'd cried.

But lately I wasn't so sure. Maybe it wasn't terrible, having a quiet life. Having a family you love that loves you back. Being happy. Maybe that would be enough.

"Don't you ever get tired of feeling angry?" I asked her, genuinely curious.

"No," she said firmly.

"Why not?" Just thinking about it was exhausting—maintaining the white-hot fury she carried with her.

"Because," she said, lighting another cigarette and passing it to me, "the moment you let that anger go, you lose the drive to fight. You accept the shitty things that people do to you." Anger was the source of her power. It was the source of all her strength.

And suddenly she didn't seem all that strong anymore.

"Well, I'm exhausted," I said. "And I'm too tired to fight."

She looked at me, disappointment written all over her face. "That's Jack talking, not you."

I shook my head. "It's not."

"It's like he's brainwashing you," she said.

"Come on," I said with a laugh, even though I was starting to get annoyed. "No one's brainwashing me."

"You're different now," she lamented. "And it's all because of him."

"Don't be ridiculous."

"It's true," she said. "You never answer my calls. It takes you days to text me back. And last week we had a thing and you were just completely MIA."

"What thing?"

"A Deadly Vipers thing," she said.

I took a final drag of my cigarette before tossing it onto the concrete.

"Don't lie, you were with Jack, weren't you? I can't believe you—"

"I wasn't with Jack," I said, annoyed. "I was stuck at home because my parents were tearing into each other again and I couldn't get away."

That stopped her. "Oh."

"And for the record, I only met Jack because you ditched me, remember?"

"Is that what this is all about? You're just mad about that?" she said, looking strangely relieved. "Oh my God. That really is it, isn't it?"

"No—"

"You want me to fight for you, is that it? I can do that," she said.

"That's not it," I said, growing agitated. "Stop. Just stop. It's not a competition! I love both of you, okay?"

"You *love* him now?" she asked in shock. I was surprised too. I hadn't known how I felt until that moment.

"I do."

She scoffed.

I sighed. "You want it to be just the two of us forever."

"And what is wrong with that?" she said. "Love makes you do crazy things. I don't mean love like ours. I mean infatuation. What we have is true love, the way we feel about each other is *real*. The way I felt about Christian wasn't. I was infatuated with him and it made me crazy. It's the same with Jack. You'll see. You're just infatuated with him. One day you'll do something in the name of love and you'll regret it."

I shook my head. I couldn't believe the things she was saying. I wasn't infatuated. I knew how I felt.

"What we have is real," she repeated. "No one else has what we have. No one will ever love you like I do."

"*No one will ever love me like you*? Are you kidding me?" Maybe I believed that too at one point. I thought Elise had swept into my life and saved me. I thought she was my one and only salvation. I thought *we* were each other's salvation, but Elise wanted more. It was how I'd ended up meeting Jack in the first place. And now she was upset because I didn't need her like I used to. "Do you even hear yourself?"

She looked like I'd punched her in the stomach.

"I want to go home," I said, turning away from her. For a while there was just silence, the two of us sitting in the Pink Caddy in the middle of an empty gas station. Finally she started the car again and drove me home.

As we slowed to the front of my house, Elise grabbed my wrist and held on tight. "What, you're just done with me?" she said.

"No." I sighed. "I'm just tired, okay?"

She eventually let me go. I got out of the car and was halfway to my front door when she called my name.

"What?" I said, turning back.

"You use people, Remy," she said. "You're a user. Cameron, Melody, and now me. We're just—just *things* to you. You feed off our attention and then you leave us behind when you're done."

And before I had a chance to respond, she was gone.

43.

I don't tell Detective Ward about our fight, or what was said, just that we had one. A bad one. "I didn't speak to her after that. I ignored all her texts, emails. I let her calls go to voicemail and deleted them without listening to any of her messages."

Elise sent me a million texts saying sorry, and a slew of emails when I didn't respond to any of her messages or missed calls. I deleted her voicemails without listening to them.

But that only lasted two weeks. Then came a string of terrifying texts.

> Elise: My dad hasn't been going to The Realtor's for a whole week
> Elise: I've been avoiding him, but I'm basically under house arrest
> Elise: I'm scared, Rem
> Elise: Please I'm sorry about what I said okay?
> Elise: I need you

The scariest thing about her messages was the fact she mentioned her father at all after pretending nothing was wrong for months. I drove over to the Pink Mansion as soon as I saw them, texted her, and waited for her to slip out undetected.

"Remy!" Her whole face lit up when she saw me. I held her tight.

"What happened?" I asked. "Are you okay?"

She was. She'd just been scared, that was all.

"This happened at least four or five times," I tell Detective Ward. "She'd call, or text, and every time she'd say it was an emergency, that she was afraid of her father. *Something*. And I'd always come." I clear my throat, try to hold back my tears. "I know I should've told someone about it. I know I messed up."

Detective Ward jots down notes, and I am desperate to see what she's written, what she thinks—if she knows it's all my fault for ignoring Elise's calls that night.

"She did it several times," I repeat. "And I always came." *You have to believe me*, I am saying. *I did everything I could*, even if I hadn't.

"No one is blaming you for anything," Detective Ward says. "You know that, right? You're not on trial here."

Still, I wonder what the folder with Elise's name holds. What Ward thinks of me, what Vera must think of me, if they think I'm a monster like I do.

44.

Nothing stood out about that weekend. No dark omen or warning, no thunderstorms or black cats. Long stretches of good days were punctuated every so often with a bad one, forming a rhythm, a cadence. It was almost predictable—*almost*.

Things didn't escalate. Or maybe they did, and we were just lobsters in a pot, the temperature rising so slowly we didn't realize it was lethal until it was too late.

It went like this: I'd meet up with Jack. An hour later, I'd get the first text. Then the calls would come, one after the other. Finally I'd leave Jack at the lake or at his place and drive to the Pink Mansion.

Sometimes Elise sported a new bruise. More often she didn't. We'd sit in my car, parked on the road where her father couldn't see us. We'd talk, sometimes cry. I'd distract her, and that's what she needed most then.

Rinse and repeat, rinse and repeat.

That night was no different.

"Elise cries wolf," Jack said flatly, soon after I arrived at his house. He had the whole place to himself, Evan and his parents at dinner with his grandparents on his dad's side.

"No, she doesn't," I said, petting Lola by my side as Jack stood by the stove, making us pasta. "She just really needs me right now."

Love is to need and be needed. Love is truest, strongest when you need each other, when you can't live without each other.

"Come on, Remy," he said, like he expected better from me. "You know it's true, and you know you don't want to go."

"It's complicated," I said, and then really heard myself. It was what my dad had said once upon a time when we were sharing an ice cream and rebelling against Mom. I hadn't understood what he meant. It all seemed so simple to me back then, so black and white. But now I understood how he felt, how he probably still feels now. How an intense shared history could make it hard to give something up. Knowing this made them more human to me.

Jack shook his head. "She wants to know you'll always come when she calls." He hadn't seen her bruises. And I'd promised Elise I wouldn't tell anyone. "She wants to know you'll always pick her over me. More than that, she wants *me* to know you'll always leave if she asks."

"That's not true!" I said. Sometimes I thought about breaking my promise to Elise just so he'd understand, but I couldn't.

"Isn't it, though?" Jack said, the frustration in his voice growing.

"It isn't," I insisted.

"Then prove it," he said, challenging me. "You know she's going to text you soon, then call with some emergency."

I couldn't deny it. I glanced at my phone, checking the time. We had forty-five minutes before the first text came, maybe an hour if we were lucky.

"When she does, don't answer," he said. "Prove to me, to her, to yourself, that you can say no to her." Jack was angry, and I couldn't blame him. We'd hardly seen each other in the last few weeks. But more than that, I'd never seen Jack angry. He was at his limit, and maybe I was too.

"Fine," I said.

"No matter what she says?" he said.

"No matter what she says. I won't go. I'll stay," I promised.

Jack's face flooded with relief and my chest tightened with guilt.

The first message came when we sat down to eat. The first call came when we snuggled with Lola on the couch and started a movie. I silenced my phone, tried not to check my messages.

> Elise: Remy, why aren't you picking up?

> Elise: Are you mad? Did I do something wrong?

I picked up my phone to answer and Jack sighed.

"What? I'm not leaving, I'm just texting her back to tell her that." He didn't look convinced.

> Me: No, I'm not mad, just busy. I'll talk to you when I'm home later.

> Elise: I need to talk to you

> Elise: I'm scared

> Elise: My dad's really angry tonight, I've never seen him like this

> Elise: Remy? Are you there?

> Elise: I think he went to see The Realtor and it didn't go well

Her texts were familiar, the same ones she always sent on nights I was with Jack. I ignored them, flipped my phone facedown, and rested my hand on Jack's shoulder, the scent of his peppermint shampoo warm and comforting. I relaxed against him. It felt good to be alone just the two of us—actually alone.

    Elise: Remy please

    Elise: This is an emergency.

My phone buzzed with another call. I bumped it away and it slid between the cushions, lost. Our kisses grew heated, our skin on fire.

We moved into his bedroom. I wrapped my arms around Jack's neck, my fingers in his hair, pulling him closer.

My phone buzzed and buzzed in the living room, buried in the couch, and I ignored it. Elise was calling and calling for help, but I didn't answer.

45.

I called you, but you never picked up. I called you a million times, she whispered to me inside an ambulance what feels like an entire lifetime ago.

When I finally checked my phone after midnight, I saw the missed calls and skimmed her texts.

I called her on the drive back to my house but she didn't pick up. She was giving me the silent treatment, I thought.

I tried her again once I got home, and then after I got into bed.

> Me: Look, I'm sorry I didn't pick up
>
> Me: Are you just going to ignore me?
>
> Me: Okay, I guess this is what we're doing now

Her silence was deafening and I started getting worried. I sat up, scrolled through her texts, reading them carefully this time. The last five stopped me cold.

> Elise: Oh my god, my dad's outside my room
>
> Elise: Remy, he's pounding on the door
>
> Elise: Rem what do I do

233

Elise: I need you

Elise: Rem

After calling her one more time, uneasiness settled in the pit of my stomach and I ran to the car, keys slipping from my hands in my growing panic. I ran a red light and blew past a stop sign, but the truth was, I was already too late.

I was too late the moment I got into the car. I was too late when I checked my phone before leaving Jack's house. I was too late, and no amount of time will ever make up for those crucial hours I missed.

46.

The door to the Pink Mansion was cracked open, light escaping from the house, disappearing into the dark of night.

I found her almost immediately.

"Oh my God. Elise, oh my God." I called 9-1-1, told them to hurry.

She was lying on the steps, limp, one arm stretched up toward the second floor, a set of bloody fingerprints, the ghost of a hand clawing for freedom.

I collapsed beside her, felt sobs being ripped from my chest. Afraid I'd hurt her, make it worse, I held back, not touching her.

"Remy?" she asked, voice weak, barely audible. When she reached for me, I held her hand gently, scared I might break her. My breath caught at the sight of her, a map of blues and greens, a map of entire territories lost in battle. Her right eye was swollen almost completely shut. A river of blood ran along her collarbone, down her shoulder. Her hair was matted with blood, her neck was coated in blood from a torn earring.

"Where were you?" she said, struggling with the words, her voice hoarse and barely audible.

I needed you.

Why weren't you there to save me?

Love is to need and to be needed. Elise needed me and I wasn't there, it's as simple as that.

I sat with her in the ambulance. The bright white lights bleached every surface inside the truck and cast a harsh, ghostly glow on Elise's skin.

"I called you, but you never picked up," she said weakly. "I called you a million times."

I couldn't look her in the eye.

"I'm sorry," I said, slipping my hand in hers, a prayer in my heart for her forgiveness.

She took a deep breath and winced from the pain.

"I'm so, so sorry," I said, and vowed to make it up to her, spend the rest of my life doing it if that's what it took.

47.

The emergency room of Emory Lyndens Creek was almost completely empty when they rolled her in from the ambulance bay around midnight. I sat alone in the waiting room, called Dad. When he didn't pick up after three tries, I cried and clutched my phone to my chest, scared, lost.

Finally, I called my mother. She picked up like she always did—a doctor's habit—and fifteen minutes later, she swept into the hospital in jeans and an old T-shirt, hair tied back in a messy ponytail. Whatever her shortcomings were as a mother, she was the best at handling real emergencies.

"What happened?" she asked, no anger or recrimination in her voice.

I told her how I found Elise curled up on the stairs. I told her what I'd known about Elise's father. I confessed my sins and asked for absolution.

"Why didn't you tell anyone?" she said, a mix of shock and anger flashing across her face.

"I didn't think anyone would believe me—believe us." I stared at my shoes and watched my tears fall to the ground. *I promised I wouldn't.*

She paused, the outrage draining from her expression. "I'm sorry, you're right. It's not your fault. It's not Elise's fault either." She never apologized, never said I was right, leaving me speechless. Then she surprised me again, this time with a tight hug, and for a moment she wasn't the enemy. For a moment she wasn't my awful mother who played favorites, who was perpetually disappointed in me, who wished I was never born. She was just my mom, and I needed her. She held me and let me cry.

Mom spoke to the doctors, saw Elise, called doctor friends who worked at the hospital, woke up a plastic surgeon to come in and sew up Elise's cuts.

"Make sure you don't leave any scars," she directed.

The police came, asked Elise questions about her father. He'd driven back to The Realtor's house after leaving the Pink Mansion, but she'd refused to let him in. Undeterred, he pounded on The Realtor's door until she called the police, and that's how they found him. He was at the station now, asking for a lawyer.

"What happened, exactly?" one of the officers asked Elise.

"Isn't it obvious?" she said, tears running down her face. With her permission, they took pictures of her in her underwear: the cuts, the bruises, the taped-up ribs, the swollen eye and bloody scalp.

In the early hours of Sunday morning, after the officers left and my mom was out in the hallway talking to Elise's doctors, we were finally alone.

"Hey," I said softly, resting a light hand on her wrist, still afraid to touch her.

"Hey," Elise said, turning her head toward me, a faint smile on her lips.

"I'm sorry," I whispered. "I'm so, so sorry."

"I know," she said with a kindness I did not deserve. The guilt grew within my heart, all hard metal and sharp edges, gutting me from the inside.

I pulled away just when Elise needed me. And I'd been so wrapped up in Jack and so busy falling in love that I didn't see how badly she truly needed help.

Maybe it was all too easy to dismiss every call, every cry for help. Even the ones I answered, because this—her father's violence—had become such a routine part of our lives. It was strange and awful, how given enough time anything could start to feel normal. As pedestrian as going to school, as mundane as breathing.

"What happened?" I asked.

Elise shrugged and then winced from the movement. "What always happens. He was on the warpath and I was in the way. I wish I—" She broke off, looked away. I felt like there was something she wasn't telling me. It terrified me: Elise's secrets were unmapped mines that exploded when discovered.

She tried to take a deep breath, but then her eyes watered from the pain of expanding lungs pushing against fractured ribs. She coughed, which only made it worse. I dropped her hand, reaching for the pitcher of water by her bed. She shook her head, refusing the cup I poured.

"But how did it happen?" I asked. "Did he and The Realtor break up again?"

Her head tilted in the slightest nod.

"I don't know. All I know is he came back home from her place angry and ready to take it out on me. It's what he does, finds something to be mad about. This time he came home and started screaming about how I'd left a mess in the kitchen. Dragged me out of my room to clean it up." Her voice sounded so far away, like she was lost in a memory—like she was still in the Pink Mansion trying to escape.

I wanted to keep her from going under. I wanted to save her from drowning in the past, but I was helpless. I didn't know what to do. Elise had always been the one with all the answers, and this time she had none.

"He said I was ungrateful after all the things he'd done for me. After all the sacrifices he'd made for me. The same stuff he always says." She was trying to hold back tears, like she didn't want his words to matter, to hurt her. "The kitchen wasn't even that messy. But I guess that wasn't really the point." I remembered what Elise told me: *If he was having a bad day, he'd make sure I'd have one too.*

"Remy?" she said, finally turning toward me.

"I'm here." *And I'll never leave,* I thought. *Ever.*

238

"Am I a burden?"

"What? No," I said. Elise didn't look convinced and I didn't blame her, not after the way I'd treated her. I promised myself then and there that I'd never, ever let her feel like she was a burden.

"No one wants me around. No one *ever* wants me around. Not my mom, not my dad. I don't have *anyone*," she said, tears running down her face, clinging to the curve of her chin. "Not even you." The words cut me up.

I touched my own face, felt tears on my cheeks as well. I couldn't remember when I started crying. Maybe I had never stopped.

"That's not true," I said. "I want you. I need you. I love you." Before Elise, I spent my days on boys who never loved me— distractions that granted me temporary escape from my parents, my life. Then Elise burst into my world, filling it with searing color, and for a while it'd been just the two of us. *Elise x Remy.*

"No." She shook her head. "You don't. Not like I need you."

"What are you talking about? Of course I do." Even then I knew it was a lie. But it didn't have to be. We were *Elise x Remy* once, and we could be that again.

"You don't need me. You have Jack, you have your parents."

"I don't have my parents. You know what they're like, never there, and when they're actually there, they don't give a shit. Or worse, they blow up at each other and drag everyone into it. They throw around divorce like it means nothing."

Elise glanced out at the hallway, where my mother was, and my face flushed with embarrassment. I knew what she was saying with that simple flick of her eye. There my mother was, here when I called.

"You're right," I said quietly. "It's not the same, you're right."

She turned away, staring out of the window at the hospital parking lot.

"But I do need you, Elise," I said, touching her wrist softly, trying to pull her back toward me. "Just as much as you need me." We were soulmates, we were forever, and somehow I'd wandered off that path.

"That's just not true," she said, voice growing distressed. "Don't lie to me, Remy. Don't ever lie to me. You're never around. I have to beg, really *beg*, to get a glimpse of you. School's one week away and you didn't have time for me all summer." Her voice cracked with anger, with pain. "Bottom line, you don't need me."

"I do," I said desperately. "I do."

"You won't even answer when I call."

Her words landed like a punch to the stomach and I could no longer breathe. Her eyes cut into me, revealing the terrible truth. I'd failed her, I'd failed us.

"I'm sorry," I cried. "I'm so sorry."

I knew the words weren't enough, could never be enough.

Trauma has a gravity of its own and it'll never, ever let you go. In some ways we are still trapped in the orbit of that night. In some ways, that night is the real beginning to this story.

48.

So there it is. The truth about that night. My failure to keep her safe. The night that haunts me, the one captured in Elise's police file.

I'm sorry, Elise, I think.

Detective Ward seems to examine me carefully. She had all the facts of the case in that folder, but never the entire story. Not until now. Only me, Elise, and Jack ever knew the truth about that night— that I was with him when she called, that I purposefully ignored her cries for help. Just thinking about it makes me want to throw up.

"I can't even begin to imagine what she went through. What her father did is absolutely despicable," Detective Ward says. "It's clear that you're devastated too, that you feel responsible in some way, but I want you to know that it wasn't your fault."

"I'm her best friend," I say, looking at her like she's lost her mind. "I'm the only one she has."

"The person responsible for what happened is her father and her father alone. Not her. And not you."

"Yeah, but—"

"What exactly could you've done?" she asks. "Okay, say you picked up the phone on the first call and drove over immediately. Who's to say he wouldn't have hurt you too? It's not your fault."

It is, I want to argue, but she doesn't understand. For all of Elise's bravado, she's just a terrified young girl, as lost as anyone else. And for once, she needed me to be the strong one. She needed me to save her and I didn't show up.

"Don't beat yourself up," Detective Ward continues. "These things don't always have a pattern that makes sense. It's not like a roller coaster, there isn't always an escalation. People always worry that they missed some sign, and sometimes that's true, but it doesn't work like that every time. Things could be going perfectly all right for them for a while, maybe they don't seem violent or they've never even been violent with a loved one. Sometimes people just snap. Violence isn't logical—it doesn't follow rules or care about your expectations."

I regard her with suspicion. Why is she saying any of this? Why is she trying to comfort me? I don't trust her. I don't know what she's thinking, what games she might be playing. Worst of all, I don't know what she's told Elise, what she'll say after talking to me here.

"Remy," she says. "Sometimes people are in a holding pattern until they're not. You couldn't have predicted any of it."

"I didn't have to predict any of it," I tell her. "I just had to pick up the phone, but I didn't." I think about the photos of Elise in her case file—every cut, every bruise evidence of my failure as her friend.

I think about all she's done for me, about the moments she's protected me when I needed shelter from the storm. I think about the promises I made to her, that I'd never leave her, that I'd always love her.

I failed to protect her then, but never again.

"You couldn't have known," Detective Ward repeats. "It wasn't your fault."

I don't answer this time, exhausted by her insistence.

"Did she ever say it was your fault?" she asks.

"No," I say. "If anything, she told me it *wasn't* my fault." But unlike Ward, Elise didn't think the only person to blame was her father.

49.

Elise was discharged that Wednesday, with less than a week to the start of school. She moved into our house, staying in my room as the legal proceedings moved forward. Criminal charges were filed against her father, and an immediate protective order was issued for her safety. A social worker spoke to her at the hospital and saw that Elise was situated in our home. She told us she'd be checking in regularly.

I never left her side. We spent every minute together, watching movies in the basement all day, going for long drives at night when she couldn't sleep, which was pretty much every night. We'd smoke and talk, or we'd fall into a steady silence, stare at the dark sky.

She had terrible nightmares. Sometimes I'd wake up to the sound of desperate whimpers. I always woke her and held her tight until she fell back asleep. "Shhh," I whispered softly, running my hand over her long dark hair.

Jack and I texted whenever I had a free moment, which wasn't often in the first week after Elise moved into my house. She knew I had to tell him, that it was too big to keep under wraps since I had to explain why I couldn't see him. She'd hated the idea of anyone knowing about the abuse she suffered, but now that those closest to her knew, it seemed like she *wanted* me to tell him, so he'd know what he'd inadvertently done. Jack felt awful, told me it was all his fault. That was also what Elise thought, though she never said it out loud. To her, it was so obvious it didn't need to be acknowledged. But it wasn't his fault. I was the one who made the decision to ignore her messages that night. I was the one who failed her.

"I know you came as soon as you could, Remy." *It wasn't soon enough.*

"Don't blame yourself, it wasn't your fault." *It was Jack's fault.*

"I know you would've been there sooner if you knew." *You only ignored my texts and calls because of Jack.*

She didn't say it out loud but the subtext was there. It reminded me of what she said to me: *Love makes you do crazy things. I don't mean love like ours. I mean infatuation. What we have is true love, the way we feel about each other is real. The way I felt about Christian wasn't. I was infatuated with him and it made me crazy. It's the same with Jack. You'll see. You're just infatuated with him. One day you'll do something in the name of love and you'll regret it.*

Maybe she was right, in the end. But the way I felt about Jack wasn't just infatuation, what we had was real. And it hurt every time I couldn't answer his calls or texts.

Jack: How is she?

Jack: I know she needs you right now

Jack: But I want you to know I miss you

Jack: Call me when you can?

The only time I could talk to him was when Elise had fallen

asleep, but I couldn't be gone for too long in case she woke up. It was nerve-wracking, and I missed him, but I'd made a promise to be there for her when she needed me and I was going to keep that promise.

"Hey," I whispered, when I managed to slip away one night.

"Hey," he said, whispering back, and it felt so good, hearing his voice. We were quiet for a moment, letting the sound of our matching breaths do all the talking.

"Miss you," he said, breaking the silence.

"Me too," I admitted after a moment. He asked how Elise was doing, told me how his swim times were coming along, but then I had to go, afraid Elise might need me.

"I feel awful," he said. "I can't stop thinking about it. I should've just believed you when you said she needed you. I—" he broke off, cleared his throat like he was staving off tears. "I'm sorry. Tell her I'm sorry."

"I have," I said. "I will. And it wasn't your fault." *It was mine.* "I have to go."

He paused, his breathing shallow. Finally, he let me go. "See you at school," he said softly.

"Yeah, see you next week," I said.

"It's going to be so weird, being back as a senior again, all my friends gone."

"You have me," I said, smiling at the idea of seeing him at school—of being able to see him every day again.

The night before the first day of school, Elise and I packed our bags and went to bed early. But after Elise fell asleep, I slipped out of bed alone. Something had been bothering me ever since she left the hospital. When we went to the Pink Mansion to pack up her things, I saw her go up into the attic. She said she was looking for a picture of her mother to take with her, but I knew that couldn't be true. I thought about it on and off all week and finally, I couldn't stand it any longer.

Most of Elise's boxes had been put into the guest room for now, and that's where I started. Quietly, I began sifting through them. It took almost an hour but I finally found what I was looking for: the gun case. Taking a deep breath, I undid the snaps and looked inside.

"No," I whispered. The bullets were there, the cleaning kit too. But the revolver was missing.

"What are you doing?" Elise asked, and I almost screamed. She was at the door, standing in her tank top and athletic shorts, rubbing her eyes.

There was no point in trying to hide it. I rose slowly, showed her the case. "Where's the gun?"

"What are you doing looking for it?" she said, snatching the case out of my hands.

"Where is it?"

She didn't answer.

"You can't be serious. At least tell me you're not carrying it everywhere," I begged.

She remained quiet.

"Please, Elise. Tell me it's not in your messenger bag, that you're not bringing it to school tomorrow."

"No, of course not," she said. "Don't be silly. I'll leave it in the car when I'm at school."

"You can't," I said, panicking. "You can't bring a gun onto school grounds." She was smart, I thought. There was no way she'd do it.

"It's my gun. I can do whatever I want with it. And you know exactly why I have it." She sat down on the guest bed and seemed very tired.

"But your dad—"

She cut me off with one look.

"Exactly. My dad. What, you think a protective order will actually protect me? It's nothing but a piece of paper, Remy. He's out on bail now and I can't stop him from coming for me if he wanted to." The fear and anger in her voice stopped me cold. For a long moment, we sat there in silence.

Finally I swallowed. I understood what Elise was saying but I was still terrified. The thought that she'd even think about bringing a gun to school was unimaginable.

"Don't worry," she said. "I'm not stupid. I'm not bringing it to school, but I need to have it near me, especially when I'm alone." She placed a light hand on my arm. "I need to be able to protect myself."

I left to take a shower, wanting to clear my head. The water ran cold after a while but I stayed, shivering. Elise was so much harder, rougher these days, and I couldn't blame her for that, but I wasn't sure what to say to her anymore. Maybe I thought I'd lost the right to challenge her, that I'd lost the right to judge her. So I let it go.

"It's going to be okay, Remy," Elise said when we were both back in bed. "You worry too much. Everything's going to be okay."

I wanted so badly to believe her.

50.

"Here's what we're going to tell everyone," Elise said to me on the way to school. "We're going to say that my dad had to move for work but I didn't want to go and your parents were nice enough to let me stay."

"Okay?"

"I'm serious, Rem. Now tell me what I just told you."

I dutifully recited it back to her, and when we split up for class, I texted Jack the story Elise had come up with. We finally met up at lunch, and it was the first time in over a week that I'd seen him.

"Hey," he said softly when I flew into his embrace. "Missed you." It felt so good, being in his arms again. But I pulled back quickly, worried Elise might see and get upset. She was the priority right now. Everything else, including our relationship, had to take a back seat to making her happy.

"Missed you too," I said.

"It's so weird," he said when we sat down to wait for the others. "Almost everyone I know is gone."

249

"Evan's still here."

"That's also weird. We've never been in any classes together and now we've got three. I feel so left behind," he said. "It's disorienting."

"It'll get better." I held his hand, intertwining our fingers together loosely.

Soon the others showed up, and I introduced Jack to Jae and Julie.

"Where's Elise?" I asked, looking around the caf.

"Maybe behind the school?" Jae suggested.

"Behind the school?" Jack asked me.

"Come on." I led us out to look for her and sure enough, there she was, sitting by herself on the curb, looking a little lost.

"Hey," she said when she noticed us. "Where's Madi?"

"She graduated, remember?" Julie said, giving her a weird look.

"Oh. Right. Sorry, I'm just tired."

We all sat down, catching up on what everyone had been up to in the last couple weeks before school started. Elise was uncharacteristically quiet and closed off, her smiles rare and her expression faraway.

"You okay?" I asked Elise when the bell rang.

"Yeah, of course," she said with a nearly imperceptible nod. *Not here.* Then, before everyone left for class, she called us all together. "I've been thinking."

"Uh-oh," Jae said, "that can be dangerous."

She smiled. "I think we should quit while we're ahead."

"What do you mean?" Evan asked.

"The Deadly Vipers, the pranks. I'm done." Then she walked away, leaving all of us in shock.

51.

"I want to pull one more prank," Elise announced one night, two weeks into the school year. She'd kept her word and didn't organize any more late-night missions. Everyone was confused, but Elise just said she'd grown bored of them—until now. "One more prank. Just you and me."

"What? But you said you were done," I said, instantly filled with dread. I believed her when she announced it on the first day of school.

"With the Deadly Vipers, yes," she said. "This would be just the two of us, though." We were in my basement, the TV on in the background.

"When?"

"Tonight," she said, and for the first time in weeks, I saw her smile, and it was so good seeing even a glimpse of her old self.

"This will be the very last one," she said, that glint in her eyes. "Promise. After this, I won't care if we never do another one. I mean it."

I was apprehensive. She was always talking about delivering justice, righting wrongs. She prided herself on her anger. She carefully nursed it like a small flame within her, never letting it die. And now she was saying she *was* going to let it go after one more mission? I didn't know if I could trust her to really leave her anger behind. "What do you want to do?"

"I want to prank my dad."

"*What*?" I stared at her, dumbfounded.

"He's out on bail and back in Chattanooga." She spoke calmly, like she'd thought all of it through. "He never put our house up for sale. I bet he's there right now."

"But—" My eyes searched her face wildly.

"All those times over the summer, I helped get justice for anyone who asked for it. Over the last year, I did it for you, for Jae, for Evan. It's my turn now. And it's not even about justice this time. It's about closure," she said, her voice emotional and uneven. "I need closure."

"I don't know," I said. It'd been three weeks since she'd been hospitalized. She'd only just started to breathe without any pain. "I think we should just let the police deal with him. I know you're upset, but—" The thought of going anywhere near him was terrifying.

"No." She seemed to deflate. "I'm not upset. That's not why I want to do this."

"This isn't a good idea. You're not thinking straight," I said. "You don't really want to do this." I was pleading with her.

"Yes. I do," she said. "This is what I need."

"No," I said, ready to argue with her. This was a bad idea and I only wanted to protect her. "You're not yourself, you're still—"

"*Yes, I am.*" She released a frustrated sigh, almost a growl. "I feel like myself. This is just who I am."

"I'm sorry," I said. "I meant there's nothing wrong with taking some time to recover. We can talk about it when you feel like yourself again." I thought that if I could delay things long enough, she might change her mind, or her father would be sent to prison after his court date.

"And that's what I'm telling you," she said. "I *do* feel like myself. You know what, this always happens. People like Elise when they meet her."

I couldn't understand then, why she was speaking in the third person.

"People think she's fun and wild and they fall for this—this *version* of her. And then they see the real her, and well—" She lifted a hand in a half shrug. "Listen, this is who I am. I'm not always fun and wild. Sometimes I'm sad, I'm angry, I'm sick of everything. And maybe that's who I am, deep down. So go ahead. Abandon me like everyone else has. I won't fight it. I won't blame you." The rawness of her voice was agonizing to hear.

"That's not true," I cried. "I love you. I'll always love you." It broke my heart seeing her like this. She had once seemed so strong, like nothing could ever take her down, but now I could see she was only human. Vulnerable like the rest of us.

"You love the idea of me, like everyone else." She started sobbing, burying her face in her hands.

"You know I'm not like everyone else!" It felt like the early days again, us against the world. *Elise x Remy.* When no one else knew us like we did. When no one was there for us like we were.

She continued to sob and I felt completely helpless, wanting desperately to make her feel better. But what I wanted most of all was to erase all the awful things that'd happened to her.

"I love you," I said, starting to cry too. "I'll always love you, and if this is the real you, then I'll love her too." Elise needed me, needed this *of* me. How could I refuse, after everything?

She reached for me and we leaned on each other, sobbing.

"I can't do this without you. Please, Remy. *Please.*"

She was the patron saint of the wronged. She was hurting. She was my best friend.

I said yes.

52.

"I just want him to have one bad night." That's what Elise had said. "Just one bad night."

It only takes two hours to drive to Chattanooga from Lyndens Creek, and in the late hours of the night, we were almost completely alone on the road. She had found another box of fireworks when she was clearing out the attic, one we'd missed, and her plan was simple—set off the last of the fireworks outside her old house, and startle him awake with explosions in the sky and the sound of firecrackers by his bedroom window. It had a poetic symmetry with the very first night we met. We began the pranks with a bang and we'd end them with one too, just the two of us.

It was supposed to be harmless. No one would get hurt, least of all Jack.

"Do you want to know what I was thinking that night?" she asked me as we drove north on 75. "That night, I was lying there in the dark after he left, head spinning, barely able to see out of my right eye, every breath excruciating—I was lying there and all I could think was, 'I hope I die.'"

I looked at her sharply, lips parted in shock. "Elise."

"All I could think was, *I hope I die*, because then everyone would know what a monster he was. He'd spend the rest of his pitiful life rotting away in some prison like he deserves.

"And everyone would miss me, and talk about how much they loved me and what a good person I was, and how sad—*she died so young*. That's what happened at my mother's funeral. She was a shitty person but everyone cried and talked about her like she was this angel who'd been stolen from us. I couldn't understand why people act like that at funerals. *Don't speak ill of the dead*, all that bullshit. And lying there, wishing I'd die, I understood. Everybody knows funerals aren't for the dead, that they're for the people who are left behind. But funerals aren't just a place for people to mourn or find closure. They're also a place for people to get a front-seat preview of their own demise." She turned to me, our eyes making contact for what felt like a long second before she looked back at the road ahead, hands gripping the wheel tightly. "Funerals remind people that they'll be dead one day, that everyone dies, and no one wants to be remembered as anything other than a saint. *That* is why people at funerals collectively rewrite the deceased's biography."

I didn't know what to say. She'd clearly been thinking about this for a while, which was devastating. I didn't want to think about Elise's funeral, *anyone's* funeral. And if she had died that night, I could never have forgiven myself. I'd been selfish. Elise was there for me at all of my low points—the breakup with Cameron, the battles between my parents—but I wasn't there when she needed me. I'd been a coward, running away from her when things got hard. The first tears hit my lap before I even realized I was crying. I couldn't believe I almost lost her. Now when I looked at her beside me, I couldn't imagine a future without her.

"I've always wanted to disappear, you know?" she continued. "Be that girl who disappears to live her life, and everyone wonders what happened to her from time to time. Then one day, they'd see me on TV or read about me and know just how extraordinary I was." She wanted to be remembered. "Except in this case, they'd wonder what *could have* happened to me." Her voice had a dreamlike sheen to it.

My tears had turned into sobs and she glanced over.

"Don't cry, Remy," she said. "It's okay! I didn't die, obviously. It just really hurt."

"I'm sorry," I said, and cried harder, unsure if I was apologizing for crying or for not being there when she needed me. "I'm so, so sorry."

"It's not your fault. If anything, it's my fault."

"What?" I whispered, breathless.

"I should never have left my room when he was like that. He kept pounding on the door, screaming he was going to break it down, and I was so scared. But then it stopped and he left and I thought it was over, that he'd sleep off the rage, or at least that I could sneak out sometime in the night. But he came back to the door an hour later, all apologetic and pleading. *I'm sorry, Elise, I didn't mean what I said.* Pathetic and pitiful. He was out there crying and saying how sorry he was for everything. He said he wanted my forgiveness." I couldn't picture him like that, groveling. In my mind, he was an unrepentant monster, pure evil.

256

She sighed heavily, her grip on the steering wheel tight. I glanced out at the road and realized she was speeding up. The lights flew by us, the trees blurring into one dark wall. It'd rained a couple days ago and the top was up, shaking from the violent wind. I put a hand against the window as if to brace myself for impact.

"He kept leaving and coming back to beg for my forgiveness, and finally I caved and opened the door." She shook her head like she was disappointed in herself. "I was an idiot."

"I'm so sorry." It was all I could say. She'd never told me the whole story and I'd never asked, not wanting to make her talk about it, relive it. But in that moment, I realized I was really motivated by a selfish desire to not have to hear her tell me. I wasn't sparing her, I was sparing myself. And now I forced myself to listen to every awful word.

"You know that lie my dad liked to tell me, about how it hurt him more than it hurt me? How he hit me out of love?" She scoffed. "He didn't even bother that night. Didn't pretend. There was just this raw anger. Half the things he screamed at me didn't even make sense! It was my fault. I should've known better."

Her voice was like the wind outside, a howl growing in force. We were still going faster, the needle on the speedometer inching toward ninety. I was frozen, afraid of cutting her off.

"I should've waited for him to break the door down." Angry with herself, she sobbed and raged, slamming the heel of her palm against the wheel. "I should've just waited."

"What do you mean, waited for him to break down the door?" I asked, confused.

Tears streaming down her face, Elise went back to gripping the wheel tightly. I looked out ahead of us at the open road and it felt like we were hurtling forward impossibly fast.

"Elise?" I said, still nervous about upsetting her, but we were now pushing one hundred. "Slow down." She didn't answer. "Please slow down." I touched her lightly on the shoulder and she flinched, jolting back to reality. Finally, she let up on the gas and the roar of the engine died down as we cruised along the highway.

"I should've waited, then he'd be gone," Elise said, every word dripping with hatred.

I was confused. He was already gone, living in Chattanooga.

"Permanently."

I stared at her. She was electric, her hair wild, her eyes dangerous. I didn't dare ask again what she'd meant. All I could think about was that line from *Kill Bill*: "I roared and I rampaged and I got bloody satisfaction."

"You know what else I learned?" She didn't wait for an answer. "In the face of total destruction, you can either spend the rest of your life trying to put the pieces back together and failing, or you can burn it all down to the ground and become brand-new."

A phoenix rising from its ashes.

53.

We stopped for gas right outside of Chattanooga's city limits. The night had cooled significantly and Elise pulled down the top. After she bought food and cigarettes from the convenience store, we drove down the street to an empty strip-mall parking lot. We camped out in the Pink Caddy, eating honey buns and sipping Diet Cokes. We were both quiet, but for different reasons. Elise seemed to be getting keyed up, a look of determination hardening on her face. I was shell-shocked, still trying to process what she'd told me, and for the first time since we started driving, I acknowledged I was way out of my depth.

After we were done, Elise gathered up all the trash, and when she went to toss it, I searched through her bag for cigarettes.

I felt cold, hard metal, but it wasn't the cigarette case I'd given her for her birthday.

"What are you *doing*?" she said, coming up to the driver's side.

I pulled out the gun by the handle, pinching it gingerly. It was heavy and gleaming in the moonlight. We both stared at it in shock.

"What were you doing going through my stuff?" Elise snatched it out of my hand and shoved it back into her messenger bag.

"I wasn't!" I couldn't believe *that* was what she was mad about.

"That's not what I saw," she said.

"I was looking for the cigarettes." I held my hands up in surrender.

She glared at me, tossing her bag onto the back seat before starting the car.

"Elise?"

No answer.

"Why do you have your grandfather's gun on you?" I asked as we waited at the stoplight for the on-ramp to the highway. I'd finally recovered from my initial shock. "Do you always have it on you?" It terrified me, the thought that she carried it everywhere she went—everywhere *we* went.

"You shouldn't go through other people's stuff!" The light turned green and she hit the gas.

"I'm sorry, I wasn't—"

"I don't go through your stuff!" she continued, voice rising.

"I don't go snooping around your room, opening your drawers or rifling through *your* bag."

"Are you taking it to school? You said you weren't going to take it to school. Come on, Elise, don't be stupid. If they catch you—"

She just sat there fuming, but I was too scared for her to hold back.

"Tell me you don't carry it to school." I was begging, *begging* her to be reasonable.

"Of course not," she snapped.

"Why do you have it on you *now*?" I said. *Now, when we're going to your father's house. Now, after you said you were going to give him one bad night.* What was she planning? I felt sick.

"For self-defense! God, Remy, what else? You think I'm going to drive up there and murder my father?" she said with a scoff. "Don't be ridiculous."

"I—"

"After that night, don't you think I have the right to protect myself? Just because I'm not planning to use it doesn't mean I won't need it," she said, voice dropping back to neutral. She sounded so reasonable, so rational, almost emotionless, like this was just a simple math problem—potential run-in with her father plus his violent history equals gun. "It's for emergencies."

I didn't respond. What could I even say? More than that, I felt like I'd lost the right to say anything at all. Though she never said it, I couldn't help hearing the accusation in her voice. *It's for emergencies*—because you didn't come when I called.

We remained quiet, letting the silence do all the speaking. What had started as a simple mission to prank her father was beginning to turn into something else entirely. I just didn't know what yet.

"The second film is my favorite," Elise said after pulling off at one of the exits for Chattanooga. Her tone was conversational but I could tell she had more to say.

"Why? Because she finally kills him?" I rolled with the change in subject although it confused me. The sinking feeling in my stomach grew with each mile as we drew closer to our final destination. Elise's father was a monster, and we were driving straight into the beast's den.

"Yeah, but it's not that she finally kills him, it's that she finally gets to confront him," she explained. "It's more than the *act* of killing him. By the very end, it almost doesn't matter whether he dies or not—I mean, okay it does matter—but it's not the ultimate payoff. It wouldn't be a very satisfying story if she showed up, killed him in two minutes, found her kid, and left." She looked at me, raising an eyebrow, waiting for a response.

"I guess." The streets became more residential. We were almost there. With the top down, the wind in our hair, we had all the air in the world, but I couldn't breathe.

"But in real life, we pretty much never get that kind of resolution." She shook her head sadly. "I'm never going to get an apology and—"

"Did she get one?" I asked in surprise. "The Bride."

Elise nodded. "Don't you remember? When he says, 'So I suppose it's a little late for an apology, huh?' and she goes, 'You suppose correctly.'"

It was a non-apology apology, but I didn't push back.

"It's his way of acknowledging he was wrong. And then

there's that moment he's telling their daughter what he did to the Bride. He explained to her that after he shot her, he was sad. 'And that was when I learned, some things, once you do, they can never be undone.'" Elise knew almost every line from the movies, and in the last few times we rewatched them, she'd sometimes whisper them perfectly in sync with the actors—every syllable, every intonation.

"We should turn around, go home," I blurted out. "I have a bad feeling about this. What if he's awake and he sees you? What if he comes outside, and—"

"He's the one who should worry," she said. "*He's* the one who should be scared." The way she said it sent shivers down my spine. Her father should be scared because she would make him fear her—that was what she was saying.

We were finally pulling into a neighborhood. It was a little past two in the morning. Dread buried me as we rolled to a stop. I checked my phone to see a few missed calls from Jack and texts asking me where I was. I didn't have time to respond, I had to focus on Elise.

"Some things, once you do, they can never be undone," Elise said softly. Then she looked at me with a sad smile. "Just because I didn't die that night doesn't mean a part of me isn't gone, permanently. He took a piece of my *soul*, Remy. He stole my whole childhood. I'll never get it back."

I thought she was going to cry, the way her voice shook, but she didn't. There were no tears in her eyes, only anger. It was devastating, hearing that. I wished I could help her. I wished I could give her everything he'd taken from her, but we both knew what she'd lost was gone forever.

"He's given me so many bad nights, Remy. Too many to count. I want him to have just one bad night," she said with such pain in her voice that I knew even then her words would haunt me forever.

54.

We parked down the street, where her father couldn't see us. All the lights were out along the row of houses on both sides. Elise popped the trunk and stepped out of the car to get the fireworks. As soon as I saw the top swing up, blocking the rear windshield, I pulled the gun from her shoulder bag and shoved it into the glove compartment like it was scorching to the touch, my heart pounding as I slammed it shut. I could barely breathe, feeling claustrophobic in the Pink Caddy.

There was no way she'd need it. I would be with her the whole time, and if he did come out, I'd call 9-1-1, scream, and wake up the neighborhood. It was better this way—the gun was a security blanket more than anything, and she wouldn't even know it was gone. Because she wasn't planning on using it.

Taking a deep breath, I walked out to join her.

"Listen, Remy," Elise said. She didn't meet my eyes, just focused on reorganizing and checking the box of fireworks she'd packed. "I've been thinking about it, and I need to do this alone."

"No, that's not a good idea. Let me help." A growing sense of dread gripped me. It was impossible to ignore all the signs—Elise's insistence on going it alone, the gun in her bag, what she'd said on the drive here. *One bad night*, that's what she'd said, but I couldn't help but wonder if that was all she wanted.

"This is something I need to do for myself," she said, her eyes finally meeting mine. "I need to face him alone."

"Him?" I asked. "You're going to *face him*?"

"That's not what I meant. Don't overreact, Remy." She hoisted the box onto a hip and shut the trunk. "I've made up my mind."

"Then what am I even doing here?" I said, panicking. "Wasn't this supposed to be *our* grand finale? Something for just the two of us?" I wanted to stop her from making a mistake. I wanted to save her from herself.

"Try to understand," she said firmly. "It's personal for me. I need to know I can do this on my own."

"No!" I said, surprising both of us with the force in my own voice. "I want to go with you. I don't want you to be alone. What if . . ." I didn't need to finish. What if she needed me? What if he came outside, confronted her? What if, what if—

I didn't want to think about what might happen.

Elise set the box down and pulled me into a hug, squeezing me tightly. "I love you, Remy. I know you're worried about me. But I can do this by myself, promise," she whispered into my ear.

Then she picked up the box, grabbed her messenger bag, and left. I wanted to follow her. I wanted to be close by in case she needed help. But I was also scared. What if she spotted me, what if we fought and woke up her father? I got back into the car and shivered even though it was a summer night.

Leaning my head back, I stared up at the dark sky, clouds scattering the moonlight. I closed my eyes, running a finger over the inscription on my lighter, over and over. I tried to center myself with the steady click of metal as I flipped the top opened and closed. I checked my phone, texted Jack back with an apology, told him that I was with Elise and not to worry. I didn't know how to tell him the truth about where we were and what we were doing. I wasn't even completely sure myself what we were doing here. And I knew Elise would see anything I told him as a betrayal. This was personal for her. This was her *father*.

I kept waiting for something to happen. I wanted to text her, to make sure she was okay, but just as I was about to, I was seized with the fear that maybe her phone wasn't on silent. That maybe a call or text would give her away.

Time seemed to stand still, everything frozen—the houses, the street, me in the car. It was taking her what felt like forever to set up the fireworks, and then I realized I didn't even know which house she was at. I didn't know if at that very moment she was climbing a tree to string up firecrackers outside her father's bedroom window. Didn't know if she'd been detected, didn't know if she ran into some kind of problem with the fireworks, didn't know if she was okay at all.

Panicking, I finally texted her.

Me: Where are you?

Another five minutes crawled by.

Me: Elise, seriously, where are you

No answer. It was almost three in the morning. The night was still and quiet as a graveyard. I couldn't wait for her anymore—I had to know she was okay. I got out to head in the direction I saw her disappear, and as soon as I closed the door, the first of the fireworks shot up into the sky, bursting. The next one shot up, a sharp whistle against the eerie calm. I leaned against the car door to appreciate the show. Then the firecrackers went off, a storm of angry blasts.

I heard the explosion before I saw the flash of light. Several more followed, like a series of bombs detonating.

I watched as the roof six houses down burst into flames.

55.

Light from the houses began to hit the street as the cacophony of fireworks and firecrackers shook the air. The fire on the roof roared to life as another explosion hit the house with the distinct sound of glass shattering. I was too frozen staring at it to notice Elise until she was five feet in front of me. Without a word, she grabbed the keys from my hand and hopped in, starting the car. I followed quickly and twisted around, staring at the fire as we raced away with the headlights off until we were down the street.

"What happened?" I asked, confused and scared. Elise's face was coated in a sheen of sweat, her hair wild and eyes panicked. "Was that—should we—"

"We need to get out of here." With great effort and shaky hands, Elise slowed down through the neighborhood, careful not to attract attention. We pulled over by the entrance of the neighborhood and Elise got out, turning back to see the glow of the fire and plume of smoke rising a few streets over.

"Oh my God," I whispered, so scared I couldn't think. "What happened? *What happened?*"

"One of the fireworks hit the roof," she said, her expression unreadable.

"Is your dad . . . ?" I trailed off, unable to complete the thought.

"It was an accident," she said, so quietly I almost didn't catch it. Sirens wailed in the distance, growing closer. "Come on, let's go."

Elise got back into the Pink Caddy. She took a deep breath, and then we shot out of the neighborhood into the dark, dark night.

56.

"Where's the gun, Remy?" Elise asked on the drive back. "Where'd you put it?"

"I—"

She'd found out. A million thoughts flooded my mind. Maybe she discovered it was missing when she looked for matches or maybe her bag felt light.

But maybe it was the one thing I didn't want to consider—that she was looking for the gun itself. But *why*?

"Where is it?" she said, and it didn't sound like a request anymore.

Sighing in defeat, I popped open the glove compartment, showing her the revolver. She glanced over, but she didn't ask me why I took it, didn't reprimand me.

As she drove, I kept peeking over at her, trying to understand her, but I was beginning to wonder if I ever would.

After we'd put a few miles between us and the city, she said, "People have this idea of a perfect victim."

"What are you talking about?" Even though we were on the highway, I kept turning to look over my shoulder, half expecting a storm of lights and sirens behind us.

"I'm supposed to take the higher road. I'm supposed to accept my victimhood, that someone did something horrible to me. Let it go, move on, put it behind me," she said, anger building in her voice. "I'm supposed to let the justice system do its job, which is bullshit. The system isn't interested in protecting people like me. The system's going to take one look at a man like my dad and let him off the hook—probation, maybe a fine, maybe a couple months in a county jail. That's *it*." She took a shuddering breath. "They let him out, Remy. They just let him out after what he did to me," she said, her voice breaking. "They issued a restraining order and just *let him out*. Like a piece of paper is supposed to protect me from a monster like him." Tears spilled over, and she quickly wiped them away with the back of her hand.

"What are you saying?" I asked. *I want him to have just one bad night*, that's what she'd said, but maybe what she wanted was him to have *only one more night*.

"I'm saying it's not fair!" she said. "I'm saying that no matter what I do—even if I play the part of the perfect victim—he'll never get the justice he deserves. That *I'll* never get the justice *I* deserve. And I just can't accept the things he did to me and forget them. I can't, Remy, *I can't*."

We were on the highway now, heading south. Elise's voice wobbled. She wiped away her tears forcefully, like she was angry she was crying in the first place.

"Everyone thinks it's my fault," she said.

"*What?*"

"Even you."

"That's not true!" I cried.

"Isn't it? They asked me at the hospital if this had ever happened before, and I just knew what they were thinking: Why didn't you ever report it? I know that's what you think too. Jack, your parents, Christian. Why didn't I just fucking say something earlier, save everyone the trouble—the doctors, the police, the court?" She was gasping, openly sobbing now, her breaths shallow.

"Elise?" I gently touched her arm and pulled away immediately when she flinched. I stared out at the road. "You can't drive like this. Pull over." She didn't seem to hear me.

"And the truth is, I'm mad too! Why didn't I say anything sooner? It seems so fucking obvious now. Why didn't I just fucking say something? What's wrong with me?" The heel of her palm hit the steering wheel over and over. "It *was* my fault."

"No," I said. "It wasn't. It wasn't, it wasn't." Tears fell, running down my face. Every awful thing that had been simmering between us was now out in the open. Her anger, my guilt. My anger, her guilt.

"I just keep thinking, if I'd only told someone, if I hadn't left my room that night, if I'd been faster, stronger, fought him off. If only—"

If only, if only.

Finally she decelerated and pulled over.

"And now I'm going to have to live with it forever. The looks of pity follow me *everywhere*. Even from you."

"No," I tried to interject.

"Every time I talk to Evan, or Jae and Julie, or meet someone new, I always think, *Oh God, do you know?* Like I can't be sure if you or Jack told anyone."

"We haven't," I said. "I swear."

She ignored me. "Sometimes I think people just *know*. Like they can smell it on me, like they take one look at me and see right through this tough-girl act and see the real me, this weak, useless thing, and I hate it. I can't stand it. This is what he's reduced me to, Remy. I'm pathetic."

"No, you're not," I said, pleading with her. "You're not."

"I'll never be anything different. I'll never be able to forget that night." She hunched forward, left arm clutching her ribs almost instinctively, like she was being kicked. "I dream about it all the time. I can't stop thinking about it. I'll never be free. Never, ever."

"I'm sorry," I said, crying harder. The whole world closed in around just the two of us in that car. The highway, the few other cars rushing past us, it all seemed to disappear into the night until it was just Elise and me and the Pink Caddy by the side of a road to nowhere.

"And now I know I'll never escape it. Now I know I'll always be that weak, pathetic girl getting the shit beat out of her." She seemed to deflate, a once-bright star caving in on itself. "I thought"—she shook her head weakly—"I thought coming here would make me feel better. I thought getting back at him, even just a little, would be enough. If I just, I don't know. But it doesn't matter. He could die and it wouldn't make a difference." The tears kept coming, but she no longer bothered to wipe them away.

That last sentence echoed in my mind like reverberations of a thunderclap.

"What do you mean?" I said, each word laced with dread. *He could die and it wouldn't make a difference.*

"I just mean, it doesn't matter whether he's around—I'm always going to be that girl. Weak, unable to protect myself. He didn't just steal one night, he stole my entire childhood! All the years and years I spent living in terror. All that fear, it's saturated every cell in my body. It feels like it's corrupted my soul. No matter what I do, I'll never be free of it," she said, her voice lowering to a whisper at the end.

No matter what I do—the fireworks outside her father's house, more revenge pranks—*I'll never be free.* Her words hit me hard, and her voice as she said them was even more haunting, like she had given up, like she was cornered with no way out.

We spent the rest of the ride in silence. Maybe there was nothing left to say.

I wasn't capable of admitting it then, but I was terrified. Jack was right: No matter how many pranks we pulled, no matter how many people we helped, none of it would make her feel better.

Elise thought if she acted now—if she drove to Chattanooga, fucked with her father—she could somehow make up for what she perceived as her past weakness. But nothing she did seemed to ease the heaviness of her anger and self-hatred.

I wanted to free her from it, I wanted to save her from drowning, but sitting next to her in the Pink Caddy, the dark night road stretching before us, I didn't have the strength. I just felt tired.

We believed our wounds made us special. We believed what didn't kill you made you stronger. We believed our tragedies were romantic.

Only I didn't feel very special or strong or romantic. I felt helpless and scared and so very exhausted.

"Don't tell anyone what we did tonight," she said when we finally got home. "Promise me, Remy. Promise you won't tell anyone, not even Jack."

"What if he asks? What am I going to say? What am I supposed to tell him?"

"I don't know, make something up. Or just tell him you don't

271

want to talk about it." I looked away. She took my hands in hers, yanking me back. "Remy, promise me." I gave her a curt nod, not saying anything.

Maybe I knew I had no intention of keeping that promise, even then.

57.

We got home a little past five in the morning. We went to bed without washing up, and Elise fell asleep almost immediately. I lay there unable to drift off, thinking about Elise's words on the drive back. Her anger, her pain.

After an hour, I gave up, slipped out, and drove to Jack's house, texting him when I got there. He came out in his pajamas, hair mussed, eyes half-open. "Remy?"

I launched myself forward and he caught me. The last few weeks had been hard on us. I basically didn't see him outside of school, and even then, only at lunch with everyone else. And in front of Elise, I was too self-conscious to so much as hold his hand. We still texted all the time but there was this distance, a strain between us since that horrible night three weeks ago. Sometimes I blamed myself, sometimes I blamed him. Sometimes I wondered if maybe Elise was right, if I should've broken up with him over what'd happened.

But now we were reunited, alone, and in his arms, surrounded by his warmth, I felt safe and loved.

273

"What's wrong?" he asked, worried.

I just shook my head, rested my chin on his right shoulder, and squeezed him tighter.

"What happened? Where were you last night? You didn't answer any of my texts or calls and now you just show up here at"—he checked his phone—"six in the morning?"

"Shhh," I said, glancing in the direction of the house. "I don't want to wake up your aunt and uncle." Quietly, we went up to his bedroom, sat on his bed with the door closed. Lola greeted me, then went back into her crate to sleep. Pulling my legs in and tucking my chin between my knees, I balled up, withdrawing into myself.

"Remy, what the hell is going on?" Jack ran a sleepy hand through his hair, expression worried.

"Can you do something for me? Can you check online for any stories about a house fire in Chattanooga?" I asked, too afraid to look it up myself.

"What?" Jack stared at me blankly, then rubbed his eyes. When I didn't speak, he sighed and pulled his laptop toward him. "Okay."

While he searched, fear rose up within me like bile and I wanted to throw up.

"I don't see anything," he said, catching me staring at him. "Can you tell me what I'm supposed to be looking for? If you gave me a little more info—"

I shook my head and hugged my legs in tighter.

"Nothing on local news sites," he said. "Okay, tell me what's going on. I'm starting to freak out. What happened? Why are you asking about house fires?"

"I can't tell you," I said.

He sighed in frustration and went back to searching.

"Nothing on Twitter or Facebook. What is it that you're looking for?" he said, tossing his laptop to the side to comfort me, taking my hands in his.

"What about hospitalizations? Burn victims?" I asked.

"I'm not helping you look until you tell me what's going on." It was still dark out but the first whispers of light were filling the sky outside. I'd always liked Jack's room, the faint scent of peppermint on his pillowcases, the small desk Lola sometimes napped under.

"Remy?"

"Elise wanted to do one last prank," I said, barely audible. "Just the two of us."

"What?" he said. "What did you do? Wait, did you drive all the way up to Chattanooga?"

I nodded.

"Why Chattanooga?" he asked, frowning in confusion.

"Elise's dad lives there," I said. "They moved from Chattanooga last year when Elise's grandmother passed away and left her the Pink Mansion. They came down to sell it and deal with legal stuff but then her dad met someone and they stayed." My voice was dull, lifeless with exhaustion. I'd been awake for almost twenty-four hours.

"I don't understand," Jack said. "What did you do once you got there?"

"We were only supposed to set off fireworks outside his house and wake him up. She just wanted him to have one bad night, you know?" Lola came up to me, sat by my feet, and rested her head on my knee. "We've done it before. Set up firecrackers outside a bedroom window, set off some fireworks. Nothing went wrong when we did it before," I said, growing distressed. Everything had gone fine the first time.

"What happened?" he asked with growing horror. "What did she do?"

"There was an accident. I wasn't there. Elise wanted to do this whole thing by herself. And—and—"

"What?" Jack said, pulling back in shock.

"One of the roman candles or something must've gone off wrong." I couldn't say it, what I feared.

"Oh my God," Jack said, eyes wide with realization. "Don't tell me you guys set the house on fire."

My silence was answer enough.

He remained quiet for a long time, then scooped Lola up and placed her on the bed with us, rubbing her head absentmindedly. I wanted him to tell me everything would be okay, I wanted him to *make* everything okay.

"If you weren't there, how do you know it was an accident?" he finally asked.

"What are you saying? That Elise set her dad's house on fire on purpose?" I didn't even want to think of that possibility, but Jack was only voicing my deepest fear.

"I'm not saying anything. I'm asking you what Elise is capable of. Only you can answer that."

"I don't know," I said, exhausted and confused. "She probably just set it up a little too close to the house, or the firecrackers hit some dry wood," I said, but I wasn't really trying to convince him, only myself.

"I'm not disputing that," he said. "What I'm asking is if she did it on purpose. If she knowingly set it up a little too close to the house. If she strung up the firecrackers where they could spark a fire. Or even angled a roman candle right at the house."

I remembered the sound of shattering glass.

"It would look like an accident, but hasn't she done this before? Set off fireworks?" he asked, and I nodded. "So she knows how to do it."

"Oh God," I said. "But—"

Yes, it was possible that it'd all been an accident. But I knew it wasn't likely.

"We have to tell someone," he said. "What she did is arson, and who's to say she won't do something like that again?"

"No, we can't," I said, panicking. This wasn't why I was here, why I told him. Getting her in trouble was the last thing I wanted. "We *can't*. She promised this was the last one."

"How do you know she didn't say that because she thought she'd finish the job tonight?" He was making it sound worse than it was. "How do you know she won't just try again?"

I shook my head as the tears fell. "I can't do that to someone I love."

Jack sighed. "You don't feel love for Elise, you just feel guilt." He ran a hand roughly through his hair. "Think back to three weeks ago, *before* her father assaulted her. You hadn't been talking much, and you didn't want to talk to her. It looks like she hasn't changed much, but you can't see that. You can't see beyond your guilt."

Had I ignored what was right in front of me because I felt awful, like Jack said? I thought of my parents then, the forces that kept them trapped in an unhappy marriage.

In one crystalizing moment, I could see it all so clearly. Maybe they had something once, but the years had taken whatever they had and twisted it into nothing resembling love. I thought about that conversation with Dad again from all those years ago. *It's complicated*, he'd said, and I hadn't believed him. But now, that's exactly how it felt between me and Elise—complicated. Jack was essentially telling me what I'd told Dad. And like him, I didn't want to hear it.

Maybe Elise and I had something special once, but whatever we had now was twisted with guilt, anger, jealousy. Maybe I was right when I told Dad it really was that simple.

Maybe it was time to let Elise go.

"Remy?" Jack asked, seeing the devastation on my face.

I only cried harder.

58.

"I want to play you something," Detective Ward says. I glance at the door and wonder how long it's been since my last break. Being in here, imprisoned in this room, I've lost sense of the passage of time. I have no sense of what an hour feels like anymore. I'm just trying to survive minute to minute. Second to second, one breath to the next. "It will probably be upsetting to hear," she continues, unaware of how I'm feeling.

"What is it?" Vera asks, her fingers rubbing her temple. She's exhausted too. I don't know how much time we've been talking but I know it's been a long day.

"A tape of the 9-1-1 call Remy made."

Vera and I stare at her in surprise.

"Why?" Vera asks. My grip on my knees tightens, my knuckles bloodless.

"Remy seems to be a little confused about the timeline the night of the murder." This is the first time she's used that word—murder. It stops me cold. I feel like I'm unraveling.

"The night of Jack's death," Vera clarifies. They're saying the same thing but there's a big difference. The way Vera says it, *Jack's death*, like it just happened. Detective Ward has used the word *killed*, but *murder* is something else entirely. It implies intent. The word is a window into her mind and what she thinks happened.

"Yes. Sunday night," she says, almost casually.

"And how will forcing her to listen to the traumatic 9-1-1 call she made help?" Vera says, leaning forward on her elbows, her voice sharp and angry.

Detective Ward shrugs. Then she turns to me. "Do you remember making the call?" It was all a blur. My silence gives her all she needs. "Well, don't you want to remember? Aren't you at least curious?"

Vera doesn't wait for me to respond. "This is a bad idea, Remy," she warns me, turning her back to block Ward and give us some privacy. It's one of the things I like about Vera, her protectiveness.

I hesitate. Detective Ward is referring to those unexplained fourteen minutes, the discrepancy in Jack's arrival at the Pink Mansion and my 9-1-1 call. It hits me, what she's been getting at— she thinks Elise and I murdered Jack, then called 9-1-1 only after we'd come up with a plan, a story to tell.

She's wrong, of course. Though she is right about one thing—I *am* curious. Hearing my call won't explain away the mystery of those fourteen minutes. Hearing my anguish won't bring Jack back, won't undo what's already been done. Still, I want to know. I remember crying. I remember my voice and hands shaking. I remember a few words here and there, "Please hurry," "There's so much blood," but not much more.

My eyes meet Vera's. "I want to hear it." Vera frowns at me in concern.

"I really don't think it's a good idea," she says softly.

"No," I say, more determined. "I want to hear it."

"Are you sure?"

I nod.

She turns back to Detective Ward, says reluctantly, "Fine, but no camera." Detective Ward acquiesces easily and soon it is just the three of us alone.

My voice, panicked and breathless, fills the small space.

"Hello?"

"9-1-1, what's your emergency?"

"Oh God, oh God." The sound of my short, sharp gasps ring out. "Oh God, Jack." My tears fall one after the other, splattering against the metal table.

"Ma'am?"

"There's so much blood." I am crying, both now and in the recording. My sobs, past and present, collide into one another. The pain in my chest is unbearable and it feels like I'm dying. I am there again on the floor of the Pink Mansion. Jack is in my arms and he is bleeding out.

"Please."

"Ma'am, can you give us a location? Where are you right now? Are you in any danger?"

"I'm at the Pink Mansion. Please hurry."

"An ambulance is on the way."

"Please, please, please," my voice begs. "Stay with me, stay with me." I remember the way his eyes looked, flickering wildly with no sign of recognition.

The recording ends but some time passes before I can stop shaking. Vera was right. This was a terrible idea and I am an idiot for thinking it would help. Even Detective Ward seems surprised by the intensity of my reaction. It takes everything for me to stay in the chair and in that room. The floor calls to me and I just want to lie down and curl into myself.

Jack died before the ambulance got there, I'm almost sure of it. I still don't remember taking my phone out and calling 9-1-1, but a few more pieces slide into place.

I was on my knees, Jack's blood pooling around me, soaking into my jeans and espadrilles, ruining his Superman tee made of royal blue and the softest cotton. I clutched him close to me like I could make him stay if I only held on tight enough.

"Remy, I'm sorry," Detective Ward says, and she looks genuinely apologetic. "I just have a few more—"

"I can't do this," I say, barely managing the words. "I can't, I can't. I need to get out of here. Right now."

"Okay," Vera says, eyes growing wide. "Okay, let's get you out of here."

"Please," I say.

"Call me if you have any further questions," Vera says to Detective Ward while ushering me out of the interrogation room. Neither of us waits for her reaction.

I was on my knees, Jack's blood pooling around me. The life fading out of his eyes. I clutched him tight, pressed our bodies close for the last time.

I was on my knees, Jack's blood pooling around me. I begged and begged for him to stay. But he couldn't hear me anymore. Sirens wailed in the distance.

282

I was on my knees, Jack's blood pooling around me. Elise put a hand on my shoulder, said, "Everything's going to be okay, Remy. Everything's going to be okay now."

59.

The ride home is silent, tense, the four of us ignoring one another. Christian is flying out to Providence tomorrow but none of us are in the proper send-off mood. At home, my parents begin to bicker almost immediately. I go straight to my room upstairs, try to shut them out. But at the same time, their angry voices bring me a strange kind of comfort not unlike the steady drip of a leaky faucet, irritating but dependable. They argue, and it's about the only constant I can rely on in my life. This I can handle.

I can't make out every word they're saying but I have a general idea what they're fighting about. Jack's funeral is on Sunday. Mom wants us to make a quick appearance at the service, then leave, but Dad says I should be allowed to go to all of it—the memorial, the viewing, the service and reception after.

They start there but quickly move on to the usual haunts, petty squabbles about time spent at the office or hospital, about who is the worst parent. Even now, after everything that's happened, they're still focused on themselves.

Something Elise said about her father comes to me now: *It had nothing to do with me. It never did. It didn't matter if I was the perfect daughter or not, because nothing was ever going to be enough for him. When I got older, I saw the pattern. If he was having a bad day, he'd make sure I'd have one too.*

My parents are not like her father, but there are some parallels.

It never mattered if I was the perfect daughter or not. Christian was the perfect son, and still they screamed and fought and waged an endless war. Still they ignored us, used us when convenient. We were never people, we were things—*their* things.

Their voices mix and clash and distract me from thinking about Jack and Elise, about the difference between *killed* and *murdered*. About what Elise said as Jack was dying.

Their voices crest and fall. I take a deep breath, stare at the ceiling. This I can do all day long.

This I can do—until I can't.

Their voices crest again but don't fall. Their rage and fury climb and climb, whipping into a hurricane. I tell myself that their anger is a strange comfort. But it doesn't help this time. Instead it feels like I'm drowning, like the weight of their words is pulling me under.

I fold my pillow, cover my ears, but I can't block them out.

I manage to fall asleep for a few hours, and thankfully, the house is quiet when I wake.

"Hey." Christian knocks on my door around dinnertime, catching me by surprise. "Come on, you have to eat."

I have no appetite but he insists, so I follow him downstairs, feeling dazed and confused about what he's doing. Sitting at the kitchen table, I watch as he makes mac and cheese from a box.

"So," he begins awkwardly, "are you—" *okay*? That's what he was about to ask. Instead he says, "I'm sorry," and I'm so shocked I just stare at him.

"Look, I know—" He breaks off again, seems to be struggling to find the right words. I feel wary, unsure what he's trying to do. "I'm just sorry. About everything."

He looks contrite but I don't buy it. "Everything," I repeat. Does he mean Jack's death? Does he mean what happened with Elise? Or does he mean literally everything, going all the way back to our childhood?

"Everything," he confirms without clarifying. "I'm here if you want to talk."

"Did Mom put you up to this?" I ask, suspicious of this uncharacteristic concern from him. "Are you going to report back to her?"

"What? No," he says, growing defensive.

"For the record, no, I'm not okay," I tell him. It should be obvious. I don't know how I look but it's probably terrible. I feel even worse.

He pauses as the microwave beeps in the back. "I didn't know Jack well, but he was a good guy from what I can tell."

"Oh." I keep forgetting that they were in the same grade before Jack had to take a year off.

"I'm sorry." Christian leans against the kitchen counter and looks at me, *really* looks at me. This could be the first real interaction we've had since we were little. He takes the mac and cheese out and splits half into another bowl and puts it in front of me. "You have to eat."

"I can't." I shake my head and push it away from me. I think about retreating to my room. It hurts, being around others when the one person I want to be with is irrevocably gone.

He takes a few bites but gives up when he sees I won't touch it.

"What are you doing here, anyway?" I ask, trying to keep my mind off Jack.

"I still live here, at least until tomorrow," Christian says, and attempts a friendly smile.

"No, I mean why aren't you out with your girlfriend? It's your last night."

He grows quiet. "Vanessa and I broke up, actually." It's a surprising admission from him. We're siblings, but we're not friends. "I don't really want to talk about it. Anyway, where is everybody?" he says, changing the subject.

"Mom's probably at the hospital. No idea where Dad is, not that you care." I don't know why he's talking to me. We don't hang out. We barely acknowledge each other's existence, but now he's acting like we do this all the time.

"I do care," he says quietly.

"Why? You're leaving for Brown in ten hours. You never liked Dad in the first place. You said you didn't care if he stayed or left because you had Mom."

"What are you talking about?" His obliviousness angers me and I hold on to it like a life raft in this ocean of grief. He's lucky he gets to even *be* oblivious because he has Mom in his corner. He never has to worry about how he'll survive our mother like I have to.

"You know what I'm talking about," I say, my voice strained. "You have Mom. You never, ever have to worry like I do."

"Come on, Mom's not that bad," he says.

"What?" I almost laugh. "You weren't there all the times Mom yelled at me to be more like you."

"Yeah? Well you weren't there all the times I watched you and Dad go off to do your own thing. He never paid any attention to me after he got home from work. He never took me on cool trips to Chicago."

"Dad only did that stuff with me because you were already Mom's favorite. You've *always* been Mom's favorite. I was basically the leftovers. *We* were leftovers. He didn't pick me. Mom picked you and we were left to fend for ourselves." I thought it'd feel good, finally getting these words out, yelling at Christian, but all I feel is emptiness.

"That's not how I remember it. Dad's always liked you more. He never spent any time playing with me. Or took me out, just the two of us. Or taught me how to ride a bike."

"That's because you never needed it! You were some kind of prodigy. You didn't need anyone to teach you anything." I can't believe this. Christian, flagship child, complaining about how he was treated.

"Bull."

"Mom says it all the time. *All the time.* 'Remy, why aren't you smart like Christian? Remy, why aren't you more like Christian? Remy, why can't you just *be* Christian?'"

He looks momentarily chastised.

"You know exactly what it's been like for me." Staring down at the mac and cheese, I lose what little appetite I had.

"It's not exactly been easy for me!" he says, and I scoff. "It hasn't. You don't know what it's like, having the weight of the world on your shoulders."

"Right, the weight of the world. What would we do without you?" I ask, rolling my eyes. "The whole world would just implode."

"That's what it feels like sometimes," he admits, surprising me. "You don't know how many times I wished I were you. You don't know how many times I wished Mom would stop treating me like I was her greatest accomplishment and leave me alone. You weren't there when I had to tell her I didn't get into Princeton. She acted like going to Brown was the same as going to a state school."

"No, she talks about it all the time, how she's so proud of you, how you're carrying on the family's Ivy tradition, because it sure as hell won't be me."

"Well, *of course* she acts like she's proud of me. She's not going to go around telling people how Brown's *barely an Ivy.*"

"Did she really say that?" I ask, a little stunned.

"Only when I was applying. She didn't even want me to apply, said I'd almost certainly get into Princeton. Said she knew all the alums in the area and would get me a good interviewer," he says, rolling his eyes. "Yeah, whatever."

It never seemed weird to me before, that we were always on opposing teams. It never seemed odd that we *had* teams. But now I realize we were all supposed to be on one team together.

Maybe this is what he thinks too. Maybe this is why he knocked on my door. I end up scooping all of the pasta he made into the trash, but I take a leap of faith and ask him something.

"What happened between you and Elise?"

His eyes widen. "What'd she tell you?"

"She said you told her you were breaking up with Vanessa and that you'd kissed her one night."

For a moment, he just stares at me, speechless. "First of all, *she* kissed *me.* And I didn't tell her we were breaking up! I just told her we were having a hard time deciding what to do when we went to college."

Something had always seemed off about the night she came back from her anti-anti-prom party and I could never quite figure it out until now.

"What happened the night of prom?" I don't want any more half-truths, only the whole truth now. "She said you showed up to her party."

"I didn't even know that was her party," he says. "I just heard from a few of Vanessa's friends that there was an after-party on the football field. We ended up going because we didn't have anything else to do." He sighed, frustrated. "What did she say I did?"

"Just said that you were cold to her, that you wouldn't even talk to her after what'd happened between you guys."

He looks down, like he feels bad. "I guess I didn't handle that very well. I was afraid she'd say something to Vanessa, and at that point, I was still hoping maybe we'd stay together." Then he shakes his head roughly as if to clear it. "You should get some rest. You must be exhausted."

It was so strange seeing Christian like this. Knocking on my door, asking how I was. Trying to make me dinner, criticizing Mom. Telling me the truth, admitting he was fallible.

"Have a safe flight," I tell him when we're upstairs. We've talked more in the last half hour than we have in the last five years. There's still a distance between us, but for the first time I can remember, I'm not sure if it'll always be there or if we can close it someday, together.

60.

Without my phone and laptop, I'm completely isolated. Mom's forcing me to take the rest of the week off, and I have the whole house to myself for the better part of each day. I don't think she knows what to do with me. No one does, me included. I can't imagine going back to school now without Jack, without Elise.

Every day I half expect Elise to show up, and I don't know what I'd say to her. I don't know how I'd even feel about seeing her again.

For some inexplicable reason, I rewatch the Kill Bill movies by myself even though I've seen them a million times with Elise already. I have no idea what I'm looking for, but I can't shake the feeling that I might find it in the Bride's story.

Five hours later, I'm a sobbing mess on the couch. It's been there the whole time, staring at me in the face, but I didn't want to see it.

On the surface, the movies are about revenge. It's even in the opening epigraph—*revenge is a dish best served cold*. But it's not a story about revenge. It's a story about love.

And abuse.

Every act of love is corrupted with it. And it's not just the relationship between Bill and the Bride, Beatrix, whose real name is only revealed near the end. Even when Beatrix goes to train under Pai Mei, his respect is only earned through her ability to withstand his abuse.

Once you see it, you can't unsee it.

We have been sold a lie. Our parents thought nothing of hurting us in the name of love. What a thing, to learn as a child, that pain is love. That love is bruises on our bodies and scars in our minds.

Elise's father told her it hurt him more than it hurt her when he hit her, that he hit her only because he loved her. Tell your daughter enough times and maybe she'll believe it—believe it so deep down in her soul that she thinks it's only love if it hurts.

That it's not love if it doesn't.

We believed our tragedies were romantic. We believed what didn't kill us made us stronger. We believed our wounds made us special, because in a strange and awful way, maybe they were proof that we were loved.

Trauma has a gravity of its own, but so does love—an invisible force, an unseen tether. How easy it is, then, to feel the pull of one and confuse it with the other.

61.

Vera comes by in the afternoon with an update. She opens with, "I have some news." She's spoken with a friend in the DA's office. "It appears unlikely they'll pursue any charges related to Jack's death."

"What?" I say, breathless with shock. "How? Why?"

"It's not official," she cautions. "And even if they decline to press charges now, they could still bring them years down the line if something changes. But unofficially, they're probably not going to press any charges right now."

I'm too stunned to speak.

"Prosecutors don't like to try cases they might lose. And in this instance, the law is on Elise's side. He was near the doorway. It was dark. It was her house. He didn't tell her he'd be there." Vera goes on for a while, explaining the technical details of the case. Apparently, Elise would make an extremely sympathetic defendant. "No jury's going to see those pictures of her beaten up and convict." She keeps going but my mind is spinning.

I did it, I think. I protected her. Collapsing to the ground, I begin to sob. Vera kneels to comfort me with an arm around my shoulders. She thinks these are tears of joy, of relief. But I don't feel any relief. I just feel like I'm drowning.

This was what I'd hoped for. This means we're free. Only I don't feel free at all.

62.

I need to see her.

It's been four days since she killed Jack, four days without my phone, without any contact with her. My car keys have been confiscated. There's talk of switching schools or homeschooling, and I'm basically under house arrest until they figure it out.

But still. I have to see her. She's the only one who has all the answers, who knows what really happened that night. So when my mom comes home late on Thursday, I wait until she's in the shower before I snatch her keys and make my getaway.

"Remy?" It's Elise, as if appearing out of thin air before I even have a chance to unlock the car door. It's surreal seeing her here on my driveway.

"How are you here right now?" I whisper, my throat still scratchy and raw. I want to run into her arms as much as I want to run in the opposite direction. I love her, but I am horrified by her.

"Oh, thank God," she says, clearly relieved and oblivious to my growing distress. "I've been basically camped out here hoping to catch you."

"What?" I look all around us in confusion. "Where's your car?"

"I had to park it on the other side of the neighborhood so your parents wouldn't see me. Come on." She pauses when she sees I haven't followed. "I just want to talk," she says. "Let's go for a drive." When I remain unmoving, she shoots me a halting smile. "Remy?"

For a moment, I think about turning back. Maybe this was a mistake. The thought of being with her in the Pink Caddy terrifies me.

But I have to find out the truth.

"Fine," I say, and she seems surprised by the edge in my voice.

"Is something wrong?" she asks as soon as we've pulled out of my neighborhood.

I know she's asking about right now, this moment, why I'm so distant and quiet, but still my mind screams: *What* isn't *wrong*? But I'm paralyzed, overwhelmed and unable to speak.

At a stoplight, she hands me the cigarette case I got for her birthday. I shake my head, refusing it. "What?" Now she sounds *really* concerned. Elise hesitates but lets it go, lighting one for herself, glancing at me every few seconds as she drives. I stare at the cigarette case, the filigree and inscription. The lighter she gave me is in my bedroom in the drawer of my nightstand. I haven't been able to look at it.

We're heading in the direction of the Pink Mansion, maybe out of habit, but there's no way I'll step foot inside it now, or ever. "Where are we going?" I ask.

"We could go anywhere. And I really mean *anywhere*," she says. "Let's do it. Let's just go tonight. We'll run away. Leave and never come back." Then she sees my expression and her smile falters. "That was a joke," she says. "But maybe when this is all over—we could go. You'll be eighteen soon, and no one will bother to look for me."

I can't believe *this* is what she's thinking, what she's *been* thinking in the aftermath of Jack's death. She hasn't brought him up at all, and I feel sick. I want to scream—for her to feel my devastation.

I want her to hurt like I do.

Elise seems to mistake my silence for encouragement. "We can sell the fancy furniture in the Pink Mansion, my grandmother's jewelry. Then after I turn eighteen next year, we'd never have to worry about money again. Rem—"

"What happened?" I ask, unable to stand it anymore. "Sunday night."

She takes a moment to answer. "I don't remember," she says slowly.

"You don't remember anything?" I don't believe her.

"I don't," she says. Her voice wavers like she might cry. "One minute I was standing there, the next Jack was down and the gun was in my hand."

"So then tell me what you do remember." She glances over at me, and I refuse to look away. I refuse to let this go.

"I told you—"

"Before the moment you came face-to-face with Jack. What do you remember about that night?" The top is down and the wind is in our faces, my hair beginning to whip around me.

"I don't know what you want me to say." Her voice turns flat, her expression tense. All the warmth is gone, replaced by a growing wariness.

"I don't want you to *say* anything. I just want the truth," I tell her. "Do you remember when we went to the Pink Mansion?"

She nods in confirmation.

"Do you remember us arguing?" I say, frustrated, and she nods again. "Then what happened?"

She remains quiet, eyes focused on the road even though we're driving around aimlessly, as far as I can tell.

"Elise—"

"We argued about Jack, about the night before," she says, referring to what we did in Chattanooga. "Why'd you tell him, Remy? You promised. You *promised* you wouldn't tell anyone, not even him. Why'd you do it?" She begins to cry. "Why?"

"I don't know," I answer, even though I do. I was scared—scared and confused. I didn't know how to process what had happened. I didn't even know what'd actually happened in the first place. Jack calmed me down, helped me piece through it.

But once he knew, he wasn't going to let it go.

I rushed over to the Pink Mansion Sunday night, trying to prevent this very collision between them.

"It was harmless," I told Jack over the phone as I drove to Elise's.

"You know it wasn't, Remy. It never is," he said, and I could just picture him shaking his head sadly.

"No one got hurt."

"That we know of. And that's not the point, you know that," he said, sighing.

"It was an accident. Fireworks can be dangerous." Elise said—no, insisted—that it was an accident, and I wanted to believe her.

"Exactly," he said. "They're dangerous. And she knew that."

Silence stretched tight between us.

"I'll talk to her."

"Remy—"

"I have to go," I said, ending the call.

"Did you talk to Jack?" Elise asked once I arrived at the Pink Mansion. By the time I'd made it back home from Jack's house, she was already up waiting for me. I had no choice but to tell her the truth. Where I was. What I said. What Jack said.

"I did." I was slipping my espadrilles off by the door, and Elise was leaning against a wall in the foyer, her arms crossed.

"What'd he say?"

"He hasn't changed his mind," I said, not meeting her eyes. "But he will. I'll explain and—" It was all just a big misunderstanding, I thought. If I could get them to listen to each other.

"You told him it was an accident?"

"I did." We walked out onto the balcony, the air thick with humidity and still warm from the day.

"Why did you even tell him?" she snapped at me. "If you'd only—" She saw the hurt on my face and exhaled in frustration.

"What are you going to do?" I asked.

"You've put me in an impossible position," she said, looking out at the water below. It'd been raining a lot recently, leaving the river swollen, its violent current a symphony filling the air.

I was trying to head off their collision but all I did was speed it up.

"What happened?" I ask her one more time. I've had enough. I want answers.

"Does it even matter anymore?" she says, shaking her head.

"Of course it does!" I shout.

"Nothing I say or do is going to change anything."

"It matters," I insist.

"No," she says. "What matters is you and me. Everything's going to be okay, Remy. Everything's going to be okay now. We're family, you and me. It's just the two of us now, and it'll always be just the two of us."

Her words knock the air out of my lungs and I'm dizzy with nausea.

It's just the two of us *now*.

I fold over myself, elbows propped against knees, hands cradling my head, clasped around my neck, my hair clinging to my face from fresh tears.

I am back at the Pink Mansion. Elise places a hand on my shoulder, says *Everything's going to be okay, Remy. Everything's going to be okay now.* What she said after had been out of reach. Jumbled, disorienting. But now I remember, her voice clear and strong, and it's like I'm still there in the living room, kneeling over Jack's body.

Everything's going to be okay, Remy. Everything's going to be okay now, she said. *You and me, we're family,* she said. *It's just the two of us now, and it'll always be just the two of us,* she said.

It's all flooding back and I hug my ribs tight, preparing for the blow.

"Remy!" Elise says in alarm, looking over at me. She reaches for me but I shrink away.

"Don't touch me!" I slap her hand away. "No, no, no," I whisper. *"No."*

I remember.

Those fourteen minutes.

I remember everything.

63.

"It was harmless," I told Jack over the phone on my way to Elise's house. It was getting late, and I'd been up for almost forty hours. I was starting to swing between moments of drowsiness and adrenaline-fueled bursts of panic.

"You know it wasn't," he said, and I could just picture him shaking his head sadly. He'd found a small piece on the website of a local Chattanooga news station detailing a house fire caused by an unlawful use of fireworks. The fire had been put out almost immediately, with some damage to an upstairs bathroom and the roof.

"No one got hurt," I said, which is what the news said, but even then, I could still see the roof catching on fire. I could still hear the glass breaking.

I knew it hadn't been harmless. I *knew*.

"That's not the point, you know that," he said, sighing.

"It was an accident." Was it? "Fireworks can be dangerous." I knew I was just repeating myself, but there was nothing else to say. Either he believed me, or he didn't.

Either I believed her, or I didn't.

"Exactly," he said. "They're dangerous. And she knew that."

Silence stretched tight between us.

"I'll talk to her."

"Remy—"

"I have to go," I said, ending the call. I still didn't want to face the truth. I wasn't ready, and I didn't want to be ready because of what it might mean for us, for our friendship.

Home was a person, and that person was still Elise, the first person who ever truly loved me for me. She sheltered me from the storm, she was my first home.

She was waiting for me, opening the door before I even knocked.

"Did you talk to Jack?" she asked, eyes lingering on my shirt—Jack's Superman tee.

"I did." We were standing in the foyer, at an impasse.

"What'd he say?"

"He hasn't changed his mind," I said, not meeting her eyes. "But he will. I'll explain and—"

"You told him it was an accident?"

"I did." We walked out onto the balcony, the air thick with humidity and still warm from the day. Elise lit a cigarette and offered me one.

"Why did you even tell him?" she snapped at me. "If you'd only—" She saw the hurt on my face and exhaled in frustration.

"What are you going to do?" I asked. What *could* she do? But then again, it was Elise. She always had a plan.

"You've put me in an impossible position," she said, looking out at the water below. It'd been raining a lot recently, leaving the river swollen, its violent current a symphony filling the air. For a while that's all there was. Then, when she was done with her cigarette, she tossed it at the water and turned to me. "You know I'd do anything for you, right?"

I nodded slowly, unsure of where this was coming from.

"And anything for us."

"I know," I said, still confused.

"Good." She lit another cigarette, passed me the case I'd given her for her birthday. *Remy x Elise.* "What are you thinking right now?"

"Nothing really," I said, lighting myself a cigarette and passing the case back. "Just tired." I was scared of saying the wrong thing, setting her off.

"You don't believe him, do you?" she asked, eyebrow raised.

"Believe what?"

"That I did it on purpose."

"I—" Maybe it was the sleep deprivation, the sheer exhaustion, but I ended up saying the wrong thing: "I don't know."

Her eyes flashed with anger. "You don't know?"

"That's not what I meant," I said, trying to backtrack.

"It was just an accident," she said. "You know me. You know I'd never do that." All I could think about was the moment I left the Pink Caddy to search for her, the moment the roof caught on fire. All I could think about was the windows shattering, her running toward me.

All I could think about was the gun she'd brought with her. The fact she knew it'd been missing from her bag when she returned.

Did I really know her?

Maybe she was looking for something and noticed it was gone.

301

I didn't want to acknowledge the other possibility—that she'd needed it because she planned on using it.

"Tell me you know I didn't intentionally set my father's house on fire," she said, pleading with me. "Tell me you know, Rem."

Maybe it really had just been an accident. A mistake. I couldn't decide. There were moments I thought it hadn't been an accident, but then there were moments like this, seeing Elise begging for me to believe her.

"Not that I would've cried if the whole house had burned down," she continued. "I was so miserable there, just seeing it again made me want to throw up. The worst years of my life, all wrapped up inside one shitty house." She shook her head, not looking at me. "And maybe it's what he deserved," she added quietly. "Maybe he deserved to lose his home, to feel a little ter-rified, to wonder if he was going to die. To know how I've felt my whole life."

"I'm sorry," I said quietly, shifting closer, placing a hand on her shoulder. Maybe it was karma, all of his crimes coming back to haunt him.

"Would you really hate me, if I'd done it on purpose?" she asked, eyes ablaze. "Would you have blamed me for wanting to?"

"Elise," I said. "Tell me you didn't."

"I didn't," she said quickly. "I'm just saying—*if.*"

I stared at her in stunned silence, dread growing in the pit of my stomach. What was she *really* saying?

"It'd be poetic justice," she said. "Or just plain old justice." She laughed, but it lacked warmth. Then she seemed to notice the hor-ror on my face. "Don't worry, Remy, I didn't! I'm just saying I don't regret it. And if I had the chance, I'd do it all over again."

I pulled back. I didn't recognize her in that moment, the cold laughter, the bitter anger on her face.

"Rem—" she began.

"No," I said, stepping back. "Just no." Poetic justice, that's what she called it, and she seemed a little too gleeful at how the night had turned out.

"Remy, come on," she said, and I shrank back. "It was just a hypothetical." That wasn't what it felt like. If anything, she seemed to be testing the waters, seeing how I'd react. A confession wrapped in the abstract.

"I need a moment." I went inside, sat on the stairs, knees drawn up, arms wrapped around my legs.

Oh God, Jack was right, I thought, my heart racing. Alarmed, I pressed my forehead against my knees, just trying to shut out the world. I remembered Jack's words from the night we met. *It feels almost like I veered off course somewhere and ended up in the wrong timeline of my life. The wrong version of myself. And now I don't know where to go.*

I felt homesick, but for a home that didn't exist anymore, one that maybe only ever existed in my imagination. I couldn't understand where I'd veered off, where *we* had veered off, but we were in the wrong timeline of our lives. I was the wrong version of myself, and now I didn't know where to go.

But maybe Jack was wrong, said a small voice in my mind. Elise said she wouldn't have cared if the house caught on fire and burned down, not that she meant to light it on fire herself. Fireworks were tricky, and she was probably tired from the drive, or too keyed up. It was easy, then, to make a mistake. An accident was almost inevitable under those circumstances.

It's amazing, what you can talk yourself out of.

Maybe I'd never really know what happened in Chattanooga. But maybe none of it mattered. Because even if Elise had done it on purpose, I could never just let her go to jail.

I glanced back toward the kitchen, the balcony doors. She was out there, expecting me to take some time and then come back to her. But I didn't know if I could, or if I wanted to any longer. Elise wanted to be the Bride, Beatrix Kiddo. She wanted to play super-hero, but none of it ever made her feel better. None of it ever helped her, and I was beginning to think that maybe nothing I did could help her either. Whether I said no or went along with her plans, it was never enough.

Dizzy with exhaustion and doubt, I pulled out my phone and texted Jack.

> Me: I don't know what to do
>
> Jack: Leave
>
> Me: I can't do that

It felt like a betrayal, to leave her in that house.

> Jack: Where are you guys?
>
> Me: Pink Mansion, why?
>
> Jack: I can be there in twenty
>
> Me: No, you'll just make it worse
>
> Jack: At least let me take you home
>
> Jack: You must be exhausted
>
> Me: I guess

Then, fifteen minutes later, I got the text.

> Jack: I'm here

Elise was still out on the balcony, so I opened the front door carefully. "Hey," I whispered.

"Why are you whispering?" he asked.

"I don't know," I answered. "I don't know what to do."

I hugged him tight, and in his arms, I felt safe. I pulled him impossibly closer, my hands in his hair. He smelled like peppermint soap and coffee, like the true home I'd been searching for, the life I wanted. And maybe together we could rebuild, and maybe with him I could be the version of myself I wanted to be, the Remy he saw in me, the Remy he loved.

"What's going on?" he asked, gently pulling my arms off to look at me. We were still by the door, the rest of the house dark and too quiet. "What did Elise say?"

I ignored his question. "Please don't go to the police," I said instead. "Please. For me."

He looked torn. Worse, he looked like he was disappointed in me.

"Don't make this harder for me," I begged. "I don't even know how she and I will recover from this, *if* we'll recover from it."

"What do you mean?" he asked.

"I don't think I can do this anymore," I said, the words bursting out, surprising both of us. I glanced back at the balcony doors. "But I don't want her arrested or anything. Maybe it really was an accident."

Jack took a moment to process what I'd said. "Okay."

"Okay?"

He nodded.

I turned around to look at the balcony doors once more. I could feel her presence, the push and pull between us, our invisible tether.

"Is she out there?" Jack asked.

"Yeah. I should go—I should say something." I started to head back there but he caught me by the wrist.

305

"Let me talk to her for you." Maybe he saw the dread on my face, or maybe I just looked completely exhausted. "You should go home, get some sleep. I'll tell her myself that I'm not going to the cops. And who knows, maybe it's better if I talk to her alone."

I hesitated.

"Go home, Remy. You look like you're about to keel over." He pressed a kiss to my forehead for the last time, though I didn't know it then.

"Okay," I said, pulling on my shoes. I *was* exhausted. And maybe if they talked to each other, they'd hash it out.

"Hey," he said before I left. "It's going to be okay."

I nodded and lingered for a moment before finally leaving. I believed him.

Standing at my car, I looked back at the Pink Mansion. Without any lights on, it looked haunted, abandoned. The house had fallen into disrepair in the year Elise and her father had lived there—the hedges untrimmed, the grass patchy and overgrown with weeds, the shutters crooked. A wave of sadness hit me at how time and neglect had turned what was once beautiful into something ugly and heartbreaking.

Getting in, I started the car, foot on the brake, ready to go when I heard it.

Not gunshots, like I later recalled, but the two of them yelling. I ran back, the car door left wide open, my keys forgotten in the ignition.

I hadn't fallen asleep in my car. I'd never fallen asleep at all.

"How dare you come to my house and tell me what to do," I heard Elise say as I reached the door, my hand hovering over the handle, frozen by the anger in her voice.

"I'm not telling you what to do. I'm offering you a choice," Jack said.

Elise scoffed. "It's not a choice, it's an ultimatum." My palm rested against the door, but I stood still, unable to move. It felt like all the times I'd taken shelter in closets, hiding from whatever storm was raging out there.

"It's what Remy wants," Jack said simply.

"No, it's not," Elise said. "She would never want that. She would never do that to me. You're lying." Her voice rose dangerously.

"I'm not." Jack sounded frustrated. "Look, I don't care if you believe me or not. Let's just leave Remy out of it. This is what I'm offering. Leave us alone and I won't go to the police and tell them you committed arson."

"I didn't commit arson!" she screamed. "What is this, some kind of power play?"

He held firm. "No."

"Don't lie. You're enjoying this, having something to lord over me. It has nothing to do with Remy. You don't care about her."

"I do care about Remy, and I'm sick of the way you treat her, the way you tell her to jump and she asks how high," he said. "That's why I'm doing this. Protecting her from you." Had Jack planned to confront her all along? After he'd texted me that he was here, he came to the door instead of waiting for me, like he wanted to come inside. And then he insisted I go home, let him talk to Elise.

"This ends now," Jack said. "Stay away from us. Stay away from Remy."

"I won't let you take her from me," she said, desperation in her voice. "Once I tell her—"

"Go ahead," Jack said, cutting her off. "Like I said, it's what she wants."

I hated the way they were talking about me, like I was some *thing* to be fought over. I hated the way I'd let them tell me what I wanted and what I didn't.

"You lie," Elise said. "You're just scared what'll happen when Remy realizes what a loser you are. You're just a scared little boy making empty threats."

"Fine, have it your way," Jack said. "I'll go to the police station tomorrow, tell them what I know."

"You won't take her away from me." She was gunpowder.

"Look, you can go to jail and lose her or you can leave us alone and not go to jail. Your choice." He was a lit match.

I touched the handle but remained still, unable to bring myself to confront them. To have to choose between them once and for all.

"You'll take her from me over my dead body." Then I heard a click, that distinct sound of a gun cocking.

"No!" I flew inside but it was already too late, the sound of six gunshots piercing the air.

"Remy?" Our eyes met for the briefest moment. What I saw wasn't anger—it was fear. I saw who she really was, who she'd been the entire time. She wasn't electric. She was just terrified—a cornered animal.

I collapsed by Jack's side. "No, no, no," I cried as I looked into his eyes for the last time. "Stay with me, stay with me." I cradled his head ever so gently as he gasped for breath. "No, no, please," I begged, holding him close as if I could keep him there if I held on tight enough.

Everything fell away. I became unmoored—from time, from

reality. Everything fell away and it was just him and me.

And then it was just me.

"No, no, no," I cried as his blood soaked the shirt he'd given me the first night we met. I sobbed so hard I couldn't breathe. My world was spinning out of control, untethered, lost.

"Remy?" Elise's voice sounded muffled, like I was underwater, drowning.

"Listen to me, Remy, listen. You weren't here," she said. "You weren't here, okay? You were in your car. Jack came in, and I thought he was an intruder. It was an accident."

Jack's eyes were glassy and lifeless. "No!" I screamed and screamed, lay my head on his shoulder. "Please, please."

"Remy, did you hear me?" she asked. "You weren't here. You didn't see anything, hear anything. You were in your car. Then you heard the gunshots and ran in. It was dark. I thought Jack was an intruder. It was all an accident." She placed a hand on me, shook me violently, but I barely felt it. "Everything's going to be okay, Remy. Everything's going to be okay now."

"No, please," I said as I cried over Jack's body. "Come back, come back to me."

"You and me, we're family," she continued as if none of this was happening, as if she hadn't just murdered the boy I loved. "It's just the two of us now. It'll always be just the two of us." She'd said it a million times.

Those words, once a source of comfort, now sounded like a threat.

64.

Home was a person and for me, that person was Elise. Only now home has become a prison, and that prison is Elise.

"You killed him." I feel faint, my collapse complete. "You murdered him." As soon as I say it, I know it's true. Maybe I've known all along and locked it away deep within me because I couldn't face what she'd done.

"That's not true," she says, shaking her head firmly. "I don't know how much you overheard, but he was threatening me. You weren't there at the beginning. You didn't hear the way he spoke." Her voice begins to tremble. "I hadn't done anything wrong. Chattanooga was an accident. But he was going to tell the police it was arson. He was going to tell the police I went there with the intention of killing my father. He was threatening me with decades in prison, Remy."

The wind whipped around us faster, the Pink Caddy speeding up.

"My dad brutally beats me and he's out of jail in less than a day, free to go until a hearing where he'll get off with a slap on the wrist, and I have an accident playing an innocent prank and *I'm* the one who's going to lose everything? It was all a ploy, Rem. Don't you see that? He wanted to take you away from me. That's what it was about. That's what it's *always* been about. You're the only thing I have in the whole world and he was going to take you from me!"

"I'm not a—a *thing*. No one can take me, not him, not even you," I blurt out. I have a choice to make now, not between Elise or Jack but between Elise and me. Between letting her take over my life or letting her go.

"That's not what I'm saying."

"That's exactly what you're saying. You're acting like Jack was *stealing* me away from you, like I'm some kind of possession." I feel trapped in the car with no way to escape.

"No, I was protecting us, protecting *you*."

"No." I shake my head roughly. "You weren't." I'm overwhelmed with anger—and regret. My stomach twists at the thought of everything *I'd* done in the name of protecting us, protecting her.

"He was making these decisions without you, like some kind of sick puppet master. He was obsessed with you, he wanted to control you. I know you can't see that right now, but it's the truth. And I was the only one who could save you."

"No. Stop it." I want it all to end. The lies, the half-truths, the manipulation.

"You have to trust me, Rem," Elise says. "He was a monster."

"Not everyone is a monster," I say. "Not everyone is—" I don't need to finish for her to know who I'm talking about. *Your dad.*

"You're unbelievable, you know that? You're acting like it happened to you," she says, cutting me off. "But it didn't. It happened to me. And you act like you're this old soul, this broken spirit, this *victim*, but you're not! You don't have wounds, you've never bled. I'm the one who's bled. Not metaphorically. Literally. And you think, what with your shitty parents and their fighting and how mean they are to you, you think that's the same?" She laughs, jarring and bitter. "It's not. Only one of us here has been truly damaged, and guess what, it's not you." She's yelling now.

"So what, you decided you'd be the one to fix it? Kill Jack, make sure I was just as damaged as you?"

"You think I wouldn't trade places with you in a heartbeat? Wake the fuck up, Remy."

Jack asked me when I was going to wake up Sunday morning, on the day he died. Have I been asleep this whole time?

"Only one of us has been truly traumatized. And in the last few months, I've been blaming myself. I lie awake at night and replay every punch, every kick, every word, every agonizing second. I lie there and think, why wasn't I smarter, why wasn't I faster, why didn't I report it?" she says, sobbing.

"Elise—pull over."

She ignores me, driving through her tears. "But it wasn't my fault! It happened because you weren't there. Because I called you and you knew—you *knew*—I needed you and you just fucking ignored me. And for what? Some guy you'd met a few months ago? Well, Remy, was it worth it?" Elise says, leaving both of us in a stunned silence.

"What do you want me to say?" I finally ask, but I'm furious. She knows I was wracked with guilt for not answering her calls that night. She *knows* and now she isn't even pretending it wasn't my fault—she takes the knife I'd sharpened for her and buries it in me with a twist. "You want everything to be just you and me, forever and ever. You say things like *love is need* and tell me that we need each other, but what you really mean is you don't want me to need anyone else. What you really mean is you don't want me to love anyone else but you."

"That's not true!" she says as the sky opens up and warm rain begins to fall, soaking us and the car instantly. "Fuck."

"Pull over!" I yell, but she ignores me, lets the rain pound on us, drench the convertible. "I'm allowed to want other things, other people. I'm allowed to need more."

The words I hold back hang between us: You can't be my whole world.

Then I shake my head. "None of this changes what you did. You—you *killed* him. You *murdered* Jack."

"It was self-defense!"

"No," I say. "It wasn't." The rain crashes down on me in waves, running down my face, but I'm no longer crying. I scream at the sky in rage.

"It was," Elise insists, her voice wild, like she's losing control. "It was self-defense."

"Oh my God," I say, squeezing myself against the door trying to get as far away from her as possible. "You don't even feel bad. You don't even care that you murdered him."

"Don't be ridiculous," she says. "Look, I know you liked Jack but—"

"Liked Jack?" I say. "*Liked* Jack?"

"Oh, please," she says. "Don't tell me you were in love. Don't tell me you wanted to be with him forever." Her voice mocks me and my hands clench, knuckles white. I look at her and I can't find the Elise that I knew, the one I loved. All I see now is a stranger, an echo of someone I once knew. "You and I are forever. You and I are soulmates."

"No. We're not."

She glances at me. "Other people come and go, but I'll always love you." Love is to need and be needed.

"You don't love me," I say in the quietest voice.

"I'm the only one who loves you," she says. "The *only* one."

"That's not true. Jack loved me," I say, the tears falling hard and fast just as the rain lets up, slowing to a lazy drizzle. "And I loved him. I don't want to do this anymore. Just take me home."

"No."

"No?" I say, staring at her in shock. Then I look all around me, confused. "Where are we going?" I thought we were driving around in circles, but I hadn't been paying attention until now. We're about to get on the highway, heading south.

"No," she repeats. Her voice is firm.

"You're refusing to drive me home? Are you kidding me?" I start to feel panicked, try to force air into my lungs.

"You don't want to leave me," she says. "You need me."

"I don't!"

"You do. You need me because there is no heroine without a villain, and you so enjoy playing the part of the heroine. Poor, poor Remy. Nothing's her fault. Bad things just happen to her. Bad people made her do it."

Her words are jarringly familiar. She sounds just like my mother.

"Like you didn't want all of it," she continues. "Like you didn't just love watching the two of us fight over you. I know you. I know what's in your heart. I know exactly who you are and I still love you. No one will love you like I do. Don't throw away what we have to punish me. It's you and me, Remy. We're family." And there it is again, those awful words like a chain around my neck, choking all the air out of me.

"Where are we going? Where are you taking me?" I'm so scared, so angry that I want to scream. I'm trapped, no way to reach anyone, least of all Elise. She's completely gone.

"We can go anywhere you want," she says. "Maybe LA or San Francisco, or maybe Portland. We could drive around the whole country, go to the Grand Canyon, see everything, do anything."

Her smile is so wide, her eyes are so bright, that hint of dangerous electricity underneath. We turn off 141 onto 285 West as I watch helplessly. It's late with few cars around. The rain makes it worse.

"Like I said, we can sell off my grandmother's things for now and when I turn eighteen, I'll have more than enough money for the both of us. I'll buy you whatever you want. You'll be free of your parents, truly free of them. We'll travel the world, go to Paris. Or Tokyo! I've always wanted to see Japan. Where do you want to go? We can take turns picking."

She wants me to be free of my parents so I'll never be free of her. She wants me to depend on her, to *need* her. She doesn't want anyone else to have any control over me—not even myself—because she wants to be the only one who does. Life with her would be an ever-shrinking prison. Inescapable.

A new wave of rain comes down hard again, and Elise slows the car. My fingers stretch toward the door handle. Our speed is slow enough now that I could maybe roll out, but then what? We're still on the highway, and I'm without a phone. I can't think straight.

"What's wrong?" she asks. "I thought you'd be happy!"

"Why would you think that?" I'm shouting now and I don't even care. I'm done silencing myself to protect her feelings. "What part of *I want to go home* said I wanted to run away with you?"

Her expression darkens. "You can act like you don't need me, but I know the truth. I know *you*. You want to pretend you're tough but you're not. You don't know how lucky you are, Remy," she says, shaking her head, her voice dismissive. "You have *everything*. But I've had to fight for everything, claw my way out with my bare hands, and it's made me strong. It's made me a survivor." She sounds deluded, clinging onto the story she wants to believe about herself. The story that turns everything tragic in her life into something that gives her power.

"I don't want to do this anymore."

"Do what?"

"Play this game. You win, okay? You clearly had it worse. You're right. Now what?"

She looks surprised. I've taken away one of her weapons. It was a mistake, letting her wounds define mine. Even now, I feel guilty for being "lucky," but I know I was never lucky. Life isn't a race to the bottom—having it worse doesn't win her some kind of prize. Her pain doesn't diminish my pain. It's a false dichotomy.

Elise is so proud of her suffering. I used to believe her when she said our battle scars made us strong because all I ever felt was weak. But that was before Jack died in my arms, before I knew what real loss was. What it meant to be truly powerless.

We found it romantic, being the tragic heroines of our own stories. But the cost to being a tragic hero was always going to be the ending. Romeo and Juliet with their poison and knife, Gatsby by his pool, Bonnie and Clyde in a shoot-out.

The ride is always grand—the rush at the beginning, the ever-mounting obstacles, and finally, the *fait accompli*, the heart-breaking conclusion.

We are careening toward it now and maybe it's too late already, but I want out—out of the car, out of this story.

"Look, I know I fucked up, okay?" she says. "I know that. But I'm different now. I'm better, I'll be better."

"Are you even listening to me?" I say.

"Yes! Are you listening to *me*?" she asks, and I shake my head.

"You're fucking unbelievable, you know that?" I say. "You're such a liar. You say we're just going for a drive and then you kidnap me. You never had any intention of taking me home, did you? You say you love me but you're so afraid of losing me that you murdered Jack. This is so fucked up. Can't you see how terrible we are for each other? We're not good for each other, can't you see that?"

Her chin trembles and she starts to cry.

"And saying you're different doesn't actually make you different. I don't want to go anywhere with you! I don't ever want to see or talk to you again."

"No, Remy, please," she says. "I am different. Killing Jack was a mistake—"

"*A mistake?*"

"Please, Remy." She's sobbing now, groveling, but I don't want to hear it.

"You're different now, less than a week after you murdered Jack? What, are you going to pinky swear not to shoot the next person I love?"

She cries harder. "Listen," she says between sobs. "Listen to me. I know what you did in your police interview. I know you tried to protect me. I know you still care about me, or you wouldn't have done it."

She's not wrong, but I won't give her the satisfaction. "Take me home, Elise. I want to go home." I know my voice is cold, but I can't crack, can't show any weakness. Yes, I still care about her, but it's not enough, not after everything.

"Fine!" she says. "You want to go home, I'll take you home." She swerves three lanes over to pull off the nearest exit, barely missing the metal guardrails. We almost crash into another car but Elise avoids it just in time.

"Oh my God," I breathe, my hands against the dash bracing for impact.

She turns right, and without slowing down, she makes a wide U-turn and then we are swerving out of control, the tires skidding and then hydroplaning on the wet road.

The Pink Caddy lurches forward off the road and shoots down a hill.

I'm screaming at the top of my lungs as she tries to regain control of the car, slamming the brakes. Finally we're slowing down, but before the tires can find purchase, we hit a tree.

The airbags discharge and I'm disoriented from their punch. But the impact is minor—bruises, not broken bones.

"Are you okay?" Elise asks beside me.

"Stay away from me," I say, freeing myself from the seat belt and popping open the door.

"What are you doing?" she asks. "Where are you going?"

"I don't care as long as it's far away from you!" My legs are weak and I'm stumbling, but I have to get away.

"You can't leave!"

I keep going.

"No one will ever love you like I do!" she screams after me desperately.

"Good!" I shout back, but I'm beginning to feel faint. The exhaustion and grief is catching up.

If this is love then I don't want it. Love isn't need, isn't holding another person in a death grip.

"Stop," she says, pushing open the door, scrambling after me.

"Stay away from me," I say weakly, collapsing to the ground from the exertion, heaving. My head hurts. Everything's spinning around me.

"You can't leave me. You *can't*," she says, catching up. The Pink Caddy is behind her, smoke and steam rising from under the crushed hood. The tree stands strong, unaffected. "I'll die without you, I will." She's beside me now, also on her knees, hands gripping the grass, tears falling.

I shake my head, try to stand again.

Even though we're off an exit in the middle of nowhere, a couple cars have passed, though none stop.

"I will," she insists. "I'll die without you."

Elise grabs my wrist and I shove her off me.

"Get away from me!" I cry, trying to catch my breath, my footing.

Suddenly she does, hobbling in the opposite direction toward the Pink Caddy. Propping myself up with hands on my knees, I can't pull in enough air. The whole world seems to tilt and sway, the ground shifting beneath me. Struggling, I manage to push myself all the way up to see Elise emerge from the passenger side, glove compartment left hanging open.

I don't notice the gun until she's lifting it. For a second I think she's going to point it at me. For a second I think I'm going to die.

But she raises it to her own temple.

"Don't leave me, Remy. Please don't leave me," she cries.

"No!" I stumble toward her, tripping and falling. "Elise, no!"

"I don't know how to exist without you, I can't do it," she sobs. "I need you, Remy. I need you."

"No, no, no," I say, finally reaching her. Dimly, I register a car finally pulling over near us. Elise squeezes her eyes shut and I lunge forward.

I knock the revolver from her hand. It hits the car seat and bounces into the passenger side footwell. She's after it immediately and manages to retrieve it.

"No," I say, trying to pull it away from her.

Behind me, more cars have pulled over and people are running toward us, closing in. I just have to keep the gun away from her for another minute.

"I can't do it," she says, crying and fighting me for control. "Just let go of me, Remy, just let me go!"

"Don't do this!"

We struggle, the gun between us.

I hear someone shouting behind me.

Only a few more seconds, I think.

And that's when it goes off.

65.

Pain explodes through me as I slip away from Elise and hit the ground with a thud. I clutch my left shoulder, crying out. It's excruciating. I can't breathe. The world closes in around me—I can't see, can't hear.

I am pain and pain is me.

"Remy, Remy," Elise says, but her voice is so, so far away.

I exist in a strange in-between state, coming in and out of focus. When I open my eyes, the sun overhead is blinding. It takes me a moment to realize it's night, not day, and I'm no longer lying outside on the grass but inside of an ambulance, strapped to a gurney and staring up at the bright white lights.

I have one last thought before I'm pulled under.

Our wounds don't make us special. They only mean we've been hurt.

Suffering isn't romantic. It's just painful.

66.

When I open my eyes, I'm completely alone in a hospital room. Vases of flowers fill my bedside table and line the windowsill. The pain in my shoulder is dull but persistent.

"She's awake," someone says, and I look up to find Christian standing by the door.

All of them walk toward me and it feels like I'm in a dream. Mom, Dad, Christian—they surround my bed and ask me how I am. No one is arguing, no one is angry or sad, only relieved.

The bullet hit my left shoulder, far away from any major arteries, they tell me. It was only a 9mm and I was very lucky, they say. I was in surgery for six hours and might need to have another operation later. I'm looking at a few months of physical therapy, and I might not regain full range of motion in that shoulder, but I'll be okay. I'll survive.

"The doctors are optimistic since you're so young," Mom tells me. Then she launches into a long and detailed medical explanation of what the surgeons did, how I now have hardware inside me, pieces of metal I'll always have to carry within me. I think of Jack and his shoulder, of the way trauma changes you forever.

"How are you feeling?" Dad asks, pouring a cup of water for me. I try to drink but can't, feeling dizzy and nauseated from the pain meds.

Lucky. They keep telling me how lucky I was, but I don't feel particularly lucky. I reach for my shoulder with my right hand. Even the lightest pressure is excruciating, leaving me gasping in pain.

"Don't touch it," Mom says, and it's not anger in her voice but fear.

"You flew back?" I ask Christian when we have a moment alone. "You just left three days ago."

"I flew back as soon as I heard," he says. I can see the concern on his face. "I can't believe she shot you."

"She didn't," I say. "It was an accident."

"You can't be serious," he says. "You're really going to keep covering for her?"

"I'm not covering for her," I say, and it's the truth. "It was an accident." None of them believe me, but that's what happened. She didn't aim the gun at me—we both had hands on it when it went off.

And when the Atlanta police arrive for a statement, that's exactly what I tell them despite the glares from my family. It takes all my effort to hold back, to not ask about Elise. I don't tell them about the memories I've recovered, but it's not because I'm still protecting Elise. I haven't decided what I'll do, if I can even recant my previous statement.

In quiet moments, I wonder where she is, how she's doing. I can't shake our last moments together—the struggle over the gun, the sound of her voice begging me not to leave.

But at the same time, I feel a strange distance. I worry about her but I don't feel responsible for her in the same way I used to—I don't feel guilt gnawing at my heart. It's not just the fight, what was said at the end. I can't explain it, but it's like the bullet severed more than soft tissue and bone. Like it destroyed every last shred of who I was so completely that I became brand-new.

Within hours I'm running a fever, but it doesn't feel like any fever I've ever had.

Instead, as I burn up, tossing and turning on the hospital bed, it feels like a cleansing fire. Like destruction but also rebirth.

A phoenix rising from its ashes.

It's a comforting thought, but then I catch myself. This is the kind of lie Elise would believe—this is the kind of pain she thought would make her stronger.

I am not a phoenix rising from its ashes. Fire does not cleanse, only burn. Death isn't rebirth.

Jack is never coming back.

67.

In the afternoon, Vera comes by. "I thought we agreed to stop meeting like this," she jokes with a gentle smile.

"Sorry," I say, returning the smile.

She tells me she's spoken with Detective Ward, who wants to talk to me again. "This specific incident didn't happen in her jurisdiction, but she wants to know if there's anything you'd like to revise in your statement."

I start crying, alarming Mom, Dad, and Christian. Vera asks them to give us a few minutes. I tell her everything. I tell her about the pranks, about our trip to Chattanooga and the ensuing argument between Elise and Jack, and finally, what really happened Sunday night.

"Will you—" My voice cracks. "Will you make sure Elise is okay?" I can still see her standing in the downpour, gun to her temple. She needs help I can't give.

"I will," she says. Vera is the one I trust. She'll know what to do. "Can I?" she asks, reaching a hand forward, and I nod, letting her squeeze my wrist.

For a while we just sit together quietly, uncertainty hanging in the air between us.

"What do you think I should do?" I finally ask.

"Do you want to know what I think as a friend or what I think as your lawyer?" she says.

"Both."

She lays out the options. There's obvious risk to recanting my entire interview. Not only could I be charged with obstruction of justice, but footage of everything I said exists and will be admissible as evidence, making it, again, difficult to prosecute. Another risk is that I could be charged as an accessory to the crime itself for my part after it happened—the lies I told at the station.

"As your lawyer, I'm not sure I'd advise changing your statement now. But there are downsides to staying silent too. If the police recover more evidence and decide to go forward with charges against Elise, you'll almost certainly be charged as well. Now that they have the murder weapon, it could change things," she says.

"What do you think I should do?" I ask again, my voice so, so small.

"I think you should let me talk to Detective Ward and the DA first. I can't say with certainty what they'll do, but I think they'll be interested in making a deal in exchange for your testimony."

"What will happen to Elise?" I ask.

Vera begins to answer but pauses. "I think you already know," she says. "I think what you're really asking me is if she'll be okay."

I nod.

"I will do everything in my power to get her the help she needs. But no one can say if Elise will be okay or not," she tells me. "But I know you feel bad. I know you feel like you weren't able to help her." All of this is true. That guilt comes and goes. That guilt may never be completely eradicated. "But I have to say, Remy, that I agree with Detective Ward for once. It wasn't your fault." Even though I know it too, it's hard for me to accept it. "A lot of people in Elise's life failed her. Her parents, her caseworker after she was hospitalized. She needed counseling. She needed things that you couldn't give her."

I let Vera's words sink in, try to process them. She stays a little while longer but eventually the pain in my shoulder becomes too strong for me to think straight. She leaves, promising to come back soon.

A nurse comes in to change my bandages, and after he leaves I click the remote attached to the infusion pump containing my pain meds and slip into a fitful but dreamless sleep.

When I awaken I find Evan and his parents there. They tell me that Jack's mother finally managed to get a flight home and that she'd like to meet me since I won't be able to attend the funeral. They seem worried about me, and not just because of the gunshot wound. Evan is the most bewildered of all, struggling to process everything that's happened, struggling with this new view of Elise, both of her past and what she's done. When his parents leave to get some coffee, he sits beside me and tells me he's sorry.

"Why?" I ask, and for a moment he looks like he's about to cry.

"Jack—I'm just sorry," he says, shaking his head.

"How's Lola?" I ask. Just thinking about her brings tears to my eyes. Jack left and never returned and no one can tell her why.

"She's confused," Evan says. "Hangs out by the door and stares out the window a lot."

"God, that's awful." My heart breaks for her and I tear up. No one will ever be able to explain to her why he's not coming back— or the fact he won't be coming back *at all*.

"My parents wanted me to ask you about her, actually." He takes a deep breath. "Jack's mom can't take her since she's almost never home, and of course Lola will always have a home with us, but she was really Jack's dog and she seemed to like you a lot, so—"

"Yes," I say immediately, and my heart breaks again at the thought of the two of us coping with the loss of Jack, but it also brings me a ray of comfort that we'll have each other.

"Okay," Evan says with a small smile. "I'll bring her over when you get out."

I cry when they leave. My parents, the nurses, and doctors all think I'm in pain, and they're right, but it's not the gunshot wound.

Jack was right. The guilt I felt for failing Elise when she needed me most consumed me, confused me. And without its oppressive weight, I am free to really mourn Jack. I cry and cry and cry. I run through all the ways I could've prevented his death, all the ways I failed *him*.

That night, when I sleep, I dream of him briefly. We're at the

327

lake, and it's a starry night, like the one when we met. This time, he's the first to jump in. I quickly follow, and even though it's dark, I can see his face, that gentle smile.

He goes under and, in my dream, I think we are playing a game. I wait and wait for him to emerge laughing, but he never does. The dream lingers long after I wake up sobbing, gasping for air.

A night tech comes into the room. "Are you okay?" he asks.

I answer honestly. "I don't know."

68.

The next day, I'm surprised with a visit from Melody. She brings me coconut cupcakes and chocolate chip cookies. She tells me about school and the things she's been up to, and it's nice to just listen to her voice, let her distract me.

"You know you're always welcome at our table," she tells me before she leaves. I don't know if it'll even be possible to go back to Riverside, if I'll be able to handle it, but it's kind of her to offer. "You're always welcome there. You and Elise both were."

"But you and Elise—" I think of what Christian said, how Elise had embellished aspects of her story. I remember what she told me the day we went off campus for lunch in that sub's car, about how Melody had confronted her about our friendship. I'm about to ask Mel but I decide not to. I have to let go of the past.

Later that day, when Mom has gone back to work, Dad sticks around for lunch. "Let's do it," he tells me.

"Do what?" I ask warily.

329

"Get out of here. For real."

"Um, I kind of can't on account of being shot," I say with a weak laugh.

"No, not this." He laughs too. "I mean you and me. Let's do it, okay?"

I shrug with my right shoulder. We've been here before. "Okay," I say, indulging him. "Let's do it."

"I mean it," he insists. "This—this was a wake-up call, Remy. I almost lost you." He begins to cry. "I want to start over. I don't want to fail you."

"Dad . . ."

"I'll get an apartment and then we can move out right away."

"Okay," I say, my smile a little warmer this time. I'm not sure I have faith in anything he says anymore, but I can't help but hope anyway.

69.

I'm sitting outside on the front steps of my house, my left arm in a sling, when Evan pulls up. Lola jumps out of his car and runs toward me, and I smile genuinely for the first time since Jack's death. I walk her around the neighborhood for a bit with Evan, and when Mom comes home, Lola's napping under the dining table.

Mom freezes when she spots her. She sets down her bag and slips off her shoes, and without a word, she makes her way over to Lola and lifts a tentative hand before petting her.

I'm ready with arguments but she begins to speak and they never make it out of my throat.

"We had a cat once," she says, surprising me. "When I was six. Princess Georgina, we called her. Just George for short." Over the years, Christian and I have gotten every excuse under the sun for why we weren't allowed to have pets. A spark of anger pulses through me, but before I get a chance to call her out on her hypocrisy, she sheds a tear.

331

"I loved George so much. Some of my earliest memories were of that silly cat," she says now, leaving me in a stunned silence. "But when I was twelve or thirteen, she got sick, really, really sick. She passed away within a year, and I—" Her eyes widen with realization.

"What?" I ask.

"She passed away within a year and I never wanted to feel like that again. We never got another cat, and I guess somewhere along the way, never getting another pet became a self-imposed rule and I stopped wondering why." Another tear rolled down her cheek as she sat on the floor next to Lola, who lets Mom gather her into her arms.

70.

Dad comes by later in the afternoon with some movers. I'd almost forgotten his promise. Mom doesn't come out of her office, so she must know.

I watch them dismantle my bed and pack it away, and I still can't believe it's happening.

"By the way," I tell Dad, "we have a dog now."

He raises a single eyebrow. "I noticed." We share a small smile. When everything is packed up, Mom comes out of the office. They exchange a few words. Dad tells her when to expect the divorce papers. They're subdued, polite even. It feels like the end of an era.

Not long ago, Mom was anger and Dad was exasperation. These were roles they'd played for years. That was the only story they wanted to tell.

Now she is sorrow and he is regret. They are no longer a powder keg about to explode now that they're separating. For the first time, I wonder what role I've played all these years, what story I've been telling myself.

That I've been nothing but a pawn in their games.

That they love me only for what I am to them, what I could be to them.

That love is the weapon they wield, the justification for everything they do.

That love is a weapon, period.

And for the first time, I am asking myself if it has to be this way. For the first time, I am asking myself if there's another story I want to tell.

Trauma has a gravity of its own, and I am forever trapped in its orbit. Try too hard to escape and it'll tear your whole life apart.

That's the story I've been telling, but maybe I'm only half-right.

Trauma has a gravity of its own, a force you can feel but not see. But it's not a black hole. It's not a large, looming celestial body. I am not trapped in any orbit but my own, and all my past mistakes and bad memories are moons that circle me, captured in *my* orbit. I feel their pull the way the tides do—high, then low. Up, then down. But in the end, I am the one keeping them close wherever I go. I am the one tugging them gently along.

I think about the lies Elise has told me, the ones I was desperate to believe. They were such beautiful lies. The best lies. But now I am ready for the truth.

My wounds don't make me special. What doesn't kill me won't make me stronger. Pain has no lesson to teach, suffering serves no purpose. I am not a tragic heroine trudging down some predetermined path set for me by someone else. I don't have to be a casualty of my parents' actions, of my past misfortunes. I don't have to become my parents, I don't have to play out their stories.

I can cut the tether, leave the past to disappear into the vast darkness of space.

I can tell another story.

71.

My stomach clenches in fear as I walk into the interrogation room again. Vera has struck a deal with the DA: In exchange for my testimony and cooperation, I won't be charged.

The camera's aimed at me and it feels eerily familiar, with Detective Ward across the table, Vera on my left. The red light blinks, but this time I'm not holding my breath, waiting for a bomb to detonate.

Tell me something true, Jack used to say to me, and it was one of my favorite things about him. Remembering it now grounds me, holds me up.

Here, for the last time, is the truth in all its awful entirety.

The truth about the night Jack died, the truth about everything leading up to that night and everything after it.

"State your name, please," Detective Ward says. The room doesn't feel like it's closing in—the light isn't too bright, and I'm not struggling to breathe. For once, the room is just a room.

335

"My name is Katherine Remy Tsai, but everyone calls me Remy," I say.

"Okay, Remy," Detective Ward says. "Can you tell me what happened?"

I nod.

"Go ahead," she says, her voice gentle.

I take a deep breath and begin again.

ACKNOWLEDGMENTS

I am so grateful to everyone who helped make my wildest dreams a reality.

To my agent, Kerry Sparks, who read the very first draft and believed in Remy's story from the start. You are a tireless champion, and I am so lucky to have you in my corner.

To my editor and fellow Batman aficionado, Liesa Abrams: I knew I was in good hands from our first phone call. Thank you for sharing my vision and for your faith that we would get there. This book truly wouldn't be the same without you. Special thanks, also, to Jessi Smith, whose perceptive insights helped strengthen this story.

To Mara Anastas and the entire S&S team: Thank you so much for all you do. I know it takes a village, and this book was raised by the very best one.

This story has also benefited from the advice of so many, but particularly Natasha Razi, Shannon O'Guin, and RuthAnne Snow.

I've been fortunate to have many wonderful teachers and mentors, but two stand out: Liz Van Doren and Jane O'Connor. Thank you for teaching me so much about books and life.

To friends near and far who always lift me up: Amanda Yao, D.S., Katarzyna Piękoś, Amy Oliver, Jean Mone, A.C. Leath, Kristin Lambert, Jennifer Fan, Alysia Campbell, Beth Branch, Anna Birch, and Tia Bearden. Jen, Anna, and Kristin also read drafts at various stages, and their enthusiasm was invaluable.

To my parents, who fretted over my decision to major in English but let me do it anyway—thank you for keeping the faith. And of course, shout-out to my brother, Tyler, who has always been proud of me. I'm proud of you, too.

To my family, who supports me in everything I do. Naga, the best dog in the world, who stayed up with me through every single late night. And my husband, Gene, whose contribution to this book is immeasurable. Thank you for reading a million drafts and always taking the time to listen to me talk out story ideas. I love you.

And finally to you, the reader: Thank you for taking this journey with me.

RESOURCES

Child Abuse
Childhelp
Phone: 480-922-8212
National hotline (available 24/7): 1-800-422-4453
http://www.childhelp.org/

Organizations related to child welfare, including a list of child abuse reporting numbers by state and a list of toll-free crisis hotline numbers: https://www.childwelfare.gov/organizations/

Survivors
Adult Survivors of Child Abuse
Phone: 415-928-4576
Email: info@ascasupport.org
http://www.ascasupport.org/

Adult Children of Alcoholics/Dysfunctional Families
Phone: 310-534-1815
information@acawso.com
https://www.adultchildren.org/

National Suicide Prevention Lifeline

1-800-273-8255

https://www.suicidepreventionlifeline.org/

ABOUT THE AUTHOR

Sarah Lyu grew up outside of Atlanta, Georgia, and graduated from the University of Pennsylvania. She currenty resides in Birmingham, Alabama, with her family. She loves a good hike but can often be found with a book on her lap and sweet tea in hand. *The Best Lies* is her first book. You can visit her at sarahlyu.com.

Two Powerful, Moving Novels from Amy Reed

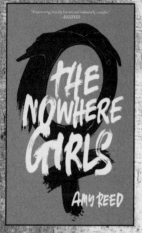

"A call-to-action to everyone out there who wants to fight back."
–*Bustle*

"Empowering, brutally honest, and realistically complex."
–*BuzzFeed*

★"Just try to put it down."
–*Kirkus Reviews*, starred review

★"A must-read."
–*SLJ*, starred review

★"Captivating . . . Fans of Rainbow Rowell and John Green who also like a bit of fantasy will fall in love with Billy and Lydia."
–*SLJ*, starred review

"Teens will deeply relate to these characters."
–*Booklist*

"Gritty, gutsy, and ferociously strange."
–Nova Ren Suma, #1 *New York Times* bestselling author

EBOOK EDITIONS ALSO AVAILABLE
Simon Pulse
simonandschuster.com/teen